Erin's Hope

The Voyage of the Irish Rebellion's One-Ship Armada

ISBN: 978-1503283572

Cover Design - Dick Blazek

Druid Hill Press

Foreword

All journalists are story-tellers – but that's a description that conceals as much as it reveals. And too many of the stories that journalists tell are hide-bound by convention, crippled by censorship, or squeezed, like the unwitting guests in Procrustes' bed, into formulae that do scant justice to the reality that they are intended to convey. Once in a while, however journalists are liberated from these constraints – by innovative and courageous editors, or by the unconquerable desire to tell a story that reflects a different and perhaps difficult genre – and settle down to telling a story that draws not only on what they know and see or hear, but on the long-hoarded recesses of their own imaginations.

Erin's Hope is such a story.

At its core is the curious tale of a brave but ultimately futile 9,000-mile voyage bringing guns from America to Ireland in 1867 to support one of the many unsuccessful attempts by Irish revolutionaries to throw off the yoke of British rule.

Its author, Tom Walsh, is a journalist who happened across this story – or at least the weathered historical skeleton which he has here endowed with blood and bone, skin and sensibility – and immediately recognised that any attempt to tell the tale in conventional factual terms simply wouldn't be worth the candle. So he blended both real and composite characters into actual and fictionalized events.

Collectively this work of what its author terms "historical faction" – a novel grounded in historical events and which also reflects detailed historical and archival research – traces the social, political, economic and deeply personal origins of 19th Century Irish-American involvement in what Britain, generally condescendingly, used to refer to as "The Irish Question" and which, then as now, has deep resonance on the American side of the Atlantic.

I first met the author quite by chance while he was in Dublin on one of his many research forays, the first of many such treks to Ireland over at least 10 years. A glutton for punishment, he even signed on as crew on a two-masted, square-rigged brigantine (a similar vessel to the Erin's Hope) on a voyage from Boston to Cork, the better to be able to convey to his readers something of the real perils that still confront those who go down to the sea in ships, especially when they include a landlubber from Iowa.

Tom and I share the craft of journalism – to call it a profession is perhaps to garland it with too much authority – which prides itself on good writing, on attention to detail, on honesty, and on credibility. Erin's Hope has all these qualities in spades, and the vividness of the narrative is testament, not only to the author's uncommon skills in all these areas, but also to the quality of his imagination.

As a colleague of his in his occasional forays to Dublin City University, and a friend for as long, I have been a fascinated witness to this book's emergence from its chrysalis over the past few years. I am happy now to wish it *bon voyage*.

Professor John Horgan
Dublin City University

Says Johnny Bull to Larcom: Oh! Tell my dear police
To watch those wicked foreigners who so disturb my
peace;
Who come across the ocean with no manifest pursuits,
Who swagger down my thoroughfares wearing square-
toed boots.

Their hats caved in and shapeless, to slight the Crown are
meant;
Their knickerbockers and gaiters show a desperate intent.
Their beards look all seditious, from the tips unto the
roots,
But there's mischief beyond measure in their square-toed
boots.

But now no more those rovers shall fright me and annoy,
I'll treat them to the beauties of Kilmainham and
Mountjoy;
For I've made a resolution, whatever be its fruits,
That my laws shall not be trampled on by men in square-
toed boots.

From Larcom to the Royals the word was sent around,
And fast they seized Americans where'er they could be
found.
They dragged them off to prison, and they treated them
like brutes,
On a charge of foul conspiracy and wearing square-toed
boots.

But now the news has traveled afar across the sea,
Old Uncle Sam has heard it, and a mighty man is he;
Through all his huge anatomy a thrill of anger shoots,
And like thunder comes the stamping of his square-toed
boots.

And Johnny Bull grows fearful, as surely well he may,
When up the giant rises and strides across his way;

For past experience whispers what no later fact refutes,
That there's terrible propulsion in his square-toed
boots.

Square-Toed Boots

By T.D. Sullivan, 1867

Most of what follows really happened.

Prologue

July, 1849
Killane, County Wexford

After watching his father's last desperate days, Sean Kenneally felt strangely pleased when they came at last with linen over their faces to haul away what little remained of him. Sean would never forget the sight of that cart moving down the lane, wheels groaning under the weight, his father atop a heap of others, all of them bloated and stinking and black with flies. There was plenty of food for the flies.

Before they arrived, Sean had taken for himself his dead father's boots, not as much in remembrance as need. His own boots were in tatters, no good against either the cold or the damp. For more than a week now, Sean survived on nettles and turnips. Yesterday brought a pain to his jaw, and since morning his mouth tasted blood.

When he spotted Father Fraher heading up the cowpath, Sean hoped the priest was bringing bread, real bread, a half-loaf at least, not some wafer that melted away on your tongue before it could find your stomach. What the priest had brought instead was a sermon on how grand life would be across the sea among the hillsides beyond a great river he said was as broad as a lake.

Talk of the old priest's dream had found its way even to these desolate pastures above Killane. Sean and what few remained in these hills thought him daft to have returned to this wretched place. Hundreds had died and hundreds more had left, but only Father Fraher had come back, all the way back from America to urge whoever might listen to flee the hunger while they still had the strength. And today he wasn't taking no.

"You will die here, boy, you must know that," the old priest told Sean. "Take a look at yourself. And have a look at this place. There's nothing here to keep alive what little is left of you. Not you, Sean Kenneally, not anymore."

Sean knew the priest was right. The black hunger – the gorta, the old ones called it – had taken his father and had taken its time. His brother, Christor, refused to watch another day and had fled for England a fortnight ago, leaving only a scribble of a note. Their Ma had been gone for some years now. Consumption, they called it. A terrible cough with a name like a sacrament.

"Come with us, boy," the old priest said. "You owe it to your dear dead Da not to end up like himself, racked by the hunger, burning with the fever, delirious at the end. How could you want that for yourself, Sean? You're just a boy. You're what now? Fourteen?"

"Fifteen now, Father," Sean said. He had known of

this priest for years, but had seen him only twice. He looked to Sean the same as he had years ago, when he came to rub holy oil onto the forehead of Sean's dead mother.

"Fifteen is it now? Well surely you understand that fifteen is too young to wind up like your Da, pitched naked into a pit with so many others. Haven't you had enough of the hunger, lad, enough of the death?"

From his pulpit at St. Michael's, the old priest preached a promised land, a place with soil so black that grasses grew taller than even a tall man could reach, a place where anything would grow and everything did, even without being planted. In spring, the priest said, mushrooms as big as a grown man's fist grew like a carpet beneath the elms, and in summer wild berries grew as thick as gorse. In any season, a man with a proper musket could feed even a family of ten just by wandering the wooded hillsides thick with white-tailed deer and turkeys the size of sows. The lakes, he said, were choked with fish, big fish as long as your leg and as fat around as a smithy's right arm.

It was more than some holy grail, the priest told anyone who might listen. He had seen it himself, having traveled there by steamer with six monks sent with gold from the Mount Mellary Abbey near Cappoquin to buy cheap land in the western wilderness of America. Three died of ship's fever and were buried at sea, but Father Fraher and the others had reached the great river and traveled by steamer to the place where they started work on a new abbey. They bought more than a thousand acres of land nearby, land for houses, land for farms. It was good land, too, he said, good thick dirt, more soil than stones.

The priest told Sean of the crossing, but not the worst of it. It had been a nightmare, but no worse than what the priest had left behind. The roadsides between Youghal and Cork had been clogged by a mix of those who had starved and those who soon would, yet the ships at Cobh harbor were swollen with fat cattle and sheep, the docks stacked with countless casks of bacon and sacks of oats. Every mouthful, he knew, was bound for tables of well-fed landlords who seldom crossed the Irish Sea. Though the London papers called it famine, the priest knew The Lord would one day call it something else.

America was all Father Fraher had hoped it might be. Beyond the stinking cities he found an endless expanse of opportunity, a land that went on forever, a place where those with ambition were sure to thrive and even those with none could surely survive. He knew it at once to be a place to which he must lead whatever might remain of his flock back in Wexford. Like Moses, he would bring them across the sea, lead them to a land of honey and milk, take them far away from slavery and certain death.

When the snows were gone at last and the roads to the west had cleared, it had taken him weeks to travel overland to New York from the land west of the river the red men called Mississippi. He sailed back to Queenstown as soon as the ice would permit a crossing, enduring the cold and rain of a North Atlantic spring. Along the roads to Wexford, he anointed the dead, mixing beeswax and shoe black to replenish his last traces of sacred oil.

"Come with us, boy, you must," the priest told Sean. "Nearly a hundred are going now, good people you know from St. Michael's, people like yourself, people with nothing left to keep them here. The Heatleys are going, with all five of their young ones. Isn't their Liam about your age?"

"What if he is?" Sean said. "I haven't the passage, Father, even if I wished to go. The crossing to Liverpool and then the passage to America must cost five quid. And even one quid might as well be fifty to the likes of me. Look about, Father. Do you see anything here worth even a shilling?"

The old priest wasn't taking no.

"God will provide, Sean Kenneally," he said. "I wouldn't have hiked this hillside and be standing here asking you to be joining us if I thought for a minute there wasn't a way. Have faith, lad, faith in yourself and above all faith in Our Lord to see that you and those like you come to more than the fate of being young victims of the old hatreds. And, if you've set your mind on staying, you will be seeing to your own ruin, and don't be blaming fate or cursing Our Lord Jesus Christ for your troubles."

Sean stared down at his boots, his father's boots.

"I've arranged for a ship, a proper ship, an American ship, not a coffin ship," the priest said. "We leave next week by steamer for Liverpool and from there we will cross to America. We will sail to New Orleans, not to New York or to Canada. It's farther across, but, take my word, we'll all be better off once we arrive."

The priest had seen New York for himself, awash in sin and temptation, preying on the weak, on young lads like this. Other priests had told him the docks of Canada were even worse, the immigrant camps festering with ship's fever and cholera. Those who endured the North Atlantic crossing drank in the smell of the pines that spilled down to the banks of the St. Lawrence River, but too few lived to leave the squalor of places like Grosse Isle.

"After resting up from the crossing in New Orleans, a grand steamer will take us six days up the great river to a land without people, to a place where I have walked for days and never seen another living soul."

"Nor will you be seeing me, Father," Sean said. "I hadn't even two coppers to cover me own dead Da's eyes."

"Are you deaf now, Sean?" the priest asked. "Did I not say to leave that to me for now. I cannot leave you here, nor can I in good conscience allow you to leave yourself. To stay in Wexford is death, to be sure. There's nothing left to sustain you here, Sean, not food, not work, and from the insolent way you speak not even hope, it seems. Open your eyes, lad. Surely you can see it for yourself? You make up your mind to come, here and now, and I'll set my mind, and my prayers, on finding the means to make it so."

He was right, Sean knew. He should go.

"Today is Thursday. You bring yourself and whatever you can carry to St. Michael's on Sunday. Come well before half nine. You can come the night before if you like and sleep on the floor of the vestibule. On Sunday morning, we'll be saying a Mass, a glorious Mass of farewell to this place and to those dear to us we must leave behind. By mid-day we will be off, the lot of us, by handcart and wagon to the docks at Rosslare."

Sean didn't say no, nor did he say yes. This hillside and this small stone house were all he knew, all he had ever known. That and the death that had come to it. Still, it was home. He looked down at the old priest's muddy shoes, but could find no words.

"You think on it, lad, but not too long," the priest said. "You should pray on it as well. Kneel now."

Father Fraher laid his left hand upon the boy's head, reciting a prayer in a curious mix of Latin and Irish. Sean understood barely a word, but crossed himself along with priest.

Two days later, when Saturday came, Sean found it easy to walk away. Just as the old priest had said, there was nothing to hold him, not a hint of fondness to cloud either his eyes or his thinking. These fields had been his world for all his fifteen years, but these last few months had left him empty and numb.

He had nothing at all to bring with him to St. Michael's parish, nothing to take to America. All that was left of his Da were the boots on Sean's feet and an old clay pipe, cracked and stained but smelling still like so many evenings by the hearth. Sean tucked the pipe into a pocket already swollen with the last bites of turnip.

From Killanne, Sean would head east on the Enniscorthy road, a road he had traveled only once before, in the back of a borrowed wagon, the time when his father heard talk of jobs at the workhouse. Da would sign on and send back what he could to ward off the squire and to keep his boys as well as a few shillings would permit. Instead, they had come home together. The workhouse was filled, its courtyard swelled with starving wretches with nowhere else to go. Sean and his father waited three hours in rain for a half bowl of cold soup then spent the night in a wood well outside the city walls. Sean and his Da had slept in turns to keep the Widow Mahon's jackass from being stolen in the darkness and roasted on a spit.

That was summer last, before things went black, before Christor left him alone to watch their Da die, shriveled, pale, clutching his dead wife's rosary, his yellow eyes fixed in an empty stare, his last breath shallow and long.

Let the greedy British bastards have this place, Sean thought, looking back one more time. Little but misery has it brought me.

Chapter One

December 13, 1862
Fredericksburg, Virginia

"Captain Kenneally…Get up."

Through the fog of sleep, Sean Kenneally heard the voice, but refused to be lured away from the peace of his own vivid visions. He was back in Wexford. Not Ireland's Wexford, but Iowa's. He was listening to the peal of the cast iron bell of the church he had helped to build.

The older men had quarried the stone, letting Sean and a few other of the strongest boys handle the oxen that dragged three hundred pound blocks of limestone to a quiet grove sheltered by a stand of shag-bark hickories.

The church took shape on a site Father Fraher chose himself, consecrating it with a special Mass. They agreed to name the church St. Mary's and to name the settlement surrounding it Wexford, though the Quigleys and others who had made the journey to Iowa from Rath Droma and other places in the Avonmore Valley would have preferred to name it Wicklow.

Sean was fishing in his dream. The prairies

surrounding Wexford were quilted together by threads of rivers and creeks that ran fast and clear and were thick with fish, even some with whiskers but not scales. Until he could save enough from his trapping to build a small house of his own, Sean lived with the Flanagans, Seamus and Mary, helping Seamus turn the heavy thick sod and helping Mary pick the bugs drawn to her summer squash.

On a trip to Dubuque with Father Fraher for supplies, a lead miner had traded Sean a long-barreled rifle for five of Sean's best beaver pelts. The old man had been drunk, his fingers shaking so hard he could barely show Sean how to wrap and tie up his own paper cartridges. The rifle, he said, was a "Mississippi" used by himself in the Mexican War. Sean kept its dark walnut stock polished to the same brightness as the brass of its barrel bands and trigger guard. Just as the old miner said it would, his Mississippi proved deadly accurate, even at impossible range.

Sean listened in his dream to the wind playing through the woods on the hillside above him. The thick stands of trees surrounding all of Wexford sheltered deer and squirrels and black-eyed balls of thick brown fur, strange tree-hugging creatures with dark rings on their long bushy tails.

"Wake up, Captain," the voice said again.

It was beginning to rain in his dream. Sean could hear the low rumble of thunder and feel a burst of thick damp wind tousle his chestnut hair. He threw aside his willow pole and headed into the tall grass, drawn toward the sound of the bell. Was it the noon Angelus, or some special Mass?, he wondered. Had someone died? He must remember to ask Father Fraher.

The old priest had been right. This was a promised land. The monks who built the new New Melleray Abbey in the hills beyond Dubuque bought countless hundreds of acres for nearly nothing from the federal government now that mounted cavalry had pushed the red men west and north. The monks resold the land to those who had followed Father Fraher back to Iowa from Ireland. In his dream, Sean was back in Iowa, sprawled on his back in the tall grass surrounding Wexford of the wilderness.

"Up with you, Captain," the voice said again, this time with enough edge to steal Sean from his dream. "Meagher wants you and the other officers up to his tent by first light."

The frantic rush began before ten, the first of six suicide charges toward the well-entrenched lines of three Rebel generals. French's troops went up first, followed closely by Zooke's.

The Irish Brigade crossed pontoon bridges over the Rappahannock River just before noon. Mounted on the opposite bank, General Thomas Francis Meagher waved his saber, urging on the boys of his Brigade with shouts of encouragement. At the morning briefing, Meagher told Sean and the other assembled officers to order their men to cut green sprigs from the woods and to plant them in their caps. Meagher set the example himself, his oak leaf looking like a St. Patrick's Day shamrock.

The Rebels commenced a raking fire as the Brigade crossed a small millstream. Little more than a ditch, it skirted the fringes of Fredericksburg, which since morning had been in flames. No artillery had been put in place to

11

support the advance. The Sixty-Ninth went ahead, the Twenty-Eighth Massachusetts close behind. The men and boys of the Sixty-Ninth moved forward, double quick, plunging into a cornfield, leaving behind blankets and haversacks before sprinting from the cover of withered, stunted cornstalks into the open pasture above.

An eerie cloud of sulfur stung their eyes as a ceaseless roar of Confederate cannonade turned the mid-day sky to dusk. Through the battle fog, a first fence line was gained at a terrible price, then another some forty yards beyond. It would be as far as the Irish Brigade would advance.

Meagher later reported a tangle of bodies, one piled on another, had slowed the Brigade's assault within sixty yards of the enemy's batteries. This was not a battle, Meagher would angrily tell General Burnside's aide-de-camp, this was wholesale slaughter. The rebel's hilltop position along Marye's Heights was tactically unassailable.

Toward the end, what remained of the Sixty-Ninth New York and the Twenty-Eighth Massachusetts was felled by a hail of oblique flank fire. Those few who escaped broke for the rear or lay low among the dead, ducking a continuous spray of shot and shell, grape and canister.

Meagher's official report had every man of the Sixty-Ninth either dead or wounded, himself included. He had taken a minie ball in his left calf and hobbled to the rear after his horse was shot out from beneath him. His old and trusted friend, Major Sean Horgan, wasn't so lucky. Horgan was shot through the mouth, the ball tearing into his brain and dropping him instantly.

Despite heavy losses at Antietam in September, the Irish Brigade arrived at Fredericksburg with five full regiments, some twelve hundred men. By sundown, a full two-thirds of the Irish Brigade was gone. More than seven hundred men were dead, or left for dead, on the hillsides above Fredericksburg city, amid the groans and the gore of a place called Marye's Heights.

Somewhere within the knee-high breastwork of broken bodies marking the front was sharpshooter Sean Kenneally. Somewhere, too, was Private Jimmy O'Boyle.

❦   ❦   ❦

Two Irish Brigade recruiters had found Jimmy O'Boyle wandering the Bronx, pissed and penniless and ducking the October winds in any public house still willing to offer a stool.

The war was going badly, recruiting worse. The New York Times, with its thirst for lengthy front-page accounts of the carnage and its long lists of dead and wounded, was hardly encouraging recruits. Still, there were quotas to be filled and bounties to be paid. Jobless, shell-shocked veterans and those hopeless or full of drink were easy marks.

James Patrick O'Boyle had been forcibly put ashore at New York, ordered off a barquentine after an ugly row with the ship's First Mate. He had joined her crew in September at Boston, claiming to be an experienced cook's helper, though truth was he had never even cracked an egg. It was a lie of convenience that took him out to sea, away from the Boston slums and the threats that surrounded a gambling debt he had no means to settle.

Jimmy O'Boyle never took to sea life, but he was well apprenticed at drink. If he lived until March he would be twenty, a remarkable feat for a man who had done little else since the age of twelve but drink as much as his bungled attempts at thieving would allow. He was a better drunk than thief, and laying hands on a bottle could prove a challenge in jail, even for a smooth-skinned boy.

He wandered off the New York docks with forty-six dollars and no plans at all, except finding a bottle and a bed. A two-dollar whore helped herself to his twenty dollar gold piece after Jimmy had passed out limp, exhausted and reeking of rum. Two days later, her body was pulled from the East River, just above Benton's Wharf, her skull crushed like a melon, one breast missing, the other hacked from her torso and stuffed between her legs.

When the money ran out, Jimmy lived on the streets and slept in the alleys. For any damn fool who would keep him in pints, he would play the veteran, drawing a well-polished litany of battlefield fictions. His account of Antietam was a favorite among the Paddies too old to enlist, most of them men with brothers, sons or nephews still off to the war.

The battle of Sharpsburg had been a great Union victory and, by Jimmy's account, he had stood with the Irish Brigade through the thick of it. Early on his horse was shot from beneath him as the brave sons of Ireland rushed into the jaws of death. When the red-haired boy who carried the regimental banner was cut in two by cannon fire, it was Jimmy himself who raised up the sunburst and harp, waving the green flag in defiance at the Rebs, encouraging the stragglers behind him to push ahead for the glory of the aulde sod.

Before his story ran its course, Jimmy would, inevitably, take a bullet, sometimes to a shoulder, sometimes to a leg. Either way he would manage nonetheless to dispatch as many as fourteen Rebs to their rightful place in hell. It was a grand tale, grandly embellished, and one usually judged worthy of a whiskey in the end.

❧ ❧ ❧

The minutes passed like hours, with not a single hour passing that Jimmy O'Boyle didn't curse the day he agreed to enlist. The recruiters' fifty dollars had bought enough dark rum to make him seem invincible then, but here, at Fredericksburg, nothing seemed invincible, nothing except the Rebel line.

The Irish Brigade's assault had been underway all day and was going nowhere. Neither was Jimmy O'Boyle. A few strides from the cover of a long-abandoned stand of wilted corn, Jimmy had thrown himself down and buried his face in the mud. Not me, he thought. Let those other daft bastards waste their lives taking this fucking hill. I'm staying put.

Hundreds fell around him, each man taking to his grave his own heart-felt reason for charging up Marye's Heights. Some reasons were deeply personal, others deeply political. Most were steeped in genetic revenge centuries in the brewing. Around fires at night, amid the boredom between battles, Private O'Boyle stayed in the shadows, drinking alone while listening as the others babbled endlessly about why they were there, about the nobility of their cause, about wee ones and loved ones left behind, at home.

Every last one of them had his own story to tell, each story more than less the same. He or his people had been forced by poverty or hunger to flee Ireland's shores, a half-step ahead of John Bull's boot. What passed at first for life in New England's shanty towns taught them all, reluctantly, how to endure poverty and scorn. Both Ireland and America had made them veterans of the depravations that came with life on the march. Soldiers went hungry, soldiers went sleepless, soldiers lived like wild beasts in the cold and the rain. Soldiers died of the fever more often than wounds. So had these Paddies. In America, as in Ireland, they had endured it all before.

For their trouble they also had learned hate, a bottomless and seething contempt for all things British and an even deeper resentment of the coloreds who, now free, dared to take what few jobs the Irish had finally claimed as their own. This war was about many things, to be certain, but to these Irish troops it was about emancipating themselves, not the coloreds.

To the Protestant hierarchy that for centuries had controlled their miserable lives on both sides of the Atlantic, the Irish were worse than the coloreds. They were lazy, shiftless, drunken, rosary-mumbling papists portrayed even in the House of Lords as living, breathing proof of the blasphemous assertion of linkage between man and ape. A pity the famine and Providence had reduced their numbers only by a million.

Jimmy O'Boyle hated Meagher and had for long before the General ordered him up this hillside. Meagher reminded Jimmy of some half-witted New York politician working the Paddy vote at a Jones's Woods picnic. The General's visits to each regiment inevitably fanned the fires of their hatred and their resolve, and each appearance required a speech. If none was planned, the men would insist, loudly, until the General finally obliged.

His men worshipped Meagher, most of them. After every oration, they would drown him in cheers, waving their hats in mad demonstrations that lasted as long as the speeches themselves. Meagher was the stuff of heroes. Through the Irish Brigade, he had made these men an extension of himself, of his legend, of the tradition of the Young Islanders, the men of '48. In this great war Meagher was their Finn McCool, they his warriors, his trusted Fianna.

After mounting a caisson or climbing onto the bed of a wagon, Meagher would begin slowly, his voice building gradually from a whisper to a shout and then back again to a whisper. He would thrash the sky with tightly clenched fists, sounding to the crush of men surrounding him like some reincarnation of The Great Liberator himself, Daniel O'Connell.

"I have heard it said, from both within and without these ranks, that you men of the Irish Brigade are overworked," Meagher told his exhausted troops a few days after Antietam. "As Heaven is my witness, it is not so. Many are the little privations. Many are the severe duties. And great is the fatigue and great the exhaustion. But, sons of Ireland, great as well is our just cause. And it is the greatness and justness of that cause that keeps us going.

"You have had no more marching to do than other brigades. Nor have you done any more duty in the trenches or on picket than other brigades. Nor have you been any more exposed to the unhealthiness of the climate, to the dampness, to the miasma, to the drenching rain of the deadening sun. What you have done more of is fighting."

It was a well-rehearsed line that, inevitably, sent a wave of cheers through the ranks.

"Well, whose fault is that?" Meagher shouted through the cheers. "If Irishmen had not long ago established a reputation for superlative ability at fighting, the Irish Brigade would not have any more fighting to do than anyone else. But it's in your blood, lads. And once we together have won this fight at hand, we have other battles that will take us home to those green shores across the sea, to raise this poor beggar of a nation to its inevitable and rightful place among the nations of the free.

"When it comes to England, lads, and come to England it will, always remember this. The man that will listen to reason let him be reasoned with. But it is the weaponed arm of the patriot that can alone prevail against battalioned despotism. Ireland is destined, as are you to make it so, to be a nation like this great Republic for which we stand today, prosperous, limitless and invincible."

🦋 🦋 🦋

As others dropped around him, Jimmy O'Boyle dragged himself toward the body of a boy without a face. A fragment of the boy's skull dangled limply from what this morning had been his neck. Jimmy moved close against the body, burying his face in his hand and burying his hands into a mix of mud, blood and the dead boy's brains.

In the semi-darkness of a quarter moon the lethal hail finally began to subside. Jimmy crawled slowly to his left, burrowing himself beneath two still-warm bodies, the blood pooling beneath him and soaking his woolen britches.

The shrieks and plaintiff prayers of those shattered and half-dead carried over the numbing chill and down the hillside to the others at the rear tending wounds of their own and the wounds of others. They carried above as well, where greyback marksmen used the moonlight to make quick work of what few brave souls ventured up to offer aid.

By first light, the Confederates agreed to give the Federals three hours to tend the wounded and cart off the dead. Jimmy awakened from a shallow doze to the sound of his own chattering teeth and the huffing of teams straining to pull burial wagons up the steep hillside. The overnight cold had left his blood-soaked britches as stiff as hardtack. Jimmy needed a wound, a head wound to account for his unconsciousness.

He groped beneath the bearded corpse to his left and came up with a bayonet. Gritting his teeth, Jimmy raked its point across his forehead, slicing the skin deeply from the crest of his forehead to base of his left ear. Blood poured into his eyes and dripped down his left cheek. Through a squint he watched, motionless, as the detail approached.

Chapter Two

June 4, 1866
Stevensville, Ontario

She slipped into the barn, inching along quietly on the balls of her bare feet. A chill rushed through her, melting into the excitement that had overtaken her exhaustion, keeping her from sleep. Over the nickers of her father's aging cart horse she listened carefully for the Fenian's labored breathing.

By morning, he would be gone. It was an unsettling realization, a gnawing fear that refused to leave her thoughts. It had coaxed her from beneath the warmth of the bulky quilt she now wore as a shawl. She would come to Sean Kenneally as he had come to her, blood-stained forbidden fruit, out of nowhere, out of a dream.

❦   ❦   ❦

It was Saturday, sometime before midday, when, through the window by the dry sink, Katherine spotted him, dazed and panting, stumbling out of their field of young corn and collapsing by the trough. She ran startled out the front door. Father was in the garden. He would know what to do.

Breathless, Katherine told her father what she had seen. A man was in their yard, around back. His boots were muddy, his face streaked with scratches and grime. One shoulder of his dark green shirt had gone brown. It looked to be soaked in blood.

Jeremias Tucker left the fork in the furrow where he was spreading manure and took Katherine's hand. Together they found the man collapsed face down. They approached him slowly. Jeremias could see he was breathing. He also could see he was bleeding.

"Help me roll him onto his back," he said to Katherine, who kept her distance.

"Who is he?" Katherine asked.

"I know him not," Jeremias said.

"Will he die?" Katherine asked.

Her father did not answer.

Katherine was startled to see the bleeding man's eyes were open. His gaze appeared to be on her as she stared down at him. What unsettled her most was that he seemed not to see her, or anything else.

"He's been shot," Jeremias said, peeling back the wounded man's shirt. "And he is bleeding still. We must move him inside."

Jeremias Tucker was a quiet man. He kept to himself and was known among those who farmed this desolate corner of Niagara Frontier only as "The Quaker." He and Katherine were new to British America, having come to Ontario in the fall of 1863, settling on a farm south of Stevensville left abandoned by a widower's passing. With his daughter in tow, he had fled Pennsylvania, reluctant to leave behind his dead wife's grave, but eager to escape the war, which he feared would spread well beyond Gettysburg. Now, apparently, it had.

All spring, the Canadian border towns had been ripe with stories and rumors of American Fenians. Not a week went by that the papers weren't peppered with items on roving bands of Irish pirates poised to violate the border and ravage the surrounding countryside. In April, they had tried to capture Campobello, an island near the Maine-New Brunswick border. The whole affair had been a fiasco.

These Fenians, the papers said, drilled openly in Buffalo, waving green banners embroidered with golden harps. They gathered by the thousands in the streets of Boston, wearing military uniforms and carrying weapons purchased openly from U.S. government arsenals. The Toronto Globe said Fenians could be found as far west as Chicago. At a recent Fenian convention in Philadelphia, they openly advocated an armed invasion of Canada, declaring they would capture enough of Her Majesty's North America to persuade the English to forever abandon its stranglehold on Ireland. The Philadelphia threats had sent the British ambassador to the United States into an apoplectic rage.

The Irish had overrun America in a single generation, and much of Canada as well. With an Irishman now in the

White House, anything seemed possible, including war between England and America. Even so soon after so many had died in the Great War of the Rebellion, brother killing brother, Irish killing Irish, the papers said a Canadian invasion and yet another war with England were not out of the question.

Jeremias Tucker hated war. He hated guns. He hated shallow human intolerance and the venom that it spawned. He hated men who hated, men who hated enough to kill, though he knew in his heart that his hatred, like their own, was just as terrible a sin.

Governor-General Charles Stanley Monck had called for fourteen thousand volunteers to repel any Fenian incursions onto Canadian soil. Members of the Queen's Own Rifles Regiment, wearing sabers on their belts, went house to house, farm to farm, recruiting a militia and offering breechloading rifles to all who signed on. No one came by Jeremias Tucker's farm. Quakers would not fight.

She came to him in the darkness, dropping her quilt and slipping beneath his woolen blanket. The Fenian wore only a shirt, the one her father had offered in the hope of never seeing him again. He slept on his side, his good shoulder carrying his weight.

She moved against him, the length of her warmth now pressing against his back. When he stirred only slightly, she let one knee find its way into the ridge between his thighs and with it began caressing him there. She moved one arm around him, slipping her hand inside her father's shirt, spinning tiny circles in the tangle of hairs on his chest.

Slowly, gently, she coaxed him from a deep and dreamless sleep.

As her warmth ebbed through him, the muscles in his back began to tighten. His body suddenly stiffened, then twitched in one quick and strong convulsion that trapped her probing knee between his thighs.

He was awake now and fully aware he was not alone. He had known dreams like this before. But, he could smell her soap, feel her hot breath on his shoulder. This was no dream.

He released her knee and rolled toward her, onto his back. He searched her features in the near darkness of the barn.

"Speak not, Sean Kenneally," she said in a whisper, running a finger across his lips. "Awaken Jeremias and you awaken the wrath of God."

❦ ❦ ❦

They struggled together to carry the wounded man inside, the soles of his heavy boots streaking Katherine's dress with mud as she strained to lift his legs clear of the three porch steps. They moved him slowly through the kitchen and into the parlor, setting him on the floor, close to the hearth.

"Put on the kettle and find a clean sheet and tear it into long, narrow strips," her father told Katherine.

The young man remained dazed as Jeremias used a bone-handled knife to cut away his blood-soaked shirt.

"Bring me a cloth and wet it from the kettle," he called over one shoulder to Katherine. "Hot, but not too hot."

With it Jeremias swiped at the matted blood. A ball from a rifle had struck the right shoulder, leaving a bloody black spot.

"Help me roll him onto his side," Jeremias said. "His left side."

Katherine could see a dirty, oozing tear in the man's upper back. The sight of it made her queasy. She turned her head away. The bullet had passed through him. Thank God for that, Jeremias thought. He might bleed to death still, but there would be little chance of new infection.

The wounded man drifted in and out of consciousness as they worked together to clean and bind his shoulder. If the bleeding stopped, Jeremias would pack both wounds, front and back, with a steaming poultice of herbs to draw off any fever within.

Katherine kept her distance, careful to do no more than her father asked.

She removed the wounded man's muddy boots and used a warm, wet cloth to wipe the smudges from his ruddy face. She felt his hot breath on the back of her hand as she tried to recall the color of eyes now hidden by sleep.

The bleeding finally stopped, and the pungent aroma of poultice filled the house. Time and tea, small sips taken unawares, eventually brought him around.

"Where am I?" he asked, emerging from his trance, drowsy and disoriented. He tried to sit up, but pain pushed him back. His right shoulder throbbed. When he turned his head to see why, the pain tore through him again.

"Where am I?" he asked again, in a voice just above a whisper.

The room was nearly dark, lit only by soft, long shadows that danced on what little firelight managed to escape the hearth. His eyes focused on a bearded man, seated an arm's length away on a stool. "Who are you?"

"I am Jeremias Tucker, a farmer, and you are in my house, in Ontario, in Canada, not far from Ridgeway," Jeremias said. "You have been shot. You wandered here through my fields."

Sean thought back to the morning, but little came to mind.

"You were bleeding, and you collapsed in my yard," the old man said. "That was hours ago. My daughter, Katherine, and I have been tending to you since."

Sean laid back and closed his eyes. With each deep breath more memories surfaced. There had been a timber, just off their right flank, a thick grove of maples surrounding a field near the fork in the road. He remembered hearing shots.

"Where's my Whitworth?" he asked suddenly. "Do you have it?

"What's a 'Whitworth'?" Jeremias asked.

26

"A rifle," he said. "My rifle. Do you have it?"

"You had no rifle," Jeremias said. "At least not when we found you, or when you found us. There was a pouch of cartridges, which I removed with your belt. It's over there, in the corner. Other than that, you had nothing, except a hole in your shoulder and an Irish look to you. You were wearing a green shirt, which is now a blood-soaked rag that I burned in the stove. From the look of that shirt I presume you are a Fenian, one of those we had been warned to keep watch for."

"That I am," he said. "A Fenian. And what's become of the boys? The others? Were the others shot up as well?"

"I cannot say," Jeremias told him. "I knew nothing of any of this until you collapsed in my yard. I know little more now. No one stops here as a rule, and neither I nor my daughter has been to town, where there might be some news. What has become of the others I cannot say."

After a long silence, Jeremias realized he didn't know this man's name.

"What shall we call you?"

The Fenian said his name was Sean, Sean Kenneally, born in County Wexford, Ireland, and since the War of the Rebellion of New York City.

❦   ❦   ❦

"What day is it?" Sean asked.

It was Saturday, Jeremias told him. The second day of June, 1866.

Sean told Jeremias he had crossed over the Niagara River with a few hundred others two days earlier, late Thursday night. He was a captain, he said, an officer in the army of the Fenian Brotherhood. It was the work of the Brotherhood that had brought him to New York and then into Canada.

What Sean didn't tell him, he hadn't been told himself: the Brotherhood was in shambles, its leadership now crippled by years of divisive infighting. By 1865, the Brotherhood's founding fathers, Stephens and O'Mahony, had gone their separate ways. Since then, a year had passed, but not the feuding rooted in what were perceived as promises too long unkempt.

For more years than John O'Mahony cared to remember, James Stephens had promised rebellion in Ireland. Again and again, whether speaking in Ireland or preaching to the faithful in America, Stephens never failed to tell the crowds that his Irish Republican Brotherhood was on the verge of military action that would liberate all of Ireland. It would, he said, be a blow for freedom and for justice made possible with weapons and funds provided by America's Fenian Brotherhood. When will it happen?, the faithful would ask. Soon, Stephens told them, very soon. But soon never came soon enough for John O'Mahony.

For too many years, O'Mahony had watched his Fenian Brotherhood smuggle monthly stipends of cash into Ireland for Stephens and his Irish Republican Brotherhood. Countless thousands in contributions were collected at Fenian picnics and bazaars, fairs and dances. It amounted to a fortune, nearly all of it amassed in nickels and dimes, the offerings of Irish chambermaids and destitute Irish laborers who, despite their dismal situations, could never bring themselves to say no to the cause.

❦ ❦ ❦

O'Mahony demanded action. He had made promises of his own, promises to Irish Brigade veterans like Sean Kenneally, men like himself who demanded insurrection now, not later. If Stephens, in all his dictatorial arrogance, wasn't willing to commit the IRB to action in Ireland, O'Mahony would send Fenians eager to fight, brave lads like Sean Kenneally, to move on Canada instead.

❦ ❦ ❦

Fully awake now, he tried turning towards her, but his throbbing shoulder refused his weight. She touched his chest, urging him with the gentle pressure of her hand to remain on his back. She threw a leg over him, trapping his heat and his hardness beneath her right thigh.

Her hand traced its way from his chest to his stomach, then lower still. She kissed his right shoulder, just where a spot of flesh peeked through the strips of white sheet her father had used to bind his wounds.

She raised her leg slightly to make way for her hand. Her fingertips seemed alive, each on its own, exploring the delicate hairs that covered his belly. Her fingers wandered further, coming together around the thickness of his shaft. She squeezed him there gently, feeling his heat now ebb through her. With each rhythmic caress, his breathing became shallow and erratic. So, she noticed, had her own.

"Katherine," he said at last, speaking just above a

whisper. "Why are you doing this?"

It seemed to her such a foolish question.

❦ ❦ ❦

Sean Kenneally had scared her at first, appearing out of nowhere, flirting with death. Katherine had never seen anything like him, so strong yet so vulnerable. He reminded her of a wounded buck she had seen as a girl, struggling wide-eyed and frantic to outpace the hunters who failed to drop it cleanly.

There was little clean about death, she knew. It was a lesson Katherine learned at her mother's bedside, watching her succumb to a slow and painful end. That was seven years ago, when Katherine was nineteen. With her mother dead, she had little time now to do much more than keep her father's house. The youngest of the Copic boys, Nathaniel, had shown some interest in her once, but Jeremias had scared him off, warning her in the bargain that most men wanted nothing more from young women like herself than to defile the temple of the Lord. The move from Pennsylvania was made against her own wishes, wishes never expressed.

After helping her father move the Fenian inside, Katherine had been afraid to be near this Sean Kenneally, yet found herself afraid to leave him, afraid he would die, alone. After tending his wounds, her father calmed her, assuring her this stranger would live and that he would do them no harm. It was, her father explained, their Christian duty to treat his wounds, to restore him to health, even if he was a Fenian on the run. Only in health, Jeremias told her, could they rightfully send him on his way.

"And what if they come for him, father?" she asked. "What if the Queen's soldiers, those who shot him, track him here, to our farm? What will they do to him, and to us for keeping him here? For hiding him?"

"We have done nothing, child, but what as Christians we must," her father told her. "They will understand."

Katherine was not so sure.

The Fenian had appeared at mid-day. By evening the worst had passed. From the kitchen she heard him tell Jeremias how Fenians had come to take for themselves a piece of British North America, just as England had helped herself to all of Ireland, many centuries ago.

Her father told Katherine to cook the Fenian something soft, porridge or broth or a peeled potato mashed in cream. She boiled two handfuls of oats and thinned the thick paste with watered-down cream before adding a small bit of honey. When the mixture had cooled, she spooned nearly half of it into a large wooden bowl.

The Fenian ate heartily, spilling at first as he trained his left arm to carry each spoonful of sweet oats to his mouth. Katherine watched from a distance, feeling somehow safer in the shadows.

"He's better now," her father told her, bringing the empty bowl into the kitchen. "The oats will do him good, as will a good night's sleep."

Jeremias Tucker began pulling on his coat.

"Father," Katherine said, somewhat alarmed. "Where are you going? You're not leaving me here, alone, with him."

31

"To the barn," Jeremias said, surprised by her tone. "To throw some hay to the horses and corn to the hens." He sensed the concern in her eyes. They were as deeply blue and as easily read as her mother's had been.

"No worries, child," he said, reaching out to stroke her cheek. "This fierce Irish warrior seems to me little more than an overgrown boy, and he's certainly no danger to you. Keep your distance if you like, but he'll do us no harm. God will see to that."

Katherine watched with concern as her father slipped through the door, taking with him the lantern that hung by a nail in the wall. She watched out the window until the light of the lantern grew dim in the darkness.

As she turned back to the dishes, she let out a gasp that was not quite a scream. The Fenian was there, in the kitchen, leaning against the frame of the doorway to the parlor, looking as if he would collapse without its support.

"I didn't mean to scare you," he said in a manner she took as sincere. Her reaction had startled him, too. "It's just that I have to, you know, go," he told her.

"Go?" she said, incredulous. "You can't go! Look at you. You can barely stand. Surely you know you have lost a lot of blood."

She surprised herself with her directness. He was a stranger, perhaps a dangerous stranger, a man some years older than herself.

"No," he said, somewhat embarrassed. "That's not what I mean. What I mean is can you direct me to the outhouse? I have to ... go."

Katherine's complexion went crimson. Now it was she who was embarrassed.

"Oh, yes, of course," she said, not knowing what else to say. "It's out this back door, down the end of the stone path that leads off to the right. But, it's dark out now. You will need some light, and Father has taken the lantern to the barn."

What am I doing?, she thought to herself. I've told him we are here alone. "Sorry, lass, but I'll chance it in the dark," he said, forcing a smile. "It just won't wait."

No one had ever called her "lass." It was a term Katherine thought Scottish. It sounded odd coming from an Irishman.

"We've an oil lamp upstairs, in the north bedroom." My bedroom, she thought. "Wait here while I run up for it. Wait here."

She moved past him, carefully turning sideways as she inched through the doorway, careful not to brush up against him.

"I'll be right back," she said, her eyes meeting his, checking their color.

They were a deep shade of green, deep green and glassy with exhaustion. "You wait," she said nervously. "Right here."

Even with the help of the door frame, Sean found it a challenge to stand. He'd taken a bullet before, the first at Antietam and another at Marye's Heights. There was hardly a veteran of the Irish Brigade who hadn't been shot at least once. Unlike too many others, at least Sean was whole.

What happened?, he wondered. How was I shot?

He remembered taking the point, leading his reconnaissance squad south from the Fenian camp just east of Black Creek toward what his map showed to be the Garrison Road. They were some miles west of Fort Erie, the settlement directly across the Niagara River from Buffalo. Only an hour out from camp, they were no more than a mile north of Ridgeway, the village on the lake where Colonel Hoey told Sean to expect some resistance.

There had been no resistance, not at first. No one confronted them when eight hundred Fenians crossed in the night on canal boats from Black Rock. No one challenged even their daylight advance as they boldly marched on Canadian soil north from Frenchman's Creek, along the River Road. They hadn't seen a British soldier until the expedition's second day, when six Fenian battalions, including one from Tennessee, began moving on Ridgeway.

Sean remembered now crossing into a wheat field, where he heard the first of the shots. Puffs of white smoke appeared behind a scattering of pine stumps at the edge of the timberline. Then his shoulder seemed on fire.

"Here you are," said a voice, a voice Sean couldn't place.

It was a woman, holding out a lamp. He stared, transfixed, as her long chestnut hair glowed in the lamplight.

"Oh, thank you," he said, remembering at once where he was and why this young beauty was offering him a lamp. Katherine, the old man had called her.

"I appreciate it, Katherine. And not only the lamp, you understand, but you and your father taking me in, under the circumstances. You have saved my life, or at least have saved me from hanging."

She looked at him with an odd expression, a look of fascination tinged with fear.

"I'll be back," he assured her. "I'll not be gone long."

Katherine studied him from behind as he made his way across the kitchen and out the back door. He was, she guessed, twenty-eight or maybe even thirty, which would make him just a few years older than herself. He was tall, at least six feet, and his shoulders were broad, though his legs somewhat bowed. She wondered if he had a family, a wife perhaps, or children, all of them waiting and worried back in America.

The dishes washed, Katherine began sweeping. A beacon of lamplight appeared in the doorway. The Fenian had returned, with Jeremias close behind.

"Katherine," her father said as he came through the door. "Bring down some blankets, or one of our quilts. Mr. Kenneally will be spending the night by the hearth."

She returned from upstairs with a gray woolen blanket and a quilt her mother had pieced together from squares of woolens and flannels scavenged from Jeremias' well-worn clothes. The Fenian and her father sat together near the fire.

"I'll change his dressings and sit up with him a while," her father told Katherine as she set the bedding on a chair near the hearth. "You best get yourself to bed."

Reluctantly, Katherine made her way upstairs, noticing as she removed her dress how it was streaked with mud from the Fenian's boots. She pulled on a long flannel nightgown and slipped beneath her quilt, the quilt she had made as a girl while learning the stitches from her mother. Sleep came slowly, even though Katherine was exhausted from what had been a most unusual day.

The Fenian's eyes had been glassy, but so terribly green. He seemed at first crude, yet he spoke with a gentleness that surprised her in a man who was clearly no stranger to guns, to war and to the horrible deaths that came with it. And when she handed him the lamp, he had looked at her in a way that made her think now that Sean Kenneally had no wife. She seemed certain no children waited at home. She knew now, like herself, he had no one.

❧ ❧ ❧

Though sleep had come slowly, first light had not. When morning came, soldiers did, too. Katherine was filling a kettle when she saw them from the window through which she had first spotted Sean. There were three, on horses. Each had a rifle and a saber.

Father was somewhere inside the barn. She had last seen the Fenian resting in the parlor, awake and dressed and sprawled on the floor by the hearth. She followed the soldiers' movements from one window to the next. All three dismounted and watered their horses. If there was blood by the trough, no one seemed to notice.

Katherine moved into the parlor, where she found

Sean crouched by the window, studying through a slit in the curtains the men he had heard outside. Through the window, they watched the youngest of the soldiers disappear into the barn, the others close behind.

"You must hide yourself," Katherine told him. "If they find you here, you'll be hung for sure."

"Give me your gun," Sean said, feeling helpless and more vulnerable than he cared to feel. "Your father must have a gun, whatever gun he hunts with."

"There are no guns here, Sean Kenneally, nor will there ever be in my father's house," she said. "And if there were a gun, it would be the death of you, what with one of you and three of them. We must hide you away until they have left. Come with me, quick now, and keep yourself back from the windows."

Sean followed her back to the kitchen. Recessed in one corner of the kitchen floor was a hinged doorway that opened to a dirt-floored root cellar. Katherine tugged on the ring and pulled back the door, revealing a short wooden stairway.

"Get yourself below and keep still," she told Sean. "I can hide this door beneath a rug."

Sean disappeared into the dark and damp. As the door dropped behind him, he sat on the bottom step, listening carefully to Katherine's every step. He could see almost nothing, even as his eyes began adjusting to the dark.

Above him, Katherine grabbed up the tattered rag rug from in front of the dry sink and spread it in the comer, pulling a chair away from the table and placing it and a pair of her father's boots onto the rug.

The soldiers checking the barn startled Jeremias, who was busy picking the hooves of his Percheron mare. A wounded Fenian was seen heading this way, the soldiers told Jeremias. They had followed a confusing trail of bootprints and blood. Had he seen the man?

Jeremias told as few lies as he could, hoping Katherine or the Fenian had seen these soldiers approach.

The worst of the fighting appeared to be over, one soldier said. Quite a few of their own regiment had been wounded in skirmishes with the Fenians, and six or eight from another regiment had been killed, some of them just boys. Among the dead were students from the militia at Queen's College in Toronto. Dozens of Fenians had been captured near Ridgeway. Word was the prisoners would be hung before the week was out.

"Most of the Paddy bastards ran off like scared rabbits," the soldier who appeared in charge told Jeremias. "They crossed back over the river, back to the States, just north of Fort Erie. We've decided among ourselves they won't be hanging this Fenian if we stumble upon him first."

Sean followed the sound of Katherine's steps as she left the kitchen and moved into the parlor to keep watch out the window nearest the barn. From a basket near the hearth, she collected an armful of kindling. She brought it back to the kitchen, nervously tossing it into the stove, encouraging the embers to consume what remained of the bloodied strips of sheet her father used to bind the Fenian's wound.

"You're free to look about, of course," Jeremias told

the soldiers. He hated lies and didn't tell them well. "As I've said, it's just my daughter and myself here. We have seen nothing unusual, nor heard anything as well."

Two of the soldiers searched the barn, peering into stalls and checking the loft above, poking their rifles into what little hay remained after a brutal winter. The third soldier headed outside, studying the ground, pacing the parameter of the yard. As she looked out again, Katherine saw him coming toward the house, his rifle off his shoulder now.

God help us, she thought, taking in a deep breath. "Be calm now, be calm," she said to herself in a nervous whisper. Though she heard the soldier's boots on the porch, his heavy pounding on the door startled her.

She opened the door and saw he was tall and dark, with two days' growth of beard and strange black eyes that burned into her own. He looked to be twenty-five, maybe younger.

"Yes?" she said in a voice even she could barely hear.

"We're here to search your farm," the soldier said. "We're with the Queen's Own Rifles, and we've tracked a wounded Fenian through your fields. Your father, in the barn, said we could have a look, which I will if you'll step aside."

He was having a look, Katherine noticed, a long look, at her. His eyes roamed the front of her in a way that made Katherine feel as if he could see right through her blue linen dress. If he touched her, she would scream.

"Your father is lying," he said at last, watching her

eyes as he spoke.

"My father doesn't lie," she said. "And neither do I. And why would we? There are no Fenians here."

"There are tracks and blood that lead to this place, and none anywhere I can find that lead away," the soldier said, looking past her at the layout of the house.

Katherine said nothing.

"You wait here," the soldier said, turning away and bounding up the stairs to bedrooms above. Like Sean below in the cellar, Katherine listened to the floorboards creak above her. The soldier was in her father's room, moving now toward her own. When he finally reappeared at the bottom of the stairway; he was clutching the thin white camisole Katherine kept neatly folded on the shelf of her wardrobe. It had been her mother's, and Katherine often slept in it on hot summer nights.

"Very nice," the soldier said through his thin, crooked smile. He pressed the camisole to his face, as if to smell it.

"Give me that, you bastard," Katherine said, her boldness surprising herself. She rushed toward this leering man, despite his rifle. "That's my dead mother's and you'll not be defiling her memory with your schoolboy impudence."

As she reached for the camisole, the soldier caught her hand, squeezing it until her fingers went red, then white. His grasp tightened until the pain brought tears to her eyes.

"Where's the Fenian, woman?" the soldier demanded.

"He wasn't in your bed, as I suspected."

He released her throbbing hand and threw the camisole over his shoulder, half way up the steps. She was crying now as she rubbed some feeling back into her hand. The soldier glared at her as he headed into the kitchen, stopping to touch the stove.

"Burning your stove in June, are you?" he said, glancing back at her, pleased to have reduced her to tears. He opened the fire box and glanced inside.

"And what have we here?" he asked Katherine in a mocking tone, carefully lifting out a half-charred piece of white cloth smudged with smoke and soot but still clearly soaked with blood. Just as he had smelled the camisole, the soldier held the blood-soaked strip of cloth up to his face.

"Looks like blood to me," the soldier said. "Looks to me like blood on bandages, on bandages you've tried to burn. Fenian blood."

"It is blood," Katherine said, her pain now giving way to rage. "Mine. Women bleed. Or didn't you know?"

He dropped the cloth at once, as if it were hot, realizing suddenly what her words meant.

"Get in the kitchen!" he shouted. Katherine walked past him as he closed the firebox. She moved against the dry sink, never turning her back to him, glancing through the window for some sign of her father.

"Sit!" the soldier said, grabbing Katherine by one shoulder and pushing her down into the chair she had moved onto the rug to hide the doorway to the cellar.

41

"Take up your dress."

"I will not!" Katherine said, her rage giving way to contempt.

"Take up your dress and pull down your knickers," the soldier said. "If that blood is your own we'll both know it soon enough."

Sean was crouched just inches beneath them, one ear pressed against the floorboards, taking in every painful word, feeling every step. Were it not for the others still somewhere outside, he would kill this English bastard with his own hands.

"I won't!" Katherine said. "What kind of an animal are you? What have we done to you? We have nothing to hide. There are no Fenians here. Leave us alone."

"Either you will take up your dress, or I will," the soldier said.

Neither moved for what seemed to Katherine a full minute. Then the soldier backed toward the door, never taking his eyes from her own. With the butt of his rifle he broke out the glass in the window of the door. The sound of it reduced Katherine to tears.

"Charles! Henry!" he shouted. "Come here, to the house, both of you." In an instant, the others appeared on the porch, peering through the broken glass.

"What is it?" one asked. "What have you found?"

"More than I bargained for, it appears," the soldier inside told the others. "Where's the old man?"

"In the barn still," one said. "He's working on his mare as if we weren't even here. We've found nothing."

"I have. These people are lying. They know more than they've said. There are some blood-soaked bandages in the stove, bandages I'm sure they used to dress the Fenian's wounds. This woman tried to burn them when we arrived to search the farm."

"The Fenian, is he still here you think?"

"Long gone, I suspect, but before long I'll know more about when he left and where he was headed. You two take the old man back to Ridgeway. We'll get more answers from him there. I'll follow with the daughter."

He gave the others a knowing look.

"Ah, will you now?" one of the others said, looking past the doorway into the kitchen. He could hear a woman, crying softly. "And knowing you, Lloyd, it shouldn't be too long."

"Up your arse," the one they called Lloyd said. "Go! Now! Head back to Ridgeway with the old man. I'll be along with the girl."

"And if he refuses to go? ..."

"Shoot him."

Katherine's whimpers built to a scream. "Leave him alone!" she shouted. "You leave my father alone!"

"Shut your face, you lying bitch," Lloyd said, raising his rifle as if to strike Katherine with its stock.

Sean felt trapped and enraged. These men so eager to terrorize those who had helped him were a few feet away, yet Sean was entombed in this cellar, powerless to intercede. "Go! Now!" he heard the voice above say again. Footsteps left the porch and silence filled the kitchen above him.

Katherine sat in silence, her face to the floor, praying silently she would not hear the sound of a rifle coming from the barn.

"There was a Fenian here," she said at last. "He was shot, in the leg, and he appeared on our porch with a gun to my father's head and said he would kill us both if we didn't tend to his wound. He left last night, but not before saying that if we told anyone at all that he was here he would have other Fenians come back here and kill us in our sleep."

"So, the blood on the rags isn't yours after all."

"No," Katherine said.

"That's good," Lloyd said, leering at her again. "That's very good."

From the window Lloyd could see the others leading the old man out of the barn at gunpoint. They had cinched his wrists together at his waist. The two soldiers worked Jeremias onto the back of one of their horses.

As they disappeared up the lane, Lloyd shouted to them through the broken window. "Don't worry, old man, I'll take very good care of your daughter."

Tears stained his cheeks as Jeremias and the soldiers headed onto the road. "For hiding a Fenian you may hang, too," one of them told him. "And don't try to run off, old man. I've a bullet for your back if you do."

Katherine sat motionless, wondering what to do. Sean was just below them and must have heard every word. Despite his shoulder, she knew he would risk himself to keep her safe from this brute named Lloyd. He blocked the doorway to the porch, but she could make a dash for the parlor, drawing him after her, giving Sean a chance to free himself from the cellar.

She looked up from the floor to see the soldier rubbing the front of his black woolen trousers, stroking himself with the hand not clutching his rifle.

"I don't suppose a farm girl like you has ever seen anything quite like this," he said through his twisted grin. He began to unbutton his now-bulging fly. "As I said before, missy, up with that dress. And down with your knickers."

Katherine felt tears coming on again. She knew the fear building within her could only get in the way of seeing her through this, but the fear refused to be ignored. She choked back tears and forced a weak smile.

"I'm not a virgin, you know," she said, lying as best she could. "I'm twenty-six, and I know how to please a man."

"Do you now?" the soldier asked in a mocking tone. "Not a man like me, you don't."

Lloyd released his belt and laid it and his saber on the kitchen table. He began fumbling with his trousers, then realized he couldn't pull them off without first removing his boots. Katherine noticed, too.

"Promise not to hurt me, and I'll do as you like," she said. "If you promise just to leave when you've finished, I'll not run off or put up a fight, I promise. I have no reason to fight you now, now that my father is away. It would kill him to know that I understand how good a man can feel."

Katherine buried her hatred and gave him a smile. She stood and unfastened two buttons of her dress, those just below her high collar. Beneath the blue linen her knees were shaking.

"Sit here, on this chair," she said. "I'll help you off with your boots. I do it for father all the time."

Lloyd gave her a curious look. Still gripping his rifle, he waddled across the kitchen, his trousers bunched at his knees. As he neared the chair Katherine had offered, the floor below it erupted, launching the chair and the rug beneath it three feet into the air.

Lloyd's legs disappeared beneath him as Sean reached out from the stairway with his one good arm and swept away the soldier's feet. The kitchen shook as Lloyd crashed to the floor, more stunned than hurt.

Sean sprang from the cellar, pushing Katherine aside before driving a boot into the back of Lloyd's head. His other boot came down hard on the hand that gripped the rifle, hard enough to break the soldier's wrist. Lloyd screamed in pain, but only for an instant as he rolled onto his back. The rifle's brass butt plate caught him in the throat, silencing his screams, crushing his windpipe. The next blow opened his skull.

Katherine watched in silent shock as the blood pooled and flowed slowly toward her feet. Sean was splattered with it, as were the walls and ceiling.

"Stay here," Sean told Katherine, using the curtains to wipe the blood from the dead soldier's rifle. "He'll not be bothering you again."

"My father!" Katherine screamed. "They've taken Jeremias. They've taken him to Ridgeway."

"I know," Sean said, scrambling out the door. "And I shall take him back."

※　※　※

The dead soldier's rifle was a lever-action carbine, a Spencer repeater with a seven-round magazine buried within its blood-stained stock. Hardly a Whitworth, but Sean could make do.

The horse left tied at the trough had an awkward gait, but was faster than Sean expected. Jeremias and the soldiers were at least ten minutes gone, but Ridgeway was a half hour's ride. Sean knew this horse could catch them. Or it might if no one took after a blood-spattered Fenian racing past them with a carbine.

Poor Katherine, Sean thought, scared half to death, scared for herself and for her father. And all because they had tried to keep him from bleeding to death. Katherine, he was certain, had seen her fill of blood.

As the gelding drove on, Sean checked the Spencer. The carbine hadn't been recently fired and badly needed cleaning. There was one cartridge in the barrel and seven others in the stock. Two soldiers, eight rounds.

The road curved through the pines as it began its

descent into the valley below the ridgelines overlooking Lake Erie. A quarter-mile ahead and slightly below him, Sean spotted three men on two horses that were moving only slightly faster than a walk. The road below them curved off to the right as it traversed a steep hill that would take them down to the outskirts of Ridgeway.

Sean kicked the gelding into a frantic gallop and then reigned him hard, off the road, up into the hillside towering above it. Staying to the tall grasses that melted into the treeline, Sean slapped the gelding's withers with the loose ends of the reigns, shortening the distance between himself and three men below.

Sean shortened the distance by another 100 yards and then pulled up the gelding, lashing the reigns to a long-fallen pine. He sprinted to the ridgeline and dropped down on his belly, pressing the stock of the carbine into his throbbing right shoulder. The Spencer's sights were crude and unfamiliar, but at least there was no wind. Eight shots. Two soldiers.

The first round whistled past Jeremias' right ear, tearing into the upper back of the soldier in the saddle. The bullet ripped through his shoulder blade and tumbled into his lung. The impact knocked the soldier forward, dropping him from his horse onto his back in the road dust, his cries muted by the froth of pink bubbles spilling from his mouth and nose.

The soldier Lloyd had called Charlie heard the shot and watched in stunned disbelief as his friend, Henry, wrestled with death in the dirt. He jumped from his saddle and put his horse between himself and the ridgeline from which the shot had come. He pulled his own carbine from its saddle mount and scanned the landscape above, searching for some sign of snipers.

Jeremias sat frozen, doing nothing for fear of doing something that might get him killed. Despite his fear, despite watching this man dying in the dirt beneath him, Jeremias could only think of Katherine. Take me, Dear Lord, if that be Your will, he prayed, but spread Your mercy to my own dear Katherine.

Sean cycled the carbine. He sighted it on the other soldier as he disappeared behind the cover of his horse. Sean sighted again, slightly to the right and down, squeezing off a round that caught the horse just behind the right eye, killing it instantly and nearly dropping it onto the soldier now cowering behind its convulsing carcass.

Charlie jumped to his feet and ducked behind the other horse, yanking Jeremias by his bound wrists from the horse's back. Sean spent another cartridge dropping that horse, too, leaving the soldier and Jeremias with no cover and little chance of escape.

Charlie put himself behind the old man, using him as a human shield. He pressed his carbine's barrel into the back of the old man's head, resting it in the ridge just above his neck. He tugged at the waistband of Jeremias' trousers, forcing him to walk backward.

Charlie shouted up into the ridgeline. "Let us walk away, you Fenian bastard, or I'll shoot this old man dead."

Four rounds. One soldier. Jeremias in between.

Jeremias and the soldier moved backwards, one slow step after another.

Sean studied their awkward gait through the

Spencer's sights, but had no clear shot. If Jeremias would only drop to the ground, Sean could take out the soldier in an instant.

Jeremias didn't know who was shooting, or why. It must be Fenians, he thought, shooting at him while his own Katherine was as good as dead back home. Just the thought of it was more than he could bear.

Forgive me, Father, Jeremias thought as he raised his bound wrists to shoulder height and quickly spun around, catching the soldier behind him just above the left ear, rocking him backward.

"You old fool!" the soldier screamed, bringing his carbine down into Jeremias' face.

Sean's fifth round came in over Jeremias' right shoulder, leaving the soldier without a left eye. The force of the head shot lifted him off his feet, putting him on his back, dead in the roadway.

Jeremias dropped to knees in stunned disbelief. Had he been spared, or was some of this blood his own?

Sean untied his gelding and made his way quickly down the hillside. Five rifle shots would not go unnoticed so near to town. Jeremias was still on his knees, his face peppered with the soldier's blood, when he looked up to see Sean in the saddle above him. Sean dismounted quickly and untied the old man's wrists, then mounted again and pulled Jeremias onto his horse, behind him.

"Hang on," Sean said, kicking the horse into a lope. "Your Katherine is a bit shaken, but I expect she'll be fine in time. The soldier didn't hurt her, I saw to that, though I fear he left your kitchen in a bit of a mess."

❦ ❦ ❦

Katherine was beneath him now, yet somewhere else, as Sean worked his lips along each recess of her sculpted neck. As he lowered his face between her breasts, he drank in the sweetness of the soap she had used to scrub away the horrors of the day. Her nipples swelled to the size of thimbles as Sean trapped each in turn between his teeth and tongue, first one, then the other, then the other once again.

Sean's shoulder throbbed, but he was having no more of pain. He shifted his weight and braced himself on one elbow, taking his time in exploring her navel with the tip of his tongue.

Her hips lifted off the straw as he moved lower still. His face now between her thighs, he moved his head from side to side, nuzzling her soft hairs with the ridge of his nose. With each small movement of his head, her legs opened slightly.

A strange wave of warmth spread up her back, causing Katherine to cry out in a way that startled even herself. It was as though these sounds were coming from someone else, coming from somewhere else. Sean silenced her by covering her open mouth with his own.

He entered her at last, in one quick movement that took her breath away.

It returned in deep gasps, joining his own as her instant of pain gave way quickly to the pleasures of an ageless duet.

Father was right, Katherine thought. It is a great sin, indeed.

Chapter Three

March 15, 1867
Baltimore, Maryland

The letter took Joseph Kavanagh back to the sea cliffs rising up from Waterford Harbor. They still must be there, he knew, those dung-stained grottos where he would sit for hours as a boy. He hadn't thought of them in years, nor given any thought at all of returning to Ireland, as this curious letter suggested.

As a boy, he would steal away and crawl into those rocks to wait on the big noisy paddle steamers. The ships that came that way were side-wheelers mostly, big smoke-belching ships taking passengers and mail across the Irish Sea to strange places with names like Belgium, The Netherlands and Russia, places a boy couldn't know.

The Sirius was his favorite. The shriek of her three-toned steam whistle would coax him away from his studies or his chores, sending him at a sprint through the brambles, hurdling stone fences so he could lay on his belly in the pasture's tall grass, studying her lines through hands cupped like a spyglass.

Twice a month, more often in spring and summer, the

Sirius would churn past Hook Head and turn into the estuary toward Waterford City to take on water for her boilers before completing the run from Dublin to Cork. Fair weather or foul, chances were young Joe Kavanagh was taking it in from some rocky perch on high.

He was just learning to write the English then. His father said he must. "No use speaking the English, Joseph, if you can't write it as well," his father told him again and again, though he himself could neither write nor read a word of it. "Irish may do fine for me," his father would say, "and it may do fine for you in cursing the cattle or jawing with your Grandfar around the hearth, but any man to be reckoned with in this world had best be readin' and writin' the English as well as any Englishman. Better yet, even better."

When the Christian Brothers at the church school checked his lessons they were as apt to find the lined pages of his workbook filled with crude sketches of tall-masted ships as tracings of the alphabet. Brother Murphy would scold him in front of the others. "Keep your head in your lessons, Joseph, and not out to sea," he would always say. "The sea holds nothing for boys but a promise of certain death and a watery grave."

But, that whistle called him still.

Waterford City had become a regular port of call for the Sirius, what with one of Passage East's own, Captain Michel Padraic Roberts, at her helm. The Kavanaghs were from Passage East, too, or a mile to the south of the village, toward the sea. Joseph lived with three brothers and their sister, Nell. With their Da they shared a small stone house near the sea cliffs, learning their lessons, saying their prayers and tending to the sheep and the pigs and to Grandfar, their dead mother's Da. Grandfar's body was crippled with age, but not his tongue. He had tales to tell and little else but time to tell them. They were tales he told in Irish, just as they had been told to him.

Joseph's father, Brian Kavanagh, grew up with Captain Roberts, attending the same school. It was a fact oft repeated as it made young Joseph proud. The Sirius seldom put in at the Waterford Quay for more than a few hours, except now and then, when the weather went foul. At such times Captain Roberts would find his way to Passage East, visiting his people there and buying too many rounds of stout and hot whiskeys for old friends like Brian Kavanagh.

Joseph begged to tag along. When his Da would relent, he stayed close to his side, straining to hear tales of the sea the Captain would share with his Da and the others over the drone of Mooney's Pub.

Joseph was just seven in the spring of 1838, the year Captain Roberts did County Waterford and all of Ireland proud, taking the Sirius across the North Atlantic to America under steam alone, never once using her sails, making the east-to-west crossing in only eighteen days. Joseph couldn't imagine it, Queenstown to America, three thousand miles in just over a fortnight.

While the Sirius cast a special spell of its own, it was the lofty ships that intrigued Joseph most. Grandfar said the topsail schooners and the largest of the brigantines, low in the water and able to sail even backward, could call at ports where heavy steamers couldn't dock.

From the cliffs above the harbor, he often imagined himself aloft in the rigging of a barque or a brig, balanced on a footrope, way out on a yard, drenched in dirty weather as he gathered the foremast royal. From eighty feet above the sea, he would hug the yard and imagine waving to that tiny speck of a boy waving back in salute from the headlands ashore.

His first time aloft came when he was but eight. Or maybe it was nine. Who could remember? He had never told a soul of it, not even Grandfar, though he wished he had before the old man died.

Da had sent him to the city to deliver some fleece and bring home some flour. After leaving the mill on Bilberry Road he wandered the Waterford docks, studying the brigs and the barques tied up along Merchants Quay. Among them was the Jasper, a four-masted barquentine, a lumber hauler in for provisions before setting out for the Liverpool docks.

Joseph waited impatiently for dusk, studying the movements of the anchor watch from the shadows. As darkness began to fall, he summoned the nerve to sneak aboard, vaulting the caprail and scrambling silently up a mainmast shroud. Breathless and full of himself, he pulled himself up the ratlines to the platform alongside the main course yard.

Thirty feet above deck the view from aloft proved spectacular and infectious. Stolen minutes passed like treasured hours as Joseph studied her rigging, trying to trace with a finger the paths of a hundred ropes that snaked up from the pinrails. Each sail had a web of its own, buntlines and braces, halyards and clewlines, all disappearing somewhere above him, somewhere beyond the topgallant yard.

He dared not climb higher. His size had saved him from detection, but even a boy's silhouette, backlit high in the rigging by the soft glow of twilight, would give him away. From the edge of the platform, he studied the quarter deck, searching for signs of the watch. When the way looked clear, he clung to the platform, dangling his toes for a foothold. Hand over hand, rung by rope rung, he worked his way quickly to the deck.

Just above the running lamp, still ten feet up the shroud, his right foot broke through a salt-rotted ratline. Joseph gasped as he clung to the shroud, his forearms beginning to cramp as his feet pawed wildly for anything solid that would support his weight. A long step below, longer still for a boy, a toe found a ratline that proved sounder than the one just above it. He stretched to lower himself and at last found solid footing on the ship's polished caprail.

His heart pounded. His arms ached. His mouth was so dry he couldn't swallow, much less speak. What if I had broken through at sea? What if the barque had been bucking and rolling in a gale? I'd be overboard. I'd be drowned.

He leapt from the ship back onto the quay, breathless and scared, ducking into the safety of the shadows. He wanted to run without stopping, all the way to the Passage East road, but his quivering legs were having none of that. Maybe Brother Murphy was right. Maybe a cowherd is all the likes of Joseph Kavanagh was ever meant to be.

❧ ❧ ❧

It was a time that seemed to Captain Joseph Kavanagh a dream, a boyhood that had happened not to him, but to someone else, before the famine, before the war, before this curious letter.

These Fenians in New York had somehow laid claim to a brigantine in a bargain the letter assured him was better left unclear. They wanted him to sail her to Ireland. Her cargo was never discussed for reasons even a fool could suspect.

Kavanagh knew well of these Fenians and their cause. Everyone did. In Ireland, such sedition was conducted only in secret circles. They hung Fenians in Ireland, but not in America. James Stephens himself had been invited by the Federal Army's generals—Sheridan, Meade, Meagher, even Grant himself—to come into their camps to recruit. Stephens promised, when the war was over, the Fenian Brotherhood would use the military skills they had learned as Federal soldiers to take all of Ireland for the Irish, leaving to the magpies any Brits who refused to leave.

Kavanagh had come to know dozens of Fenians in the war. He himself had been encouraged to sign on, to swear their secret oath. But, oaths were not for him. He had sworn an oath once, an oath never to return to Ireland. It was to him a forsaken place, where people starved in a country brimming with crops and fat cattle they themselves had raised. God had forsaken Ireland and so had Joseph Kavanagh. The last he had seen of Ireland was from the stern of an overcrowded four-masted topgallant schooner. He remembered spitting into the water off Mizen Head as the Irish coastline disappeared in the fog at Cape Clear.

The summer of '48 it was, when Joseph and poor sickly Nell arrived in Boston Harbor half-dead from the crossing. Six weeks of entombment in the wretched leaky hold of what had once been a slave-trader left him too delirious to even speak his own name. It was left to his sister to tell the port authorities her bother's name was

57

Joe. Hunger fever had taken their Da and two of their brothers, Liam and Sean. The other, young Daniel, had stayed behind, near crazy with rage over what had become of the family and others around them.

Joseph later learned in a letter from Danny that he had sold the house and the small rocky pastures to a barrister in Waterford for little more than the price of a Liverpool passage. There was nothing left by then. The cow and the pigs had long been poached and devoured by wandering wretches worse off than Danny could find words to describe. What had become of him, in England, Joseph never knew.

Now, nearly twenty years later, this letter was calling him home.

Kavanagh kept the letter in his sea trunk, inside a sheath of charts. He had read and re-read it dozens of times. Written in a careful hand, it had arrived out of thin air. How its author knew of him or exactly where to find him he couldn't say for sure.

March 12, 1867
To: Commander Joseph B. Kavanagh

Sir,

I trust the courier who was under the strictest orders to deliver this message directly into your hands has found you to be in good health. I have learned a great deal about you in the past few weeks, including, as you see, your exact whereabouts. We are lucky, indeed, to find you ashore.

You and I have never met. I am hopeful we

shall and very soon. I am told you are a Waterford man. My own people are from the West Cork crossroads village of Derreeny Bridge, where I was born and, not too long after, very nearly buried. The blight was most severe throughout our area and many died. Like yourself, the hunger forced me to leave Ireland as a boy.

That crossing to America was my first experience at sea. It was not to be my last. Like you, I became a creature of the sea. At present, I serve as Chief of Naval Affairs of the Fenian Brotherhood, which is headquartered here in New York. It is in this capacity that I now seek your able assistance.

You have been portrayed to me as an honorable man, as a highly skilled seaman with much experience in handling square-rigged vessels in times of conflict. You served your adopted country with great distinction in the recent rebellion, I am told, as a lieutenant in the Federal Navy, aboard ships running war cargoes from Maine to Virginia. I have heard from others of your close encounter with the rebel frigate Alabama. From the sound of it, only your skilled seamanship saved your cargo, your crew and yourself from being overtaken and burned to the waterline by the Confederate pirate Semmes.

I can say little of what it is we desire of you in a dispatch such as this, except that we have a ship and have a cargo and now require a proven captain. I and others here are convinced that man is yourself. If you prefer, you need not be oath bound in this matter. It is your skill and experience at sea that we seek, not your sworn devotion to our cause.

The courier who delivered this proposal to you today will return to you tomorrow, precisely at noon. Into his hands, please deliver your reply. If you are with us, you must make your way to New York within a fortnight, the quicker the better. More specific instructions will be forthcoming, if you agree.

Given the sensitivity of any expedition of this nature, I must entrust to your strictest confidence the few specifics of this letter, even as vague as you may find them. The work of rebellion is rife with informers. Those whose judgment I trust explicitly assure me you are a man of proven honor and unimpeachable integrity and that the Brotherhood need not fear your betrayal. However, I do suggest you put to flame these few pages, committing to both memory and to ashes the arrangements I have proposed herein.

Yours,
John Powell
Chief of Naval Affairs, F.B .

Kavanagh wrote a response, but kept Powell's letter. A letter like this could put a man in jail, but might keep him out as well. Nontheless, he was intrigued. He had grown weary of coast hopping, tacking through steamer traffic, putting up with half-witted harbor pilots who acted as if they did him a favor to take his money to navigate harbors from Norfolk to Bangor that he knew in his sleep.

A North Atlantic crossing might do him good, whatever the risks.

If the price was right, he told Powell, he would take the Fenian brigantine and its contraband cargo to whatever Irish port the Fenians could secure. He would take on the ship, he told Powell, but not the Brotherhood's oath. He could neither forget nor forgive what had happened in Ireland at the hands of the English, but being hung for a Fenian was not a fate that he would choose.

Never before had he given a thought to ever going back. It seemed absurd, the idea of spending his last days back in Passage East, wrapped up in a shawl, pulling on a pipe while watching the schooners ride the tide. But, was it?

I might see my last days with these Fenians so eager to die for a place and a people some have never known themselves, he thought. And if my fate is to one day go down with my ship, what better place than in the sight of some stony head along St. George's Channel? Perhaps, he thought, I am one of them, one of these Finnini.

Chapter Four

March 25, 1867
New York

Kavanagh despised New York. It was an outdoor asylum.

Wherever he wandered, whores and pickpockets seemed as thick as the sewage that fouled the streets. An early spring chill choked the air with coal dust and smoke, leaving Kavanagh with a hacking cough even whiskey wouldn't tame, or at least what passed for whiskey at McSweeney's Public House.

The dirtiest night at sea in a leaky ship being tossed about in the clutches of a howling gale is better than the best night in a hellhole like this place, he thought. From the beggars to the barristers, those who make this Godforsaken place their home are damned fools, indeed.

Why he had come he still wasn't sure. Perhaps it was the money. In all his years at sea, he had been paid what, to some, would seem a small fortune, but now had little to show for his troubles, even nearing forty. For a voyage such as this, given the risks involved, he would set a high price and stick to it.

A lifetime at sea had left Joseph Kavanagh as fit as a young man of 20. His dark auburn hair had begun to gray, flecks of white salting his mustache and the tuft of beard at his chin. Even so, he was strong as a draft horse, and despite his age, he considered his wits to be quicker than most. His blue eyes still sparkled whenever he laughed.

He had arrived by train from Baltimore, just before four. It felt strange to approach New York by land instead of threading some packet or barquentine through the chaos of the East River harbor, only to be forced to tie up at some over-priced berth.

He had brought many ships into New York, but had seldom gone ashore.

Armed with his Savage revolver, he would supervise the deck watch, keeping at bay the thieves and the desperate wretches who plagued the wharves, always eager to sneak aboard and make off with whatever they could carry or eat.

The train platform had been crawling with newsboys, half-starved street urchins, hands black with ink, faces streaked with grime. When one of them shouted "Fenian army in retreat, read all about it," Kavanagh dug into his trousers for four pennies.

Fenian army?

It was a concept that baffled many a reader of The New York Times, especially the Germans, the Dutch and the Swedes. They and others who had been here first now found themselves reluctantly living and working amid the hoards of Irish who had overrun New York like vermin over the last twenty years.

To the countless thousands who fled Ireland to the port cities of America and Canada, an army of Fenians was a notion long embraced and longer denied. The very idea of armed Fenians rising to confront the British in England's first colony was sweetened by a vengeance born of too much remembering, a vengence bred and bred again over seven centuries of horrors that had visited Ireland and driven so many from her shores.

Among the British, whether in London, Dublin City or New York, the word "Fenian" was a pejorative, a derisive term synonymous with "bastard." British or Irish, few knew the word's true meaning, with its origins steeped in the hero tales of Celtic mythology.

In their own minds at least, the Fenians were incarnations of the legendary Fianna Eirann, the ancient militia whose warrior skills protected Ireland's pre-Christian kings from wave after wave of invaders. The Fianna had taken their name from Fionn Mac Cumhaill, the Celtic warrior and Irish king whose valor and bravery were standards by which Irishmen in arms would forever measure their worth.

Kavanagh left his sea trunk in the care of a railroad porter. By half six, he had made his way on foot to the Bowery. An old woman hawking salted fish pointed the way to McSweeney's, down around the next corner. Through the dim light and tobacco fog, Kavanagh found an empty table beyond a crush of noisy patrons, more than a few half tore. A barmaid brought him the dram he asked for as he thumbed through the paper, drinking in what news of Ireland its pages contained.

Throughout New York and all New England, across the St. Lawrence into the Irish enclaves of British North

America, the thirst for news of the Fenians had become insatiable. The Irish talked of little else since the first weeks of March, when the first advices by overseas telegraph reported all of Ireland in a state of wild excitement.

Though details were scarce, The Times reported the previous week commencement of active military operations. Fenian agitation was said to be "renewed" and "increasing." Within the next week, Atlantic cable dispatches had the Galtee Mountains swarming with Fenians and the railway line between Dublin and Cork in Fenian hands. Armed bands of men were said to be moving through Clare and Limerick. Tipperary was reported to be threatened by a Fenian army numbering fifteen hundred, which The Times described as "probably the largest force the insurgents have ever gotten together."

Cheers went up at McSweeney's, and in countless barrooms throughout New England, as accounts of a proclamation of an Irish Republic were read aloud. The Fenians in Ireland had delivered a statement to all the major Irish papers: "After ages of outrage and of vain appeals to reason and justice, the Irish people have at last resolved to appeal to arms to rescue Ireland from serfdom and to establish national unity, public safety and political freedom and to bring about the consequent separation of church and state. As Republicans, they appeal to Republicans throughout the world for sympathy and support."

Just when this so-called rising had begun no one seemed to know for sure.

News traveled slowly, when it traveled at all. One dispatch reported the Irish wires down and blamed the situation on a snow storm. The Irish who frequented the dockside alehouses confirmed the reports of a storm, but not one of nature's making. It was, they proudly proclaimed over too many pints, the raging storm of poor people too long denied.

The stories Kavanagh studied at McSweeney's reported little but setbacks.

At Tallaght, eight miles southwest of Dublin, eighty prisoners had been taken, captured with six wagons of ammunition. An army of a thousand men that once threatened to overrun Killarney had, the paper said, dwindled to only a hundred and was now being hunted down in the mountains of Kerry by British troops armed with artillery. Nine Fenians captured near Dundalk had been tried for treason and quickly sentenced to prison terms from seven to fifteen years. Under a headline that read "The Fenian Failure in Ireland" was a story that claimed that reports of an insurrection were exaggerated and that "the will of the Irish people has been broken."

Was there a rebellion, or was there not? Kavanagh found it hard to know from what he had read or what he had overheard. The Fenians were the main course of conversation, at least at McSweeney's, but who knew the truth?

❦ ❦ ❦

Just past half eight, a short man with a blackthorn walking stick and a limp to match came into McSweeney's and wove his way to the bar. He whispered into a barman's ear and was directed to the corner table Kavanagh had claimed as his own.

"Kavanagh is it, Captain Kavanagh?" he said in a

heavy brogue, extending his hand in welcome. "My name would be Timothy Sheehy, known to me friends as Chipper."

"You have the look and the tongue of a Kerryman," Kavanagh said. "And I suspect with a name such as Chipper you've done your share of working wood."

"Aye, that I have and am still," the old man said. "My people were dirt poor hill farmers along the Dingle peninsula. Raised a fine crop of rock, we did. Such a fine crop that, as a young man, I went to Dublin, leaving the stones in the fields to me brothers."

Kavanagh offered the old man a chair and ordered him a hot whiskey with lemon and cloves, which disappeared near as quickly as delivered.

"I starved at first in Dublin, but then found work as a cooper's apprentice at St. James Gate. Made a sideboard or two as well. I scrounged enough to make the crossing in '55 and, right off the boat, began making coffins. The Paddies in this God-forsaken city might be the poorest of the poor, except, of course, for the coloreds, but at least here in America we Irish can scrape enough together to properly bury our dead."

Chipper said he had been sent to McSweeney's on orders from John Powell himself, dispatched to fetch Captain Kavanagh and quick bring him round to the Fenian Brotherhood's headquarters.

Kavanaugh settled up with the barmaid and followed Chipper's limp out of McSweeney's. Once out the door, they headed east, back toward the docks.

It was nearly dark. The chill in the air was gone now,

replaced by damp cold. Small fires burned along the streets and down the alleyways, belching black smoke and casting long shadows of those huddled around them for warmth.

The two men crossed a busy street, careful to step around steaming mounds of manure left by the teams. As they reached the other side a young girl, shoeless and in rags, approached them from behind and tugged on Kavanagh's coat.

"A copper, if you please, kind sir," she said to Kavanagh, the better dressed of the pair.

Chipper lurched at the girl, putting himself between the beggar and Kavanagh. He raised his blackthorn, as if to strike her dead.

"Be gone, little one," he barked.

She raised her hands in front of her face, turned and ran. At a safe distance, she shouted back, "Go fuck your mother."

Six blocks from McSweeney's, at 19 Chatham Street, Chipper led the way inside. "Follow me," he said, routing Kavanagh one flight up a steep narrow stairwell to a half-closed door. With two raps on the door frame, Chipper slipped inside, gesturing to Kavanagh to join him in the small lamp-lit room.

Nearly lost behind a massive wooden desk cluttered with papers and charts was a man much older than Kavanagh had imagined Powell would be. Through tiny half-glasses, he was studying what appeared to be a drawing of a small ship's hull. Hearing them enter, he stood and gave Kavanagh a once-over glance. Chipper slipped back through the door and closed it behind them.

"Captain Kavanagh, welcome," the man said, shaking Kavanagh's hand and gesturing toward a chair. "I am John Powell. Please do sit down. I am most happy to meet you at last. In times such as these, it does one good to make welcome those offering solutions, instead of more problems."

"Not knowing of your problems, it's difficult to say if what I represent are their solutions," Kavanagh said, sizing up Powell, discerning what he could from the clutter of this room. "I will need to learn much more before knowing if I can do you some good."

"That you will, and that you shall," Powell said. "Now that we are face to face, I can tell you virtually all I know of the situation. You have seen the papers no doubt, the news of the Fenians, the stories of the rising?"

"A rising is it?" Kavanagh said. "From some accounts, it never happened. From all accounts whatever is happening doesn't appear to be going too well: men arrested, tried and jailed for treason. I cannot tell from the newspapers, nor from the rantings in the pub where you sent me, just what it is that is happening."

"Nor can we, I'm afraid," Powell said. "Not from the papers at least. But, do keep in mind, as do we, that the British control the underwater cable and so control as well the flow of information that passes over it. We can hardly expect our enemy to accommodate the spread of news that rebellion is sweeping over the Irish countryside."

"Is it now?" Kavanagh asked.

"It is," Powell said. "And has for weeks now, ever

since the fifth day of March. We have men and weapons
in the field from Sligo to Wicklow, trained officers oath
bound to the cause, men dispatched from here and from
Boston, and from other Fenian cities."

"These men are Fenians, American Fenians?"
Kavanagh asked.

"Aye, veteran officers of the Irish Brigades, most of
them," Powell said. "They are men who served under
Meagher and Corcoran. They include veterans of the New
York Sixty-Ninth and the Massachusetts Ninth and other
units as well. Each is a man of proven ability, a man who
has led others into battle. Though news is scarce, we have
no reason to believe they aren't faring well."

Powell was lying. There was little point in being too
candid. For more than a week, the Brotherhood's
leadership had studied the papers and their own coded
dispatches. Powell knew more of the truth than most, and
knew too well that what passed for news in the papers was
usually the thinnest of lies. He knew as well that what
passed as dispatches from the front were too often wishful
thinking at best.

One undeniable fact was that, since February, when
the British extended the suspension of habeas corpus,
hundreds of actual and suspected Fenians had been
rounded up and locked away at Mountjoy, Kilmainham
and other Dublin jails. Hundreds of others had been
chased into the hills beyond Dublin city. There was little
word at all from the west of Ireland. Nonetheless, days of
meetings had left Powell with his orders. What he needed
now was Kavanagh to carry them out.

"News is hard to come by," Powell said. "We know
not all that is reported is truth. – The London Times - had

a policeman shot and mortally wounded in Tallaght, with James Stephens, our own Fenian Head Central Organizer, pulling the trigger. This we know for certain is a lie. Stephens remains a fugitive in Paris, where he has been since his escape from Richmond. Like Wolfe Tone before him, we expect he's been busy courting French support for the rising."

Kavanagh knew of Tone. Another rising, another debacle, this one in 1798. A French fleet, carrying three thousand men intercepted off Donegal. Tone later cut his own throat while a guest in an English prison.

Kavanagh knew almost nothing of James Stephens, only what little he had seen over the years in the papers: Stephens had organized the Irish Republican Brotherhood in Ireland, while John O'Mahony had come to American to piece together its Yankee counterpart, The Fenian Brotherhood. Stephens was a clerk from Kilkenny, O'Mahony a farmer of some means from Limerick. As younger men, both had taken part in the Young Irelanders' insurrection in '48 and had avoided arrest only by fleeing to Paris. It was in Paris the two had flipped a coin. O'Mahony lost and sailed for America.

Powell noticed Kavanagh staring past him, his gaze fixed on the wall behind the desk. Hanging there was a hand-colored poster, an engraved scene of two women posed before two flags, one a stars and stripes, the other a flag of deep green. The figure dressed in red had a sash draped between her breasts. She clutched the standards in one hand and a shield of red, blue and white in the other. Seated on a rock before her was a woman with a harp, her golden hair falling to her back. Her green skirt flowed to the ground where it mingled with shamrocks of the same verdant shade. Behind them both were rose-colored sunbursts, radiating like halos to make them seem like goddess twins.

"I see you are taken by our newest engraving," Powell said. "It was commissioned for the Brotherhood as the cover for a pamphlet, a small book that has proven most useful in selling bonds to raise money for guns. The figure in red is Lady Liberty, who appears out of the west, fully armed and fully determined to bring to the Irish people the same freedoms she was able to wrest from the English in 1776. Look her over, Commander Kavanagh. It is my hope that it will be you who delivers her to dear old Ireland."

"I have the feeling, Mr. Powell, that what it is you want me to deliver to Ireland's western shores is more than this mythical goddess," Kavanagh said.

"Let me be blunt," Powell said. "It is the resolve of Fenian Brotherhood in America to come to the aid of this ongoing rebellion by delivering to those who have risen up the weapons and the officers needed to deliver Ireland to independence. It is our destiny, a destiny I encourage you to embrace as well."

Kavanagh said nothing. He had his price, which was more than patriotic pride.

"What I propose to you, Sir, is this. The Brotherhood has secured a ship, a small ship of 150 tons gross. She is rigged as a brigantine, 124 feet in length and 23 feet at the beam. She is copper-clad and carries two sets of sail. She was built in Bedford in 1861 for a Haitian merchant, a man named O'Gill. Or was it McGill? I think it was McGill, Harry McGill. She was known as the *Jacnel*.

"She has spent virtually all of her sea life in the West Indies. McGill used her to run coffee and cane from

Jacnel, Haiti, to New England ports, including New York, bringing back hogsheads of whiskey and barrels of salt pork and beef. At least he did until your old friend Raphael Semmes put the *Jacnel* and hundreds like her out of business, the owners afraid their ships would be run down and fired at sea by Semmes or some other Confederate pirate.

"Our Mr. McGill was concerned enough that sometime during the war he sold the *Jacnel* to a man named Dawes, who used her to run cargo to Mexico. Seems much of that cargo was heavy guns and surplus rifles being smuggled to Benito Juarez for his war against Maximilian. When the cargo was discovered in Panama, the ship was seized."

Powell pushed back his chair and crossed the room to a cupboard. "Are you a drinking man, Captain?" he asked, producing a cut glass decanter from behind a small hinged door. "Can I offer you some fine French brandy?"

"Never at sea, but I don't mind a drink to calm my nerves in a place as unnerving as New York," Kavanagh said with a hint of a smile. Some people liked New York. He didn't mean to offend. "Yes, please."

Powell poured two long drinks into small pewter goblets. "Where was I?" he asked, handing Kavanagh a brandy.

"You were saying the *Jacnel* was seized in Panama," Kavanagh said. "How did she wind up here in the hands of your Brotherhood?"

"She came to us in a round-about way, in an arrangement involving a Fenian named Blake, a man highly placed in the Customs," Powell said. "She was seized by the Customs sometime last year for non-payment of wages and pilot fees, and she was soon sent our way as a favor owed to someone up the chain of command, perhaps even to Stephens himself. I really don't know, and it's no business of mine, nor any of yours for that matter. Take my word, we're both better off not to know the particulars. She has no papers, as you might expect."

"And where is she now?" Kavanagh asked.

"Moored in a back bay on the lee side of the Long Island," Powell said. "I sailed her there myself from North Carolina, where we took possession. She's much quicker than she looks. She has a good grip on the water and runs into the wind as well as any brig I've yet handled."

"How many will be aboard?" Kavanagh asked.

"Thirty, more or less, not counting her captain and his crew."

"Has she berths for a cargo of so many men?"

"Berths enough for a crew, not nearly enough for all these men," Powell said. "I've put carpenters on board, including Chipper, the old gent who brought you to me from McSweeney's. They are building more berths below, enough for forty men all together. The master and mate accommodations are aft, down a passageway from the quarterdeck. We will put the necessary provisions aboard for the crew -- bread, butter, coffee, hard tack, beef, salted bacon, beans, and some whiskey if you like. And fresh water, of course. We've told the officers they must bring their own provisions. The Irish Republican Brotherhood has agreed to arrange for fresh provisions for the return trip, as well as additional crew, men whose situations as fugitives require transport to America. Such men will bring with them food of their own, and the IRB will provide sufficient fresh water for all."

"These thirty officers, these Irish Brigade men, can any one of them sail a ship?" Kavanagh asked.

"Likely not," Powell said, "at least not without a bit of instruction. I will have to leave that to you, Captain, if you take on this task. And I will leave it to you to personally select your own permanent crew or, if you prefer, we can provide you with an experienced crew - a first mate, a boatswain and others known to us as able seamen, each oath bound to our cause."

"I would bring my own first mate, if I can find him, but would likely leave it to you to select the others," Kavanaugh said.

"The crew of able seamen will supplement the efforts on deck and aloft of the Fenian officers, who've been told there will be no idlers," Powell said. "We can find you sailors you can rely on, men with the experience and the patience to head up the watches and to show these officers the deck work and sailhandling that needs doing. It will be a green crew, indeed, but these are brave men, men who I assure you will learn the ropes quickly."

"And when will she set sail?"

"The sooner the better," Powell said.

Just yesterday the Brotherhood de-coded a message from Dublin, a dispatch from Colonel Thomas J. Kelly. With Stephens now in France, Kelly was the highest ranking American Fenian in all of Ireland. It was a plea for quick assistance, urging the leadership of the

Brotherhood not to believe even a tenth of the accounts of complete suppression of the rising.

Powell passed a hand-written copy of Kelly's message across his desk to Kavanagh. "Read this," he said. "Perhaps the tone of urgency here will help you understand why we are so eager to undertake this expedition."

Kavanagh set down his goblet and began to read.

"What do our countrymen in America want?" Kelly had written. "Will they wait until the last man shall be slaughtered before sending aid? I hope the American people believe now that our people meant to fight. If they do, let them work like beavers. Fit out your privateers. There is immense work to be done. A landing at Sligo at the present time would be of infinite service. That section has been reserved for such an event, and if Fortune should only guide your ships in that direction, it would just suit our purpose."

Kavanagh handed Kelly's message back to Powell. "Why Sligo?" he asked. "Won't the British have gunboats patrolling the coast between Galway and Donegal?"

"Not as many as they have on patrol between Galway and Cork," Powell said. "Outside of Dublin, most of the Fenian activity in the last few weeks has been in the southwest. Last week, we landed twenty American officers on the coast near Dingle, in County Kerry, with a fishing smack. Kelly and others say most of the British warships have been ordered to the south and west. With Stephens so long in Paris, there may be real concern about a French landing there, between Dungarvan and Kinsale. Stephens has told us that the French have no real interest in coming to our aid, but the English don't know that.

They may still live in fear of the ghost of Wolfe Tone."

Kavanagh doubted that.

"The Brotherhood's intent is to have the *Jacnel* set forth from Sandy Hook within a few weeks, or as soon as the officers gather and all necessary arrangements can be made. The distance involved is some three thousand nautical miles. With fair weather and winds, a spring crossing should require four weeks, under the worst of conditions no more than six. Upon arrival in Ireland, her cargo of men and guns will be off-loaded in an area where weapons are scare, but enthusiasm high. After taking on new provisions and men, the ship will be ballasted for the return passage to New York, her mission completed, her captain a hero."

Or dead, Kavanagh thought to himself.

"My hope, Captain Kavanagh, is that hero will be you. You have been recommended to the Brotherhood by persons we trust, persons who speak highly of you as a battle-tested naval officer of great skill and daring. We must talk later of your close encounter with Semmes."

"We can if you like, but it's a story overblown," Kavanagh said. "At the time not one of us aboard had ever heard of Raphael Semmes. The truth of it is that I was as scared as the next man to see a ship as imposing as the *Alabama* race over the horizon with her course set for us. We only escaped out of desperation and the fact that her steam was down and her screw was triced up. We were lucky is all."

"Just as I've been told, you are too modest, Captain," Powell said. "The truth, as you know now, is that yours was the only ship the *Alabama* encountered that she didn't overhaul. What was it at the end, nearly seventy ships in thirty eight months? Even Semmes himself admitted in the papers after his arrest that the only reason one ship -- yours, at it turns out - escaped him was that he was outsailed. His term, not mine."

"With a crew of foot soldiers and a hold full of weapons, it appears to me that a voyage such as you propose is likely to be as filled with as much risk as any run-in with Semmes," Kavanagh said.

"So it may be," Powell said. "Which is why we have set aside sufficient funds to provide you with generous compensation for your time and your trouble. I am authorized to offer you one thousand dollars in gold when you sign a commission and an additional thousand upon your successful return."

It was twice what Kavanagh had decided to hold out for. Still, he had some doubts.

"And if I do not return?" Kavanagh asked.

"The gold will be delivered to whomever you designate. Of that you have my word."

"If I were to accept responsibility for this expedition," Kavanagh said, "which port is it I am to deliver this cargo of guns and men, and into whose hands?"

"That is for someone else to decide," Powell said. "My job is to provide a ship, a shipmaster and a crew capable of getting officers and munitions to the western headlands. Your specific orders will come when you sail, directly from the expedition's military leader, General James Kerrigan. You have heard of him perhaps, a member of the U.S. Congress?"

Kavanagh hadn't.

"Those orders are to be opened by you and read aloud to all those aboard when you are a few days safely at sea."

"And what are we to do if we are confronted by the British, either on the North Atlantic or along the Irish coast?" Kavanagh asked.

"Your standing orders will be to do whatever you must to ensure that not a single weapon aboard, not even one cartridge, winds up in British hands," Powell said. "Outrun the bastards if you can, heave to and fight if you must. You soon will meet a man called Clark. He will be on board as the expedition's chief engineer. He's a clever one, you will see. He has devised a method that will ensure the complete destruction of the vessel if all is lost, once all aboard have taken to the boats and rafts. You must not allow this cargo to be taken by the British."

"And tell me this," Kavanagh said, not sure if his question would seem out of line. "Why is it you're not making this passage yourself? You know these men. You've sailed this brig."

"I wish that I could, and that's God's truth," Powell said. "I am afraid I am like you, a creature of the sea, restless ashore, eager to feel the deck beneath my boots and a gathering breeze at my back. But understand, Kavanagh, this expedition is just the start. The *Jacnel* is but the first of many ships that will make this crossing, bringing to Ireland whatever is required to chase the damned English out at last.

"Between you and me, we expect to acquire a steamer, but negotiations are now bogged down, to say the least. I must stay behind, for now anyway, to work on this and other matters and to work with those finding the weapons and recruiting the men these other ships will carry.

"History has shown that the chief difficulty of the Irish in every effort to overthrow English rule has been lack of arms. Be they pikes or cannons, there has never seemed to be enough weapons on hand to equip all who were willing to fight. But understand, Captain Kavanagh, this expedition is about more than running guns and men to the rising. Your success will prove to these scurvy Irish millionaires whose arses the Brotherhood have been kissing for years that weapons can get through, that Fenian ships can slip the Royal Navy's coast patrols. With that lesson learned, there should be no stopping the flow of the money we need to buy more ships and fill their holds with more guns. That's why you're here, Captain Kavanagh. That's why we have made you an offer no sane man could refuse. You've outrun these bastards before and we're eager to have you do it once more.

Chapter Five

April 17, 1867
39° 23' north latitude, 66° 32' west longitude

Sean Kenneally hadn't known sickness like this since Antietam. September 17, 1862, it was. Twenty-three thousand dead in a single day.

What was left of the Irish Brigade was in tatters. What little was left of Corporal Brian Curry, a brave lad to the last, was all over Sean in one blinding spray of blood and bone and brains.

The shell that left Brian in pieces dropped Sean to his knees. With hollow stares, the dead who shared the muddy trench watched in silence as Sean wiped Brian from his eyes with the back of his hands. He stared at his fingers, transfixed. Then the retching began, bringing up bile from the deepest pits of his empty stomach.

The papers all agreed it was a great victory.

The strong following breeze that sent the midnight watch aloft to crowd on sail had built to a near gale by dawn. The brigantine *Jacnel* shuddered as she slammed through high seas, making northeast by north. As the winds grew stronger, the troughs grew deeper. The brigantine's black hull was listing heavily, seawater flooding her decks each time the starboard caprail dipped beneath the angry green swells. As she rolled back to port, the decks flowed with a current eager to knock a man down or sweep him over the side as he tugs on a downhaul or takes his turn at the helm. In seas such as these, Sean thought it safer aloft.

Four times in the last hour, he and most of the others on deck had been ordered into the rigging to quickly gather and reef sail before this howling wind left the topsails and the fore course in shreds. In calmer seas, while explaining the mix of ropes belayed at the pin rails, the first mate had warned this green crew of foot soldiers about some of what they were facing now. Too much sail in too much weather, he told them, would snap the *Jacnel's* yellow pine masts like a pullet's neck, leaving the ship and all aboard adrift in high seas.

This tangle of lines and cables was a somewhat baffling web of buntlines and dewlines, sheets and downhauls , but it would keep them all alive, he promised, but only if they did what needed doing exactly when it needed to be done.

In the four days out from Sandy Hook, Sean felt queasy, but now he was sick. He had been to sea only once before, and then on a much larger ship. It was years ago, when he was only a boy. The crossing from Queenstown to New Orleans had been an ordeal, but no worse to be sure than the horrors left behind in the rocky hillsides above Killanne.

Sean clung to the topmast like a black bear scaling a hemlock, gripping the big mast tightly with both arms and his knees. Whether making way in gentle winds or plodding through cavernous swells such as these, the two-masted square-rigger rocked back and forth, bobbed up and down, and swayed side to side, all at once, all the time.

Aboard this ship, Sean grew tired standing still. Below deck, when he climbed into his bunk and closed his eyes, his head spun with the motion of the ship, side to side, fore and aft, up and down. Sleep proved elusive. The first few days under sail left him bruised and sore from bumping into bulkheads, into capstans, into others who, like himself, struggled to keep their footing as they stumbled from place to place.

Over the shoulder of the helmsman, great green mountains of sea rose high above the quarterdeck, lifting the stern high into the ashen sky. As the swells grew, the *Jacnel*'s bow plunges became more severe. As she surfed to the bottom of each foaming trough, Sean felt his cheek being pressed to the mast, and then pushed away as the ship reared back.

From the foremast's second platform, Sean was seventy feet above the sea. Never himself budging an inch, he made awkward circles above the deck as if strapped to a pendulum gone mad. One second the deckhouse was directly below, the next nothing but churning sea.

As his stomach worked its way up his throat, he closed his eyes. Just as he began to gag, a hand touched his boot, then grabbed his cuff. "Move on out, man, there are others close behind."

It was Benny, the boatswain, sent aloft to show these soldiers how sailors gather sail in a hurry. "Take the starboard and be right quick about it," Benny shouted over the drone of the wind. "These sails need furling now if we're to have any sails left at all"

Sean could barely make out the words, but understood what was expected. Rain laced with ice stung his face as he worked his way slowly out onto a tarred footrope dancing in the wind below the upper topsail yardarm.

"Stepping on," he yelled over one shoulder, feeling for a foothold with the slippery toe of his square-toed boot. The footrope shifted wildly under his weight. He could make only a few inches at a time, clinging with both arms to a rain-slickened yardarm as big around as a hogshead.

The bowsprit rose as the *Jacnel* reared for another plunge. Sean felt his balance shift and gripped the yard until his forearms burned in a knot of pain. In an instant, the yard tried to rip free of his grasp, dropping in an eye's blink from Sean's chest to his knees. His feet had left the footrope. His shoulders were heading over the top of the yard. He was falling.

In one clear moment, Sean became aware he was being thrown from the yard. He would plunge down, either through the rigging and onto the deck or cast forever into the raging sea. It didn't matter which, he thought. He was a dead man either way.

Just then a hand grabbed Sean's soggy woolen britches from behind, yanking him down hard. As the yard recoiled it caught Sean squarely on the chin, driving a tooth through his lower lip.

"Get your boney Irish arse out there and furl that

feckin' sail, you eejit." Benny had no time for this nonsense. This storm had no patience, and neither did he. Forty-two men on board, able-bodied all, and only nine who knew a binnacle from a barnacle. This was madness. If they managed to survive this crossing, Benny knew he would be forced to commit it to song.

The blow from the yard left Sean reeling. In the Federal Army, he'd had his head opened by the butt of a carbine and been kicked in the chest by a paymaster's mule, but he had never taken a blow like this. It hurt, but it helped. His throbbing head, the bitter taste of his own blood, took what little was left of his senses off his dancing stomach. He clung to the yard and, somehow, regained a foothold, slowly moving out along the footrope to make room for Benny and two others behind.

With four all in place, the slack gone now from the footrope, Sean followed Benny's lead. Hanging on with one arm, he reached down over the yard with his free arm, straining to gather the foot of the fore upper topsail, which had been drawn toward him by those doing rope work on deck.

Keeping together with those on the port side, Sean and the others aloft gathered in the heavy wet canvas, piling each bight atop the last. When all were at last in place, they lashed every six feet of the dripping sail snug to the yard, using a half dozen short ropes, tying each gasket off with the knot Benny had forced them to practice again and again on deck.

"Down with you now," Benny screamed, signaling to the man nearest the mast to head down the shrouds. "The three of you worthless curs go down and furl that lower topsail just below us," he yelled. "I'll head up and do the t'gallant meself."

Benny disappeared barefoot into the rigging. Sean and the others carefully worked their way around the mast and onto the windward shroud, choosing each foothold as if it might be their last. The force of the gale pressed their weary bodies against the icy rope ladder that took them to the lower topsail yard, 20 feet below.

As the first out above, Sean was the last out below, feeling somehow secure to be close to the spinning mast. The rest passed like a dream. When he came to his senses, he was back on deck, his forearms throbbing with cramps, the fingers of his left hand frozen into a claw. His lower lip was split and bleeding from the yardarm's stinging uppercut, and salt spray burned his face. In all his days, he had never felt worse.

The deck was awash now to the tops of his boots. The strength of the wind was straining the stays and had opened the planks where the chain plates were bolted to the hull. The bilge was taking on water.

"Get below and take yourself a turn on those pumps," the helmsman told him as Sean stumbled onto the quarterdeck. "And mind the water on deck. In this wind, they'll be no coming about to fish you out if you disappear over the side."

Holy Mother of God, Sean thought to himself. What in the name of Sweet Jesus am I doing here?

Chapter Six

April 21, 1867
41° 20' north latitude, 62° 35' west longitude

Sean Kenneally hadn't slept but half the night and only wanted to be left alone.

"Up with you, Captain Kenneally. We're all to gather on deck. It's all hands."

It was the cook's helper, a man named Buckley, an ugly man with an ugly scar from his forehead to his ear and breath that reeked of stale rum and tobacco. Someone on deck was ringing the ship's bell.

"Yes, alright," Sean said, quickly turning his face away. "I'll be up directly. What's the time?"

"Nearly noon," Buckley said. "We had porridge at eight, sweetened with molasses. Biscuits, too. The holiday you know. But I was told to leave you be, that you said you would rather sleep."

"Aye," Sean said. "That I would."

Sean tried to swing both his legs over the lip of his

bunk. His knees were stiff and his back was sore. The pain jogged his memory. Five times in four hours, he and the others had been sent aloft to crowd on sail as a brisk following breeze died to near calm between midnight and dawn. Since they had left Sandy Hook he had learned more about sail handling than he could ever want to know, but finding footholds in the dark remained a challenge. The *Jacnel* now seemed becalmed. Good for sleep, perhaps, but not for making way.

Up on deck, Sean saw the others clustered in small groups between the deckhouse and the companionway to the fo'c'sle, where Buckley and the other crew kept their bunks. There was no wind at all, none he could detect, but the sun was bright and warmed the back of his neck as he made his way toward those gathered at the bow.

One group of men had gathered near the foremast, six or eight standing around a small cannon. It was one of three field guns Sean had seen below in the hold, wedged between crates of rifles and girded with rope to secure it in high seas. It was a small gun, but still, Sean was glad to have slept through the job of winching it onto the deck.

Up from the helm came General Kerrigan, walking just ahead of the ship's captain, a man named Kavanagh. The General looked as if he were about to lead a parade. Across his topcoat, he wore a white sash delicately embroidered with golden threads. He also was wearing a hat not unlike the hat Sean had seen on General Meagher during the war. One side of its exaggerated brim was pinned up and decorated with a long white ostrich plume. On his belt, the General wore a saber, its silver scabbard throwing off darts of light as he strutted through the bright noon sun. In his hands, he carried a bolt of green cloth.

General Kerrigan nodded greetings to the men as he made his way toward the bow. He climbed up onto the box that kept the anchor chain out of the weather. It allowed him to tower above Sean and the others.

"Good day, gentlemen," he said in a bellow. "Allow me to wish each of you the best on this glorious Easter Sunday and to thank you all for the hardships you have together endured over what I'm sure you will all agree has been a most difficult week at sea."

The men on deck glanced at one another, acknowledging among themselves it had been a long week, indeed.

"Today the Lord Almighty has bestowed upon us and our vessel this fine weather in which we offer not only our thanks to Him for the miracle of the Resurrection of his only son, Our Lord Jesus Christ, but also reflect upon our own holy mission. I need not remind you this Easter Sunday finds us all many miles from the comforts of friends and family back in America. We have come a long way in just eight days, but we face many more miles ahead. Captain Kavanagh tells me he is greatly impressed by the courage and ready pluck you have demonstrated already in assisting his crew in taking this ship toward the destiny that awaits us."

"On to Ireland!" someone shouted, his lone cheer breaking into a group chant as it spread through the ranks.

"Each one of us has pledged our hearts, our souls, our fates to Ireland," Kerrigan shouted above the swell of enthusiasm. "Each as well has dedicated himself to the noble cause of that great Brotherhood that has brought us together on this Fenian warship. And each of us has his own reasons for being aboard. Like you, I myself am eager to avenge not only the many hardships and cruel injustices visited upon the Irish people throughout this century, but in centuries past by British tyrants who must be driven from the shores of Ireland as a humble slave named Patrick drove out the snakes before them."

"Death to the English!" came a shout.

"I am a Kerrigan," the General said. "I am descended from a proud and mighty clan of Kerrigans that extends back to the time when William of Orange first ravaged Ulster, and even before. My people went toe to toe with Oliver Cromwell at Drogheda. Much of my family died there, trapped in the tower of St. Peter's, when Cromwell put it and them to the torch. My grandfather's great-great grandfather's grandfather gave his at Drogheda at the hands of that butcher. He was among those who, as they said then, was 'decimated.' You have heard the term, no doubt. Now it means 'destroyed.' What it meant two centuries ago, during Cromwell's reign of terror, was that every tenth Irish soldier captured while in defense of Drogheda was put to the sword as an example to the other nine. One of them was my great ancestor, Brian Kerrigan. That was 1649, lads, but we Irish have been blessed with long memories."

"And even shorter tempers!" came a shout, prompting both cheers and laughter.

"My intent," Kerrigan said, "is somewhat different. It is my intent to send every nine Englishmen I encounter to their graves as a lasting example to the tenth, who I expect to see running scared, well ahead of the nine corpses behind him. It's our turn, lads!"

The cheers erupted again.

"Each of us has cut his battle teeth at places like Antietam, places like Marye's Heights and Chancellorsville. The gutless British bastards offered aid and comfort to those who were our enemies then, but through God's grace righteousness prevailed. Well, lads, it's the British who are the enemy now, not their allies, the Rebs. And now it's our turn to go toe to toe with these greedy heartless bastards. We will have our way with those who have helped themselves for too long to our fields, to our cities, to our faith, to our way of life, indeed, to all that we held dear within the homeland to which, with God's blessing, we together now return."

Sean thought back to Killanne. Whose fields were they now, he wondered. Could they ever be his own again?

"Gentlemen, do not forget that the precious cargo we carry to Ireland's shores is much more than the weapons below, much more than your own will to fight," Kerrigan continued. "To teach the Irish people to fight and die for their country is an ever-present duty and an easy task. It is, in fact, a lesson already learned by them. What you must do, what we together must do, is teach them that revolution is more than enthusiasm, teach them that numbers in themselves do not ensure success. We come not to teach them to fight, but to teach them how best to fight. It is a difficult and necessary thing we have come to do, but do it we must."

"And do it we will, General," came a retort drowned in cheers.

"Our fathers and theirs before them, back to the time of Cromwell and beyond, have fought bravely for Ireland. But, in losing victory they lost hope, leaving the contest to be renewed by their children and their grandchildren. As

Americans, we know that revolution is a matter of education and persistency, as well as devotion and courage on the battlefield. And, because God has blessed us with this wisdom, we must use this knowledge and not leave the contest to yet another generation.

"Freedom and independence are the rights of our race, and, as Irish Yankees, we must share with the forlorn masses of Ireland our determination to win those rights. Those beyond hope in Ireland must be compelled to join us in our determination to win these rights, to include them among the heritage we pass on to our children and they to theirs.

"This struggle for what is our destiny has been too long and too often denied. Through too many ages has it been handed down. It is time that the struggle and its transmission to future generations should cease, and, as God is our witness here on the day of his only Son's glorious Resurrection, so it shall."

The cheer that went up resonated like thunder. Sean noticed some men in tears. Sean had no more tears. He had spilled his last in Killane, watching the cart that had come for his father.

As the General stepped down, the men rushed him, clapping him on the back, pumping his outstretched hand. Captain Kavanagh shook the General's hand, too, and then took his place on the anchor chain box. The ship's bell quieted the buzz of excitement.

"Rest assured," Kavanagh said with a smile. "The eloquence of your commander will not be matched by the likes of an old salt like me. In the last week, I have made a point of having at least a few words with each of you. But, today, as master of this fine brigantine, I would like now to more formally welcome you aboard the *Jacnel* and to thank each of you for your efforts on her behalf. Her demands, as you've seen, can be both unpredictable and many, but if you meet her needs she will meet yours as well. God and the British gunboats willing, she will be seeing us safely to Ireland's shores."

Amid more cheers, General Kerrigan handed the bundle of folded green cloth to the Kavanaugh.

"In discussions with General Kerrigan, I have arrived at the conclusion that the name *Jacnel* is somewhat less than suitable for a vessel as important in the history of Irish independence as this one shall become," Kavanagh said.

The men cheered again.

"After consultation with the General, I have decided she will require a new name and, with it, a new ensign. I trust I have been forgiven by you all for the need to fly the dreaded Union Jack as we set out from New York on what was then a diversionary course. As you might expect, given our mission and the nature of our cargo, this ship has no papers, so we must do whatever is necessary to minimize suspicion."

"And what shall she be called, Captain?" a voice asked.

"After much deliberation," Kavanagh said, "I have decided this Fenian gunboat should be rechristened as exactly what she is: *Erin's Hope*."

Sean found himself joining the others in cheering and chanting the brigantine's new name, while Kerrigan and Kavanagh unfolded and displayed her new colors, a flag of deep green with a sunburst embroidered in gold. It reminded Sean of the Irish Brigade's regimental banner. It reminded him, too, of those who had followed it into battle.

Sean thought back to the war and back further still to those in the Iowa wilderness who he allowed to become the family he had no more. He remembered Mary Flanagan, who had mothered him since the crossing, who had pleaded with him through wet eyes to stay in Iowa, to work the land with her husband, Seamus, not to run off to get himself killed in some war for the coloreds. Sean hadn't listened. It wasn't only a war for the coloreds, or even a war to preserve the Union, he told her. It was Ireland's war as well. America had been grand, but it wasn't home, it wasn't the home the English had driven him from as a boy. Everything this war could teach him, he and thousands others like him would take back. "Only if you live, Sean," Mary Flanagan had said.

Sean avoided her tears just as his brother, Christor, had avoided Sean's own. Just as Christor had said goodbye with only a note when he fled Killane, Sean left a note of his own for the Flanagans. In it he thanked them for the years they had been like his own Ma and Da. They could do with his little stone house as they wished, he said. He didn't expect to return.

Sean walked most of the forty miles from Wexford to Dubuque, where he crossed the big river and signed on to push an ore cart in a lead mine near Galena. From two months of wages he saved back enough for the train east to Chicago, where he shoveled manure in the stockyards. From there he pushed on to Cleveland and finally on to Buffalo, where an Independence Day fair forever changed his life.

For a dime, he entered a turkey shoot, taking home not only a plump young hen, but an invitation to enlist in an elite corps of sharpshooters being assembled for the war. His years of dropping game in the Iowa wilderness had taught him skills with a rifle not lost on the New York Sixty-Ninth's recruiters, who found his abilities truly remarkable. Looking back now, his skills with a rifle had seen him through some days that, without them, could have been his last.

Four shots rang out, startling Sean out of his daydream. Then four more. Amidships the Stars and Stripes had been hauled down from the mainmast gaff. The shots continued as the green ensign of the sunburst was raised to take its place, a salute of thirty-two rounds, one for each of Ireland's beleagured counties.

Chapter Seven

April 24, 1867
Stevensville, Ontario

His Samaritan encounter with the wounded Fenian had brought Jeremias Tucker more than any man's share of troubles. He had never witnessed so much death, and he prayed each day he never would again. The raw violence of it left him changed and shaken, even though nearly a year had passed.

Late at night through closed eyes he would see it all again, hear and feel it, as well, the cries of those shot down around him, the warm spray of another man's blood burning into his cheeks. In the darkness he could smell the smoke as he watched himself leaning dazed upon a rake, staring into blue flames as they consumed his jacket and britches, his blood-spattered curtains, his daughter's blue linen dress.

Blame, he knew, was useless, but in his weakness Jeremias blamed Katherine for her own weakness, though not as often as she did herself. Katherine had gone to the Fenian, not him to her. Of that she had assured him, again and again. Still, it made no sense to Jeremias, the two of them wallowing in their lust, locked together naked in the straw, two strangers fornicating like barnyard beasts.

The child came in late March, and Katherine named her Sarah. She was green-eyed and beautiful, oblivious in her innocence to the chain of madness that brought her into this world of pain and trial. Jeremias had taken no small comfort in seeing for himself that the only grandchild he would ever know was not of that dead man's seed.

Sean Kenneally had not prepared Jeremias for what he discovered at home. His kitchen was a slaughtering pen. The horror of it had left Katherine dazed and weeping, sitting in the grass, mumbling and rocking. When her father and the Fenian rode into the yard, Katherine clung to them both, finally collapsing in sobs. "It's over," Jeremias remembered the Fenian assuring them both. Truth was, this test from God had just begun.

Jeremias had slept little that first night after the killings, finally giving in from sheer exhaustion. The Fenian was gone by morning, as he had promised, and with him the dead soldier's horse. Jeremias found Katherine sleeping fitfully in her room and found the dead man still sprawled in the kitchen, as he had been the night before. When Jeremais awakened Katherine, she clung to him like she had as a child, when lightning streaks on spring nights brought both thunder and fear.

"What shall we do, Father?" he remembered her asking. It was then Jeremias realized the lying would continue and that each lie must be believed. They told each other what they would tell the others, those in town, neighbors, others who might ask: A wounded Fenian held them at gunpoint and killed a soldier who tracked him to their farm. They knew nothing of the others. Jeremias was sure no one had seen him on the road bound like a criminal. They would say they had ridden to Ridgeway for help just as soon as the Fenian disappeared on the dead soldier's horse.

Jeremias had burned the clothes and the curtains while Katherine saddled the horses. They rehearsed their stories on the ride into Ridgeway. The bodies of the soldiers and the remains of their horses had been removed overnight, although Jeremias saw the spot where he had last seen them was dark and damp. Only that morning had he realized how close he soldiers had come to bringing him into Ridgeway as a Fenian sympathizer.

The garrison commander had offered them tea and had jotted notes as each of them spoke. Could they describe the Fenian? Katherine said yes: He was an older man, forty-five or fifty, heavyset and nearly toothless, with bright blue eyes and very little hair. Jeremias knew then the lies would never end.

They had ridden home with an escort of two mounted soldiers and two others who followed in a wagon, all heavily armed. They had been assigned to search the Tucker house and barn and to return the dead soldier's body to Ridgeway for a proper Christian burial. Katherine shied from the kitchen, but did manage to show the soldier in charge the charred remains of the Fenian's blood-stained bandages. Jeremias learned later that Katherine had kept one bloodied square for herself, hiding it within a book of poems given to her by her mother.

Much of the kitchen floor had been ruined by blood that had soaked into the deepest grain of the yellow pine flooring. It had taken Jeremias weeks to rip and shape new floorboards and to remove those stained black without causing too much damage to the others. The soldier's blood also had seeped through the flooring into the root cellar, which Jeremias carefully dusted with a half-barrel of crushed lime.

In the days and weeks that followed, Jeremias found Katherine more than a little preoccupied with news about the Fenians, imploring him to bring back newspapers from his infrequent trips into Ridgeway. She would be waiting at the door when he returned and would spend hours with The Toronto Globe and The Buffalo Express, piecing together accounts of Fenian arrests and trials. The first group of Fenian prisoners arrived in Toronto on the same day as the funerals for the student soldiers who had died. Even some American papers said the Fenians should be hung.

By September, Jeremias could see for himself what Katherine hadn't found the courage to admit. Yes, she said through tears, she was with child, the Fenian's child. Jeremias hadn't been able to bring himself to speak to her for most of a week.

What became of this Sean Kenneally he didn't know, and Jeremias wasn't sure it mattered. He didn't expect to see the man ever again, but, like Katherine, was curious enough to watch the papers for some hint as to his fate. Among the prisoners in Toronto was a Kennedy and a Kelly, but no one with a name like Kenneally, whatever its proper spelling.

The papers said all of the Fenians arrested by the American authorities as they crossed the Niagara River back into New York had been released after being detained briefly on barges tethered to a naval steamer. Those captured by the Canadians had been moved throughout the summer from crowded jails along the frontier, one group to a larger prison in Toronto, another to a jail in Sweetsburg. Some held in Toronto were later released, but the papers said fifty six others would stand trial for levying war against Her Majesty. Jeremias read in The Globe that any of the Fenians found to be British subjects would also be charged with treason, including anyone born in Ireland.

The trials began in October, and Jeremias was as stunned as Katherine when two of the first Fenians to be tried were sentenced to hang, one a man named Robert Lynch, the other a Catholic priest named Eamon McMahon. By mid-December, five others were added to the list of those sentenced to die.

As Jeremias had prayed they would, their lives were later spared. The papers said the American government had succeeded in persuading Governor General Monck that hanging the men would only make them martyrs to the Fenian cause, and that their deaths would incite a new invasion by an even larger Fenian army. In January, the Canadian government, at the urging of Her Majesty, announced those sentenced to death would instead spend twenty years in the Provincial Penitentiary at Kingston.

Jeremias watched the new year bring with it many changes, not the least of them this child. Katherine spent much of the winter sewing tiny blankets and nightgowns and other things a baby would need. Over Christmas dinner, Jeremias told Katherine she had never looked prettier, despite her size. Katherine insisted she had never looked or felt worse and disappeared up the stairs in tears.

As the last traces of snow melted away, so it seemed to Jeremias had Katherine's interest in news of the Fenians. The final efforts in London to formally confederate England's four North American colonies dominated the newspapers, making stories about Fenians harder to find. Early in March, some weeks before royal assent created the new Dominion of Canada, Jeremias had seen stories early about a new Fenian rising, this one in Ireland. The stories that followed over the next few weeks claimed little had come of it but mass arrests.

A new wave of Fenian trials was expected to begin soon, in Dublin, Cork and elsewhere. A Fenian rising thousands of miles across the sea in Canada was one thing, this quite another. Leniency, one paper said, was not expected.

Chapter Eight

April 28, 1867
43° 28' north latitude, 43° 17' west longitude

"They will be here soon," the Druid said, peering over the caprail down into the green water off the starboard quarterdeck.

"Be here?" Sean Kenneally asked, perplexed. "Who? Who will be here?"

"The dolphins," the Druid said. "The big steamers that come this way frighten them, but the bow wake of a square-rigger is an invitation they never refuse. When a ship as sleek as this fine ship calls out to them, it's like a song they too must sing. You will see."

Sean had been on watch many times with this curious man everyone called "the Druid." As often as not, when he spoke at all, the Druid spoke in riddles.

"Why have they not come before?" Sean asked. He had seen a dolphin only once, when he was a boy, making the crossing.

"Too cold," the Druid said. "We've just come upon

this warm current. The dolphins like this warm water for the fish it breeds. They're not fish themselves, of course."

"Not fish?" Sean asked, beginning to sense he was being toyed with. "Of course, they're fish."

The Druid smiled at him in a knowing way.

"You have much to learn," he said. "Dolphins are more like yourself than like a fish. They breathe air, as do you, not water like a fish. And, like yourself, these are curious beasts. They'll hear our bow song and be by to have a look at us. And when they come, look into their eyes, man. You'll see they have not the eyes of fish, but the gaze of creatures with souls. And, should they like what they see in your eyes, they may stay awhile, playing in the foam beneath the bowsprit. There may be two, or there may be twenty. Young and old ones both. You will see. They will come."

Dolphins, the Druid told him, were a sign of luck. It seemed to Sean the luck of the *Jacnel* had changed after her Easter Sunday transformation into *Erin's Hope*. Today she was standing nor'east, riding the Gulf Stream current that pushed her crew and her cargo ever so slowly toward Ireland, adding at times three knots to the momentum of this warm following breeze.

The drenching squalls that plagued the crossing throughout the diversionary West Indies tack had given way to fair days, clear nights and gentle swells. The changing skies had proven an antidote for the sickness that settled over Sean and so many others not accustomed to ships. The warm winds came none too soon for Sean. He had seen enough of damp and fog and numbing cold. He wouldn't miss soggy boots and fingers left aching and stiff from clinging to the ratlines while going aloft in a bitter gale.

Like the others new to ships, Sean's hands had gone red and raw from rope work and salt spray. His shoulders ached still from working the pumps. In the worst of the weather that had passed their way, seawater poured into the bilge at a rate of ten inches an hour, requiring the pumps to be manned twice each watch. To himself and the others ordered below to do the work, it had gone on for what seemed like days. The first week out Sean had no appetite at all and kept down little of what he forced himself to eat. The deck work now left him more hungry than tired, hungry even for meals that were little more than a few boiled potatoes, a few crusts of slightly molded fadge and a few mouthfuls of salted pork.

These sunny days were much too bright for Sean, whose fair skin blistered easily. Even with a broad hat that cast a wide shadow, the sun off the water burned his face. The others on night watch teased him that his nose glowed like a portside running lamp. To avoid the blisters, Sean asked the first mate for night watches and for daytime duty below. With all this damp, the long barrels of the rifles packed in flimsy crates were badly in need of oiling.

The cold-weather squalls were now behind them now, bringing nights so clear that a reading man could make out words beneath the pale white glow of the clustered stars. Not all the stars were in the sky. Some, it seemed, had been swallowed up by the sea itself.

Sean saw it first a few nights back, this milky trail of cloudy light, blinking and glowing, just below the waterline. First white, then green, then sometimes blue, it started in the bow wake and split apart, hugging each side of the brigantine's black hull before coming together in a burst of brightness just behind her rudder. In a trailing line of soft silver light, it marked the ship's path through the moonless night. Sean watched it for hours, entranced.

One black night, he scooped up a bit of it, using a leather bucket tethered to a coil of rope. He set the bucket in his lap, cupping the glowing water in his hands until the light slowly faded away. It seemed such a miracle.

"It's alive," the Druid told him, amused to see Sean trolling for light over the side.

"What's alive?" Sean asked.

"The sea," the Druid said. "It's alive. And not just the creatures in it, mind you, but the very water itself. These lights you see are the sea's way of letting sailors know that for a fact. And a way of making sure they never forget it."

Sean wouldn't forget. Not a miracle like this.

The next night, again on watch, Sean found the Druid silently pacing the deck. The Druid never seemed to sleep. "Tell me something," Sean said, not knowing if the Druid would take offense. "Everyone calls you 'the Druid.' Why is that?"

The Druid said nothing.

"I remember my father speaking of Druids," Sean said. "It was when I was a child, back in Killane, before the hunger. But, in his stories, Druids were pagans and sorcerers, magicians and evil-doers. Druids were wicked heathens who burned humans in baskets at Lunasa as sacrifices to the pagan harvest gods."

The Druid said nothing still.

"So, are you a Druid?" Sean asked. "Why should a Druid be making a voyage such like this?"

"You ask too many questions," the Druid finally said. "But I guess such a thing is to be praised in a man who knows so little as you. As to why I'm here ..." The Druid said nothing for a minute, then closed his eyes and spoke very slowly. "I am the sea. I am the wind. I am this ship. And they are me. As are you as well."

More riddles, Sean thought. More silence passed between them. "You are a young man, as are these others," the Druid finally said. "Perhaps one day you will grasp the connections and understand that things do not exist unto themselves, not men like you, not the creatures of the sea, not the clouds that do battle with the sun. Each lives each day and passes each night within a realm not made by the hands of man nor seen by the eyes of most. We live in the eye of the sun, in the eye of the wind, connecting through time who we were with who we are with who we will one day be."

Sean said nothing. There was nothing to say. A few minutes passed like hours. Sean found the silence grew painful.

"Benny, the boatswain, says the Old Man never sets out without you," Sean said.

"Aye, and likely won't again," the Druid replied. "I know these winds and these waves like no man you've known before. I know things that others don't, in ways that others can't. I see things not as they happen to us, but as we happen to them. I have a keen sense of good and an even keener sense of evil that is as much a part of me as your green eyes are a part of you. Like you warriors and your weapons, I am seen by Captain Kavanagh as a valuable cargo."

The Druid was no larger than a boy. Sean seemed half again his size. How old he was he couldn't tell, but Sean knew he must be old enough to have grown boys of his own. Truth was he had no one. Benny told him last night the Druid's real name was Dooley and that he hadn't set foot on land in years.

"He has a gift, I guess 'tis," Benny told Sean while finding him the tools he needed to uncrate rifles. "I have no doubt of it. He listens to the sea and he tastes the wind. You'll see him climb into the rigging and stay up for hours, breathing in the mist, studying the stars, watching the petrels and the puffins. It's been said the Druid feels change in the air, both change for ill or change for good. The Old Man won't set out without him. They've been together now for years."

Though Captain Kavanagh had never mentioned it, Benny once heard that during the war the Druid saved the Old Man's ship from being overhauled by Raphael Semmes. "Kavanagh had a barque, then, or so the story goes," Benny told Sean. "September of 1862 it was, somewhere near the 38th parallel. The Old Man was making northing slowly, hauling saltpeter to the Federals from some backwater port in Cuba, when out of the blue, for no reason at all, the Druid appears at the helm and tells the Old Man to quick throw on a mass of sail, both alow and aloft to give her even the trysails, with bonnets off. For no reason mind you.

"Why he listened, who's to say, but the Old Man did. The crew thought he'd gone daft. They were making ten knots when a Confederate raider, the *Alabama* it was, appeared off her port beam, heading straight for her. A chase of sixty miles it was. Lasted half a day, but that pirate Semmes couldn't get even the biggest of his deck guns within range. The Old Man outsailed that grayback rascal, the only quarry who ever did, or so it's been said. The Old Man's ship wasn't boarded and burned, and he believes to this day the Druid was the reason why. Kavanagh and the Druid have been together since, on every cruise."

Sean felt himself on a slippery slope already. He dared not ask the Druid if Benny's story was true. After another long and uncomfortable silence, the Druid posed a question of his own.

"I know the facts of what you and the others are doing here, but why is it you made the trip?" the Druid asked. "You clearly never set foot on any ship's deck, much less spent time in any ship's rigging. And neither have your mates. Even a blind man could see that."

"True enough," Sean said.

"So what penance am I paying for being stuck with a crew not of sailors, but of foot soldiers?" the Druid said. "Men as green as your likes can easily prove the death of a ship in seas as temperamental as these can be. Do you hate the English so that you would not only drown yourselves, but me along with you?"

"It'll do us no good to drown ourselves nor you with us," Sean said. "But it'll do all of Ireland some good indeed to put this cargo aboard to use. We are Erin's hope, you see. Dochas Eireann, as the old ones say. And that hope lies not only in these crates of rifles, mind you, but in the hearts and souls of these men."

Sean knew too well that some Boston Irish millionaire could always buy more rifles, but never again would Ireland see the likes of men like those on board. "These men are precious few," he told the Druid. "These are men who know what it is to lead other men into the hell of battle, to stare death down against incredible odds. Fewer still are men who live not merely to tell the tale, but to seek out new battles, battles that must be fought. Baptized in blood, most of us, our own blood and that of our brothers. Those on this ship have seen and lived things that others could imagine only in a nightmare."

"Aye," said the Druid. "And so they may again."

※ ※ ※

By late afternoon, the breeze that came up with the sun died away to near calm. The wake off the bow was reduced to a trickle, the sound of it giving way to the groans of the main boom's gaff jaws and the flap of luffing canvas. Like a few many of the others, Sean dozed in the shade of the deckhouse.

The Druid heard them before he saw them, forty or more, their shiny dorsal fins glinting black in the sun as they cut bow wakes of their own through the glassy calm. "Dolphins astern," the Druid yelled over his shoulder. "Astern and to port."

His words passed quickly through the ship, bringing Sean to his senses.

"Dolphins, is it?" he said to no one, jumping to his feet, blinded by the brightness. By the time he reached the port rail, twenty men had gathered, hooting and laughing and pointing out to sea.

"Just look at them!" said Mickey Green. "Aren't they glorious?"

A head taller than Green, Sean looked over the young lieutenant and squinted into the blinding glare of sun and sea. Not more than ten feet off the beam, half in and half out of the water, were three long sleek black fish, bigger by far than the biggest tuna he'd ever seen hanging in a fish market. A white stripe ran along their sides and across their bellies. Two were large, one quite small, a young one no doubt. They seemed close enough to touch.

"More, over here, to starboard!" came a voice beyond the deckhouse.

"Must be fifty of 'em."

Green and the others made their way to starboard, leaving Sean alone on the port cap rail, mesmerized. They've holes in their heads, he thought. Holes that spray water like fountains.

The trio moved even closer to the ship's black hull. They were two feet below him now, kicking their tails in an effortless harmony that maintained their speed and tight formation. All at once, the largest of the three raised its nose toward the sky and, in an instant, caught Sean's gaze in its own.

"She likes you," said a voice from behind.

It was the voice of the Druid. "Look into those eyes, Sean," the Druid whispered. "What you see in those eyes is yourself, just as she sees herself in your own. It's the eyes that tell you this is no ordinary fish, just as your eyes tell her that she sees no ordinary man."

Sean stood transfixed. When at last he turned to answer, the Druid was gone.

Turning back, the three dolphins had vanished as well.

Chapter Nine

May 15, 1867
54° 39' north latitude, 10° 25' west longitude

A gannet confirmed what the Druid already knew:
With these winds, the headlands of the Irish coastline
awaited them little more than a day beyond the dawn. The
giant bird appeared at first light, a scout from some
offshore island colony, spiraling down on *Erin's Hope* in
the false hope she was a fishing boat willing to part with a
plaice or maybe a small squid.

Erin's Hope was on a starboard tack now, sailing full
and bye. The wind had shifted overnight, from southwest
by south to north by northwest. Despite this new brisk
breeze, the Druid could detect the faintest musk of land to
the east. Benny the boatswain would be pleased. A week
and a day out, he had joined most of the others in putting
up two dollars, each man, the winnings to be divided
among those who correctly guessed the number of days
between Sandy Hook and the first sighting of the Irish
coast.

Those new to the sea sought the advice of those on
board who had made west-to-east crossings before. The
predictions ranged from a wishful twenty-one days to a

drink-induced fifty-four. Benny figured landfall in thirty-three days, what with the diversionary West Indies tack and the North Atlantic's changeable spring winds.

For two days now, all aboard had been in a state of high alert. Clear skies allowed sextant readings that put *Erin's Hope* in waters likely patrolled by English frigates. Her Majesty's gunboats would be on alert for privateer barquentines, brigantines and schooners sent from America to resupply the Fenian rebellion. Standing orders required any such Fenian ship be overhauled, boarded and burned. Those on board resisting arrest were to be put to death. Prisoners were to be brought ashore in irons.

Twice each day for the past two days all on board *Erin's Hope* had been ordered to drills. Pikes brought up from below were distributed to all hands, each man shown how to use them in repelling boarders. Empty wooden crates flung overboard served as bobbing targets in small arms drills. Sean Kenneally put on a show from the foremast platform with a Whitworth he had brought with him from New York, dissolving into splinters four empty fresh water casks as they drifted astern from view.

Taking a brigantine from New York to Ireland had proven no great challenge for a shipmaster as adept as Joseph Kavanagh, even with a crew as green as this one. He had cut his teeth aboard topsail schooners and perfected his craft at the helms of the long string of square-rigged barques and brigs on which he hauled cargoes during the war. In fair weather, a schooner was Kavanagh's ship of choice, but the job of reefing massive topsails in a storm was a difficult one at best, requiring a large and experienced crew. Square sails like these allowed maneuvers not possible in a schooner.

Her brigantine rigging was similar to that of a barque,

but with a simpler mainmast rig. Her foremast had the usual square rig with foresail, topsail, topgallant and royal, with a trysail bent to a trysail mast abaft the foremast. Her mainmast was both a lower mast and a topmast and carried a large fore-and-aft mainsail, a square topsail and a topgallant. With three headsails and three studding sails, *Erin's Hope* had shown she could make just over eight knots under the best of conditions.

What Granfar had told him when he was only a boy had proven exactly right: A brigantine could sail backwards, once her square sails had been braced so their front sides caught the wind. With a symmetrical rig, standing still in the water was an easy maneuver, as was turning on the spot. And, if the need arose, a brigantine could be handled by a skeleton crew.

Kavanagh found the cut of *Erin's Hope* unmistakably Yankee and knew lookouts aboard English gunboats would find her such as well. From the curves of her counter to the delicate wave lines of her bow, an educated eye would see her American character in every plank and spar.

This crossing of three thousand miles had required just more than thirty days. On her best day, the fifth of May, *Erin's Hope* had made one hundred eighty-nine miles. On her worst, Easter Sunday, a mere fifty-two. Remarkably, no hands had been lost, though one man had a foot crushed by a crate of Enfield rifles that broke loose in the hold during a blow.

"These men have done better than I feared they might," Kavanagh told the Druid as they huddled over charts of the rocky Irish coastline. "There's not an able seaman in this bunch, mind you, but for a group of foot soldiers they've done better than most would expect."

"Even so," said the Druid, "the real test is ahead."

"That it is, my friend," Kavanagh said, "which is why I've asked Benny to put them through some paces before this building breeze takes us any nearer to shore."

As the morning watch stepped down, the Druid took the helm, allowing Benny and the other watch commanders to gather all hands amidships.

"Listen carefully, now," General Kerrigan said. "As you have no doubt heard, we expect to spot land before too much longer. And you should know that we expect to be spotted as well. It's anyone's guess what is happening ashore, or what course the rebellion has taken in the month since we set sail. Whether the rising is a success, or whether the British have by now succeeded in putting it down, we cannot know. For our own sakes, we need to expect the worst and be ready for the worst. Your attention now, please, as the Captain has asked to speak a few words to you."

Kavanagh stepped forward and produced from his pocket a much-folded sheet of paper. "Gentlemen, good day to you," he said. "Our crossing is near complete, though your expedition is just beginning. I expect to be in sight of the western headlands of Ireland before the sun sets tomorrow, perhaps long before then if this west wind holds up. It's my hope, and I'm sure yours as well, that we will find a warm welcome and that we will learn as we at last drop anchor that the English have been routed by this rising we have come a very long way to support. This may, however, not be the case, and we must be prepared for, as General Kerrigan put it, the worst.

"As sleek as she is, a ship such as this is no match whatever for a British man-of-war. My orders are to not allow this ship to be taken. Each of you must do all you can to preserve her and her cargo and to preserve each other as well."

Kavanagh held up the paper in his hand.

"Upon leaving New York, I was given this letter," he said. "It contains my orders from Captain John Powell, chief of naval affairs for the Fenian Brotherhood, and from Anthony Griffith, the chief of the Executive of the Fenian Organization of America. I think it is appropriate that I now read these orders aloud to you."

The cluster of men on deck inched closer, eager to catch every word.

"It is dated twelve April, eighteen sixty-seven, and it reads as follows," Kavanagh said. "'Sir. You will proceed with the vessel under your command to Sligo Bay on the coast of Ireland or to any other part of the same coast of Ireland where you may more safely land your cargo and passengers. You will use every precaution to ensure the delivery of the cargo and passengers to the persons authorized to receive them.

"'If possible, after you land your cargo and passengers, you will return your vessel to New York and turn her over to the proper authorities; but, in case you see no chance of escaping with her, destroy her if practicable. You will, in all cases, use your own judgment. God bless and speed you."

Kavanagh refolded the letter and returned it to a pocket of his waistcoat. "So, there you have it, gentlemen," he said. "It is to Sligo I am to deliver you and the weapons below. As we make our way into Sligo Bay we will be looking for certain shore signals there and have been directed to use our jibs to make our identity known to those ashore we have been told will be awaiting our arrival. But, there may be others awaiting us as well, namely Her Majesty's coast guards and the Royal Navy's gunboats.

"We are not, as you can see, a vessel equipped to do naval battle. Any close encounter with a British man-of-war, or even a well-armed corvette, might prove a brief one, indeed. That is why, in these orders I have just read to you, it is stipulated that this ship is to be destroyed should capture appear to me to be unavoidable. As I presume most of you know already, your own Colonel Clark has been making plans to do just that, although be assured you will all be ordered into the boats well before the Colonel is given any order by me to send *Erin's Hope* and her cargo to the bottom.

"Be assured as well that I, like you, have not come all this way to scuttle this fine ship," Kavanagh said. "And each man here must do all he can to see that doesn't become necessary. You men have done quite well in working with my crew in taking this vessel across the North Atlantic, but your apprenticeships as sailors now take on a new level of urgency. The time you have spent so far on deck and in the rigging has involved only simple ropework and what sail handling was required to change our heading or to ride out what few storms and squalls that have challenged us. In the next few days, perhaps even sooner, we may be forced at a moment's notice to run. And, if we must run, we can expect to be pursued by larger ships of greater speed in wind and weather that may not favor our escape.

"That is why I have asked Benny and some other

crew to work with you throughout what is left of this day in familiarizing you thoroughly with the ropework required to wear ship should we need to reverse our course to escape pursuit. By now, most of you know, at least, a downhaul from a clewline. Rest assured that those who do not will have no doubt which is which by the time the sun now above you sets.

"These maneuvers you will undertake today may seem complicated at first. They are not, but they do require each of you to listen carefully to orders. You must all work together. Doing the wrong thing at the wrong time will spell disaster for us all. As Benny will remind you, this is deckwork you may very well find yourself confronting in the black of night or the teeth of a gale, so each man among you must make use of today's fine weather to learn his specific task. So, Benny, have at it. These men are at your disposal for the rest of the afternoon."

As Kavanagh returned to the helm, those on deck traded in whispers what little they knew of Sligo. One among them, Johnny FitzSimmons, had been born in nearby County Longford. As a young boy he visited an elderly aunt who lived at Rosses Point, on the sea, just beyond Sligo city. He was very young then, he said, and remembered little, except for some great table mountain with an odd name he couldn't recall.

"Quiet now," Benny said at last. "We have much to do and much to learn and little time for both."

Benny split the six watches into four new groups. Two he assigned to the pinrails - one group to starboard, the other to port. The others were to muster at the fife rails, one group below the foremast, the other below the main.

"The task at hand, gentlemen, is to wear ship. You need to turn this ship around and to get it about damn quick," he said. "When you hear the order 'Stand by to wear ship,' you will report immediately to these posts I have just assigned you. As we turn the ship to lee and begin to sail free, you will hear the order 'Square the main yards.' Those of you at the aft pinrails will do just that, just as you've squared the yards when changing tack. As the Captain has said, you must work together. Too much tug on one side can bend and shatter a yard, which will do us no good at all."

With the Druid at the wheelbox, they went through it for real, dropping off the port tack, squaring the mainyards, hauling round the foreyards. As *Erin's Hope* came about, running briefly with the wind, the order was given to gybe the mainsail and shift the head sails and staysails. As she began to sail free, those on deck began bracing the mainyards and trimming all sails.

"You've done it," Benny screamed. "But, you've done it damned slow. We'll be doing it again, and again still, until you can do it in your bloody sleep."

For the rest of the day, five hours at least, *Erin's Hope* slowly traversed the blue-green swells in lazy, awkward figure eights. By evening the men were exhausted, their hands ropeburned and raw. By the time all but the deckwatch headed below to their bunks. To a man, backs and shoulders ached. Most were too tired even to eat.

"It's Benbulben," the Druid told Johnny FitzSimmons as he reported to the helm for the watch change.

"Who's Ben Bullen?" Johnny asked.

"Not who, what," the Druid said. "The table mountain above Sligo, the one you remembered seeing as a child. They call it Benbulben."

The Druid had been nowhere near Johnny when he had mentioned the mountain to those curious about Sligo. In fact, the Druid had been well astern, taking the wheel while everyone else was gathered forward to listen to the Old Man read aloud his orders.

"And how did you know that?" Johnny asked, more than a bit baffled. "How did you know I had seen this mountain as a child? Did someone tell you?"

"There are ways of knowing without being told," the Druid said.

So, this strange little fecker is a bloody mind-reader now, is he? Johnny thought. Is he reading me thoughts right now?

"What was it, again?" Johnny asked. "Benbullin?"

"No," the Druid said. "Benbulben. You will be seeing it again before long now. It will appear out of the fog, looking still as it did centuries ago to the invading Milesians, looking like a sow swimming in the sea."

What's he mean, a sow in the sea? Johnny wondered.

"It is more than a mountain, boy," the Druid said.

"Benbulben is as sacred a place as to be found near Sligo."

"Sacred? You mean sacred like St. Bridget's Well?" Johnny asked. "A place of miracles?"

"Some miracles have occurred on Benbulben. Others should have perhaps," the Druid said. "But not miracles of the type you have in mind."

"Of what type, then?" Johnny asked.

"You know of Fionn mac Cumhaill, do you not?" the Druid asked.

"You mean Finn McCool?" Johnny said. "Yes, of course. He was the leader of the Fianna."

"The other was the name he used himself," the Druid said. "A great warrior, he was. Fearless at first. But, near the end, Fionn proved himself a mere man. And, like most mere men, he allowed himself to be consumed by jealousy, rage and revenge."

"You speak of him as if you knew the man," Johnny said.

"And you as if you never will," the Druid replied. "True enough, Fionn was an old man by then, but it was on Benbulben he proved himself less of a god and more of a mortal than the legends would have you believe."

The Druid stared out to sea, saying nothing more. In its lazy descent, the sun had painted the sky the color of salmon. The first chill of night was overtaking the warm following breeze that continued to bring both petrels and puffins. The Druid studied the birds carefully, for each had its story to tell.

The Druid's long silence made Johnny FitzSimmons increasingly uncomfortable. "Go on, man," Johnny said at last. "What of Finn McCool and Benbulben? And what miracles? Tell me."

"More magic than miracles, it was," the Druid said. "And it's a tale more about Diarmaid Ua Duibhne, the warrior some bards call 'Dark Dermot.' He was the greatest of the Fianna's warriors and, through a charm bestowed upon him by the daughter of a shepherd, he proved irresistible to women. But, it would be a curse."

The Druid explained that among the women who could not resist Diarmuid was Grainne, the beautiful daughter of King Cormac mac Airt, the High King of Tara, a daughter he had promised to Fionn mac Cumhaill. So taken was she by Dark Dermot's charms, she eloped with him from Tara on her wedding night while Fionn and the Fianna were stupid with the strong mead served at the wedding banquet."

"Finn Mac Cool's greatest warrior ran off with Finn's bride on their wedding night?" Johnny asked in disbelief. "Was he daft? Finn must have been in a killing rage."

"That he was," the Druid said. "And so he remained for years."

The Druid told Johnny how Fionn and the Fianna had searched from the glens of Antrim to the Caha Mountains in frantic pursuit of the fugitive lovers. Through Diarmuid's cunning, they successfully eluded the search. At last, the Druid said, Fionn mac Cumhaill's rage gave way to his weariness, but only after sixteen years had passed.

"After many years, he called off the search and

finally agreed to forgive them both," the Druid said. "In truth, he never did, a fact later revealed atop Benbulben."

The Druid peered toward the darkening horizon, fixing his gaze on the point where he knew, come dawn, the Milesians had seen the sow in the sea. The Druid wizards of the Tuatha De Danann had shrouded the Irish coastline in a cloaking fog, hoping to hide its richness from the invaders from Spain, hoping all they would see above the fog was the sow, swimming in the sea.

"Go on, man," Johnny said, sounding like an impatient child.

"Not long after Fionn sent word to the fugitive lovers that they had been forgiven, he invited Diarmuid to join him and the Fianna on a hunt. It was to be the great hunt of the magic boar of Benbulben, a hunt for a beast that wasn't a boar at all."

"If not a boar, then what?" Johnny asked.

"Truth be known, and Fionn knew more than he let on, it was a boy turned beast, a boy transformed by bad magic, magic bred of rage," the Druid said. "It was Diarmuid's half-brother, born of his mother, a queen, fathered by her husband's steward. On his deathbed, the old steward begged his master's forgiveness. In a rage of betrayal, the king grabbed up the child, by then a boy the king had loved as his own son, and dashed him again and again to the ground. But, the bastard child refused to die."

Johnny FitzSimmons was entranced.

"Diarmuid's father, the king, used magic to transform the boy into a boar, a boar with no ears and no tail," the Druid said. "He ordered the beast banished into the woods

123

of Benbulben where it grew strong and fierce and ravaged the land at will. It grew hateful, as well, blaming its fate not on the king, but on pureborn Diarmuid. The Druids in his father's court sensed the danger this beast posed to the prince and used their magic to make geassa upon Diarmuid, a bond that forbade him from hunting boar or eating boar's flesh."

"So, did Dark Dermot go with Finn and the Fianna on the hunt?" FitzSimmons asked.

"He knew it was forbidden, but he did, despite the Druid's bond," the Druid said. "Fionn knew he would. Diarmuid brought to the hunt his best wolf dog and his spear. And when the Fianna flushed the boar from cover, it came right for Diarmuid, its eyes burning with revenge. Diarmuid loosed his best hound, but it fled in fear. When he launched his spear, it bounced harmlessly off the beast's back. The magic boar of Benbulben was on Diarmuid in an instant, tearing into one shoulder with one of its tusks and knocking him to the ground.

"When the beast charged again, Diarmuid leapt onto its back. He was riding a nightmare, but was able to draw his sword and slash the raging beast's throat. The boar threw Diarmuid to the ground and gored him with its tusks, opening his belly. Dying himself, Diarmuid watched as the bleeding beast, gasping and thrashing, regained its human form as it drew its last breath."

"And did he die? Dark Dermot, I mean," FitzSimmons said.

"That he did, no thanks to Fionn, who could have saved him," the Druid said. "As a young man, Fionn had tasted of the Salmon of Knowledge and among the gifts imparted to him was the gift of saving lives by drawing water from a spring in his cupped hands and delivering it to those near death."

"And was there a spring on top of Benbulben?" FitzSimmons asked.

"There was," the Druid said, "and the Fianna urged Fionn to run to it and cup his hands and fill them. He did, but upon returning, Fionn's thoughts of saving his old friend gave way to the black memories of his betrayal by Grainne. As Fionn was lost in his thoughts, the water trickled through his hands.

"The Fianna urged him to return to the spring, which he did, but again his rage prevailed, and he opened his cupped hand, letting the water spill to the ground. At last Fionn decided to spare his old friend, but when he returned from the spring again, he saw it was too late. Diarmaid lay dead amid his own steaming bowels."

The two men said nothing for what seemed near an hour.

"Off with you, now," the Druid finally said. "Get below and get some rest. Tomorrow will be a day the likes of which you will not soon forget."

By midnight, even Kavanagh could smell the musk of land. The coast would be in sight by noon, by sunset at the latest. The Royal Navy's gunboats likely sooner.

"Luck is a Lord," Kavanagh told the Druid before turning in. "Let's hope some is with us from here on out."

"It will be and it won't be," the Druid said. "Luck is a fickle friend, at best. We would do best to work at making some luck of our own."

Kavanagh slowly studied the horizon one more time.

"You'll be giving me a shake should you spot any lights," he said.

"Aye, sir," the Druid said. "A shake it will be."

Chapter Ten

May 26, 1867
Off the County Mayo coast

The news awaiting them in Sligo had not been good.

Shore signals agreed upon went unacknowledged for days. The two men General Kerrigan sent ashore to find out why their signals had been ignored had failed to return as ordered. They had taken with them the cook's helper, Buckley, who badly needed a doctor. Not long after dropping anchor in Sligo Bay, he had put a bullet though his own left foot with a revolver even Buckley admitted he had no business handling.

That was hardly the worst of it.

Thursday last, as the sun burned through the last of the morning fog, *Erin's Hope* appeared in Sligo Bay. The coast guard took note of this curious ship, laying at anchor with all sails furled, except, curiously, her outer jib. The jib configuration was a signal agreed upon in New York. Fenians ashore awaiting her arrival were to respond with green banners to signify all was clear. But the only signals received were coast guard flags, asking what business had brought a black-hulled brigantine with an unmistakably

Yankee cut to the outer reaches of Sligo Bay. Those signals, too, went ignored.

In the anxious days that passed, a cutter and a few small boats selling fish and fruit had come and gone. What little news they offered had all been bad. A pilot named Gallagher invited aboard by Captain Kavanagh knew nothing of Fenian activities ashore. He was not, he said, a political man, but would gladly bring their ship and its cargo - fruit from Spain, is it? - safely into port for two sovereigns and a box of lemons.

What Gallagher told them was later confirmed by none other than Colonel Ricard O'Sullivan Burke, no amateur at smuggling weapons to the Brotherhood.

The rising in Sligo, as everywhere else, had failed nearly as quickly as it began. The weapons aboard *Erin's Hope* were too little, too little and too late, Burke said. As vital as it was, their cargo could not be safely landed, not in Sligo, nor in any other port he knew of nearby.

From what few IRB men remained in Sligo, Burke learned the March rising triggered only a few brief skirmishes. They and the handful of Americans who took part had quickly realized that the poorest of those living in and around Sligo would not risk what little they had at the whim of the Fenians. But neither did they turn out against them or seem eager to betray them. The rewards offered by the government for information on the Fenian leaders were having no effect. As desperate as they were, Burke said, these people wouldn't touch blood money, but neither would they fight. Those loyal to the cause who managed to escape arrest had long since vanished into the safety of the countryside, scattered now like windblown leaves, most licking wounds never suffered.

Burke had been waiting on the *Jacnel* for more than week, coming overland from Dublin and posing as an American factory owner. Throughout Sligo City he was known as Charles Edward Russell, a Protestant millionaire vacationing in Sligo after inspecting the tweed mills of Donegal. While waiting and watching, Burke learned all he could from the local gentry of the coastline defenses, facts freely offered over cognac and mussels at the Victoria Hotel.

The Royal Navy expected the worst. From mid-March to mid-May, English gunboats summoned from the Blacksod Bay station had patrolled Sligo Bay, positioning themselves to confront any attempt to reinforce the Fenians by sea.

Captain Kavanagh had heard enough. Three days at anchor was tempting both fate and the patience of an uneasy coast guard. Clearly, there could be no landing at Sligo. Colonel Burke presented General Kerrigan with a new set or orders from Dublin, signed by Colonel Thomas Kelly himself, the highest-ranking Fenian in all Ireland. *Erin's Hope* would run.

Head south beyond Galway to the west Kerry coastline, then east toward Skibbereen, Kelly's orders said. Sail the waters between Toe Head and Galley Head with jibs down, but not furled on the boom. A craft would approach them, Kelly promised, with her jib down but unfurled as well. Those aboard would be IRB men who would guide them to safe harbor or offload the weapons at sea.

Burke disappeared over the rail into the darkness and headed for shore, wishing Kavanagh and Kerrigan godspeed. Word of new orders spread quickly through the ship, leaving the men feeling grim and morose. They had come so far, for so little. Now they were to be off again, leaving behind three of their own.

Captain Kavanagh ordered the windlass muffled before the anchor was hove in. The binnacle was screened, the lamp in the chartroom fitted with a jacket. Those who smoked pipes were told to keep them below, and old Jenkins was told to leave his fiddle in his bunk. A reel on this moonless night might quickly become a dirge.

In the stealth of darkness, the men took their places on the yards and began dropping sail. Orders were passed in whispers, not shouts, as *Erin's Hope* slipped her mooring and began searching through the night for a breeze that could carry her from Sligo toward friendlier seas. Kavanagh laid the head of his ship west. As she neared Aughris Head he took the helm himself, at first keeping her as close to the rocky shoreline as the darkness allowed, then tacking northwest by north to make a wide berth around Killala Bay, where the French had come ashore in 1798 and where British cruisers were likely on patrol.

As the sun broke through the headland fog, *Erin's Hope* tacked into the wind, making west along the Mayo coast. Burke had delivered charts of these waters when he came aboard at Sligo. They were old and stolen and Burke had paid far too much for them, but, in these rocky waters, Kavanagh found them preferable to no charts at all.

By mid-morning the last traces of fog had melted away. The seaside pastures along the Mayo coast grew smaller on the horizon. When Kavanagh ordered all hands to stand by to wear ship, he was amazed by how quickly these foot soldiers responded. The long North Atlantic crossing and Benny's short temper had managed to make competent crew of all but a few. They took their places quickly, half along each rail, releasing and hauling the braces in unison as they squared each of the mainyards. Moving quickly to the forward pinrails, they hauled round the foreyards and shifted the heads ails and staysails.

The mainsail gybed smoothly as she came around. With the mainyards braced and the jibs properly trimmed, *Erin's Hope* churned south by southwest, now making good time toward a destination unknown to all but a few.

The Old Man ordered the watches doubled, knowing the Coast Guard at Sligo would have reported this curious, black-hulled brigantine gone now for hours.

Chapter Eleven

May 27, 1867
Off the South Cork coastline

The Druid had been high in the main mast rigging for hours, scanning the bays, searching the seacliffs for any shore signs of Fenians. The coastline from Dingle to Kinsale was thick with rocky islands, some inhabited by more than birds. He knew of the Druid clans that once lived upon islands such as these, all along the Irish coast.

Sailors left becalmed and bewildered would often pull ashore in dinghies, seeking out among the Druids old women selling baskets filled with wind. When will the Druid winds come? Soon, the old women would say. Keep watch for a blast of wind at sunset, a blow from the east.

Since first light Captain Kavanagh had kept *Erin's Hope* a mile or more off the shoreline, cruising in a long tight ellipse between Cape Clear and Toe Head. Her jib was down and left unfurled, just as Colonel Kelly ordered, but no boat appeared. Kavanagh was not amused.

An urgent dispatch from Sligo had put the entire British channel fleet on notice of suspicious activities involving a vessel suspected of being in the command of

American Fenians. The black-hulled brigantine had slipped its mooring in Sligo Bay overnight. Two reports Sunday had her running west from Killala Bay. The Royal Navy commander at Dingle wired a report of multiple sightings of a brigantine hovering well out to sea between the Blaskets and Cape Clear. He asked that warships based at Queenstown be placed on alert.

Kavanagh called all hands together at mid-morning, reminding them again *Erin's Hope* was not a warship. It was likely a matter of hours before her presence in these waters would be challenged.

"These guns we have brought this far will not be surrendered, not while they remain my responsibility," Kavanagh told them. "Should it seem improbable that we can deliver them into the hands of Fenians ashore, the guns and this ship will go to the bottom."

If the wind was right, Kavanagh said, *Erin's Hope* could run. If not, the expedition's fate would be in the capable hands of their own Colonel Clark.

🎝 🎝 🎝

Timothy Clark hadn't come to the Fenian Brotherhood. It had come to him. He wished he could join such a worthy expedition without compensation, he told Captain Powell when they met in New York, but he was not a wealthy man. And of course, there would be expenses.

Timothy Clark knew Fenians in the Union Army, he told Powell, and had met some even at West Point. Though he was Irish and certainly sympathetic to their cause, he had been far too busy with his work at West

Point to become a Fenian himself.

How the Brotherhood had found him he never was told. Though he gladly accepted the military commission Powell was offering, the whole affair became for "Colonel" Clark a business proposition that was certainly more lucrative than bookbinding. He had named his price, and the Brotherhood had paid it, in gold.

Powell knew Timothy Clark was a genius with explosives. Late in the war, as each side grew more desperate to bring the war to an end, Clark was in constant demand. In a well-equipped Federal Army ordnance laboratory he fabricated land mines and developed new techniques of floating naval mines to enforce the blockade imposed by the Federal Navy on countless Confederate ports.

Timothy Clark was nineteen, a printer like his father, when he mustered into the Federal Army at Pittsburgh. The war was going badly, and the Federals needed infantry, not typesetters. He was issued a rifle and assigned at once as a replacement for the Forty-Eighth Pennsylvania Volunteers, who were in the fight somewhere near Richmond.

On the very day he reported for duty, Lieutenant Colonel Henry Pleasants was seeking volunteers for what he would describe only as a "highly dangerous" and "very secret" mission behind enemy lines. The Colonel was true to his word. Clark and the others soon found themselves behind the graybacks' lines, and beneath those lines as well. The digging was done mostly at night, all of it by hand. They carried the clay and sandy soil excavated from below the rebel lines through a maze of timbered shafts in hand barrows built from cracker-boxes. The work continued for six full weeks, until the main shaft extended six hundred feet.

An important rebel breastworks near Petersburg, Virginia, had proven unassailable and remained a significant strategic hurdle. Word came down directly from Major General Meade at Army of the Potomac headquarters: Take it out, at any price. Colonel Pleasants was a mining engineer who worked before the war in the Pennsylvania coalfields. He offered an unusual plan. It was, he said, a strategy he could guarantee, presuming his superiors could buy him some time.

Toward the end, while carefully positioning each of three hundred and eight kegs of black powder, Timothy Clark could hear the enemy moving above him, separated now by only twenty feet of clay and sand.

The papers said the pre-dawn explosion scared horses as far away as Richmond. It left behind a gaping, smoking crater two hundred feet long, fifty feet wide and half again as deep. Those inside the rebel works not killed in the blast fled in a desperate panic.

Though General Meade himself would later pin a medal on Colonel Pleasants, the Colonel knew the credit for the Petersburg mine was hardly his alone. Corporal Clark had devised a clever new fusing device that assured simultaneous ignition of each of the mine's eight powder magazines. Clark was promoted and quickly recommended for reassignment to upstate New York, to the busy West Point Armory. Lieutenant Clark's new orders were to invent new explosives, small devices that could be easily built and effectively used by troops at the front.

The first of his creations was a flaming grenade, a

device he called a "fireball." Six inches in diameter and ten inches long, it involved affixing cotton balls soaked in turpentine around a new style of grenade, using a web of copper wires. On one end he mounted a percussion cap that would fire on striking anything solid. On the other he attached a wooden handle, two feet long. On the test range the Lieutenant and his assistants had flung fireballs at targets as far off as three hundred feet.

Clark's first torpedoes were fifty-pounders, equipped with waterproof contact fuses and designed to be anchored in eight feet of water, at the mouth of rivers and shallow harbors. Later models could be used at sea. They were floated with whiskey casks and carried slow fuses that could be configured to burn for up to an hour.

The Lieutenant worked all hours, seven days a week. His experiments consumed him. No new challenge went ignored, no problem unresolved. His reputation as a clever, self-taught engineer and incendiary chemist spread quickly through the Bureau of Ordnance.

❧ ❧ ❧

The Druid kept watch on three ships now, all merchants from the look of them. Two were steamers putting out to sea, likely from Queenstown. The third was a hermaphrodite brig that set heavy in the water, a coaler from her look. Traffic in the sea lanes might provide *Erin's Hope* with some daylight cover for her curious course of long figure eights.

Colonel Clark had been at it now for hours. Six men assigned to do precisely as the Colonel ordered built wooden crates, boxes half as wide as coffins and nearly twice as long. Three others worked below with Benny, cutting and stitching sailcloth into small canvas bags. Still others filled each bag with sand, sealing them with heavy thread.

The crates the Colonel left on deck, securing them to the facing of the deckhouse with nails before filling each crate with black powder tamped solid with a thick wooden block. For the greatest effect, as much powder as possible needed to be above the water line.

Each crate's cover had been built to a tight fit. Once in place the Colonel smeared the seams with pitch to ward off the damp. When the pitch had set, the Colonel had the men cover each crate with sandbags, both to deflect any premature enemy fire and to confine the gases of combustion.

Eight men lost their bunks when Clark ordered them removed. Powder in bags was stacked amidships in the berth deck, directly below the crates secured to the deckhouse. Bag after bag of powder was stacked as tall as headroom would allow. Small holes Benny had been told to drill in the decking allowed fusing cord to be run from one level to the next.

The best means of firing the powder would be an electro-magnetic machine, the type Clark had devised at West Point years before, exactly for this purpose. Nothing but electricity would produce the instantaneous explosion needed to scuttle a ship quickly, before she could be boarded.

Though Timothy Clark would take no pleasure in blowing up this ship, he had shown himself adept at such a task, though blowing up a fort had proven something else. In their hefty requisitions the anxious brass at the West Point Armory had characterized the whole sorry affair as an "ordnance experiment." Lieutenant Clark told them, again and again, it was an experiment doomed to fail.

The generals in Washington, even Lincoln himself he was told, envisioned a lightning bolt, a hurricane of flame, a lethal wind that would bring the earthworks surrounding Fort Fisher tumbling down like the very walls of Jericho. The strategic objective was to devastate and then storm whatever might remain of the brigade manning the forty-four heavy guns within the Confederate stronghold at the mouth of the Cape Fear River. An armada of Federal war ships would await the blast offshore and immediately commence a bombardment to cover the shore assault. The fall of Fort Fisher and nearby Fort Caswell would put an end to Confederate blockade running, placing Wilmington in the same desperate condition as the city of Mobile.

The iron gunboat U.S.S. Louisiana, once employed in the Atchafalaya cotton trade, was commandeered for the mission. At Norfolk her battery, masts and most of her deckhouse were removed. Her engines, boilers and one of her coal bunkers were left intact. At one hundred fifty feet, she could be loaded with as a many as three hundred tons of black powder, yet would still draw only nine feet.

Over Clark's objections, the Louisiana had been destined to become what the strategists termed a "powder boat" - a massive, floating bomb that would be towed to Fort Fisher and beached before detonation. It was a plan that wouldn't work, Clark told them. He could guarantee a blast that reduced the Louisiana's iron hull to filings, but not a blast that would do any significant damage to the fort. At best the Louisiana would be grounded in the sand some three hundred yards from the Fort Fisher earthworks, at worst four hundred fifty. The distances involved were just too great. He was, of course, right.

Nearly sixty Federal warships gathered on a bleak Christmas Eve, 1863, each carefully positioned in a long slow arc in the choppy seas off Fort Fisher. Though the gunners expected a midnight bombardment, the *Louisiana* didn't go up until just before four.

Though Fort Fisher's commander would later report the explosion shook his bunk, the powder ship, just as Clark had predicted, caused little damage, proving only a rude call to battle. The naval bombardment went on until fifty thousand shot and shell had rained down on Fort Fisher from offshore.

When the fort finally fell, there was little to be found of the Louisiana, but the earthworks were solid. Three hundred tons of powder had failed to do a fraction of the damage done the next morning, when thirteen thousand pounds of powder went up inside the fort, killing or wounding more than a hundred of the invading Federal troops.

A powder reserve shielded by a mound of dirt was covered even in December with luxuriant turf that proved a too inviting bivouac for the One Hundred and Sixty-Ninth New York Regiment. While Colonel Alden's weary troops lounged atop the powder magazine, two sailors from the fleet, bent on plunder and stupid with drink, were seen entering the structure carrying lanterns, a minute at most before the explosion.

❧ ❧ ❧

The Druid spotted the light draft British steam ram making way for the sea lane. The Old Man saw it, too.

Kavanagh took the helm and ordered Benny to send

all hands aloft to crowd on sail and then to ready the boats, once underway.

Off the deck of the British ram came a series of rocket signals that asked coast guard spotters on shore which of three ships in sight was the suspected Fenian brig. Their question answered, their quarry identified, the ram turned toward *Erin's Hope*.

Kavanagh saw the maneuver and made for mid-channel, tacking into a breeze that built slightly but still remained light. *Erin's Hope* wasn't making more than four knots, not even half the speed of a ram. Now under full steam, the ram took up pursuit, pulling closer by the minute.

"Tell Colonel Clark that, with this light breeze, I can buy him twenty minutes, if that," Kavanagh told Benny. "Have the men stand by the boats."

The Druid remained in the mainmast rigging, checking the force and direction of what little wind there was by studying how the wind scattered the steam ram's thickening tail of smoke.

As the ram drew closer, she signaled the Fenian brigantine to heave to.

Kavanagh was having none of it. He responded by adjusting Erin Hope's heading from southwest by south to a course of west by southwest.

A warning shot fired from the ram fell harmlessly behind her, the contrail of the shell tracing an arc of sparks through the darkening sky. *Erin's Hope* was out of range of the ram's heaviest deck gun, but wouldn't be for long. If little else, Kavanagh's new heading provided the ram only the narrowest of targets.

Colonel Clark was below, alone now while the men stood by the boats. He had tested the magneto and now awaited some signal from the helm to trigger his tangle of fuses before getting himself to a boat. Such a waste, he thought, this ship and this cargo. They had come so close.

Suddenly *Erin's Hope* surged, nearly taking Clark off his feet. It was as if she was riding the crest of some massive swell. At the helm, Kavanagh felt it, too, a strong gust at his back that stretched taut sails that minutes ago were luffing in what seemed an indifferent breeze. *Erin's Hope* was now sailing large, the wind not quite at her stern. Slowly she was putting some distance between herself and the onrushing ram.

The windburst continued, staying steady and growing stronger, now coming directly from the east. West it will be, Kavanagh thought, letting her rudder drift to port as *Erin's Hope* ran free. The British ram grew smaller, as did the headlands, both disappearing into the cover of the windblown darkness that quickly consumed the dusk.

Chapter Twelve

June 1, 1867
An Ring, County Waterford

Peig Ni Chuirrin was feeling each of her seventy-four years. The knuckles of her right hand throbbed from the damp, even as she warmed them around a cup of hot milk. Her knees would complain for hours now, having been coaxed up the path that led from the sea to the small stone house she kept in the headlands overlooking Helvick Head.

She had slept late this morning, the sun muted by fog so thick she could scarcely make out her own feet on the path to the sea. It was steep in places and littered with stones that would hobble a goat, but she had traveled it often, in fair weather and foul, to gather up seaweed left behind by the receding tide.

Peig had rested a bit before venturing onto the slippery rocks. Each weed she placed in a basket, the same basket once used in the same way by her mother.

She made the long climb home slowly, emptying the seaweed in a pile by the dung pit. Into the pit she pitched half the weeds, covering them with a layer of sand before adding what remained, then covering them as well. The oily seaweed would rot there, melting with time into a soupy, foul-smelling mud that helped to encourage the thin, sandy soil. Manure was preferred, but Peg kept but one aged cow.

If her knees would permit she would head to the rocks again tomorrow, back for more seaweed to add to the pit. Her descent to the rocks left her more hungry than tired and wanting more than a bowl of Indian meal porridge.

Two bricks of turf encouraged the fire as she thinned some milk with a dipper of water. She poured it into a pot and added an onion, cut in two, and five small potatoes, jackets and all. Into the mix went a small salted herring, left to float on top to soften in the steam. It would be more than the hungriest of old women could eat in three days, but just the smell of it would be company in itself.

As blue fingers of flame began caressing the pot, the chowder took on a slow boil. Peig backed it off the fire, letting it simmer just slightly between occasional stirs. Where was that clay pipe? she thought to herself. Perhaps she left it on the table, next to her bed.

Sean Kenneally was wet to his shoulders and eager to put himself well out of sight. The feel of solid ground seemed remarkably odd at first, stranger still for this solid ground to be Ireland.

The years had taken him so far from this place, so far from the death and despair at Killanne that drove him away. Now he was back and must hide.

His arrival and that of the others would not go unnoticed. The coast guards would know the old fisherman's smack and those who tended her. They would notice their unlikely catch of two dozen strangers. They would have questions for which there were no good answers.

The youngest of the fishermen said in Irish, then again in English, they would put into a place called Baile na nGall, a fishing village on the south shore of Dungarvan Bay. There was a coast guard station less than a mile from the pier, just above the road to Helvick pier. A company of Royal Irish Constabulary was less than six miles away, garrisoned in Dungarvan.

The old fisherman named Whelan was furious at first, but, with time, his rage gave way to worry. He had cursed the Fenians in Irish, *na Finini,* he called them, as they poured over the rail of the brigantine and crowded his smack, nearly swamping her in the chaos. He had agreed for two sovereigns to take two men ashore, not the hoard that scrambled aboard.

After meeting with the officers, General Kerrigan had decided to put only two men ashore, Colonel Warren and Captain Kenneally. Word of his orders spread quickly, and he soon deferred to the pleadings of others grown weary of cruising but still eager to fight. Stocks of food and fresh water were dangerously low. Each man aboard had done just as ordered: arrive in New York with enough provisions to see yourself through a thirty-day crossing. That was early April. Today it was June.

Captain Kavanagh assured the General that *Erin's Hope* could linger offshore in the hands of only a skeleton crew, at least for two days, maybe longer in this fog.

Colonel Clark would remain on board should they encounter more gunboats. Those going ashore were to take no weapons. The guns, the General assured them, would follow in a day, maybe two.

"Have the men scatter and speak directly to the people," Kerrigan told Colonel Warren. "Find those we can trust and coax them into taking the arms, or at least hiding them away until others can put them to use."

Those going ashore were given forty eight hours to make their case and finalize arrangements for a landing and provisions.

"Regroup in two days at the crest of Helvick Head," Kerrigan told the Colonel before sending the men over the side. "This ship will return by midday and await your signals. Should there be no sign of us, consider the expedition a failure and do whatever is required to avoid arrest. Should there be any trouble, head north and west, through Youghal, toward Cork. There's no shortage of Fenians in Cork."

Erin's Hope would sail east, he said, drawing attention away from the landing. She would linger tomorrow well out to sea and then head back toward Helvick Head. General Kerrigan's final order was to make sure the smack lingered at sea until dusk, and that the men go ashore only under the cover of night.

While the fog remained thick, the patience of the nearly thirty anxious men crowded together on the smack grew thin. We're wasting our time out here, they told Warren. Why wait for dark when we have the cover of fog? Over Sean's objections, the Colonel ordered Old Pat Whelan to make quick for shore, a distance he estimated at four miles or less.

In the time required to get the overloaded smack ashore, the cover of fog had dissolved to a translucent haze. With the tide well out, Whelan was forced to run her aground in chest-deep water, still some four hundred yards from the strand. Some of the men removed their boots, others even their britches before slipping over the side, holding them over their heads while wading to shore. On the strand the men scattered like minnows, some alone, others in twos and threes. A few dropped to their knees, kissing the sand and crossing themselves. Patrick Roche told Sean he had been to this place before and set off to find some cousins, his mother's people.

Sean stayed close to the shoreline, working his way along the rocks. After a mile or more he came upon a path that disappeared up the hillside. The sun was burning clear and a meadow of thick green grass spread out to the ridgeline above, inviting him to linger or, better still, to sleep.

Sleep must wait, Sean thought, heading up the pathway into whatever cover these hills might offer.

❦ ❦ ❦

Her cottage smelled like herring now, like fish salted with tobacco.

A filthy habit it was, but one Peig Ni Chuirrin had come to thoroughly enjoy. The smell of her pipe always brought back memories of her father, who smoked a pipe every day she had known him. The smoke from his pipe often awakened her as she dozed in the loft at night. The sweet smell of the smoke assured her that her Da was home, safe among them after checking his nets or gathering oysters from the bay with Uncle Liam.

Coming up the path, now well above the bay, Sean smelled it too, an odd mix of aromas that coaxed him further along the hillside. The curl of smoke escaping from the chimney of the small stone house brought with it a rush of memories, some bitter, some sweet. Turf was unknown in America, where coal was plentiful and cheap. Sean thought back to the shirt he had put on in Killane for the crossing, how it had reeked of peat, a smell he cherished until constant wear reduced the shirt to a rag.

What was the rest of it, this mix of smells? Food perhaps? God, he was hungry.

A stone barn near the house was nearly empty, just one cow inside. She complained only slightly as Sean helped himself to a few sprays of milk. It felt sticky and warm in the cup of his hand, its sweetness a reminder of how long it had been since any real food had passed his lips.

Stay here or go on? he asked himself, content for the moment to be out of the wind, his clothes still clammy, seawater damp. Should he make himself known, or hide himself here, in this barn?

This is lunacy, he decided at last. He had come thousands of miles, risking his life in the rigging, crossing the North Atlantic on an expedition to help these people reclaim their own souls. Why was he now cowered in a barn, afraid even to make himself known? The door to the house was shut tight, the window beside it opaque with grime.

His three strong knocks gave Peig quite a start. No one came by here, not any more.

"Cé 'tha ansan?" she demanded, asking in Irish who it

was at her door. Sean heard her, yet didn't. She sounded old and was speaking Irish, he knew, but not Irish of any type he had heard before.

"My name is Sean, Sean Kenneally," he said in English, then once again in the Irish he knew as a boy. "Sean Ó Cionnfhaolaidh is ainm dom."

Peig laid her pipe on the floor and coaxed herself from the rocker she had pulled up close to the hearth. The warmth of the chowder had made her quite sleepy, and she had permitted herself to doze off by the fire. Perhaps all this commotion was only a dream.

"Cé 'thá ansan?" she demanded, asking again who it was as she made her way slowly to the window by the door.

"Ni baol duit mé," Sean said, telling her in his own broken Irish that he meant her no harm.

Peig had meant to wash these windows, which were grimy with cobwebs and soot. She could make out only the vaguest outline of a man, a young man from what little she could see. It was a young man she couldn't remember ever seeing before.

"Is amhlaidh athá mé caillte," Sean shouted at the heavy oaken door, telling her he was lost. Caillte. It was the first word he had spoken that she could clearly understand. Lost, indeed, she thought, to be way up here hammering your fist on an old woman's door. She opened the door, just enough to peer out.

"Cé h-e tú fein?" she asked, wanting his name. He understood her, at least well enough to respond.

"Is mise Sean, Sean Ó Cionnfhaolaidh," he said, repeating his name. "Tháinig mé dé'n árthach, árthach Finin Ó Shasana Nua," explaining that he had come from a ship, come from America, come ashore with the Fenians.

Na Finini? Jesus, Mary and Joseph, she thought to herself. Those letters, those letters from America passed around the village, they must have contained more than boasts and bald-faced lies. There really were Fenians, she thought. Na Finini in Ring. And one of them was knocking at her door.

❦   ❦   ❦

Two Royal Irish Constabulary men armed with carbines drove their cart as best they could around the deep ruts in the steep lane leading to Peig Ni Chuirrin's farm.

Both men lived some miles away in Dungarvan, and neither had been up to Helvick Head before, nor even knew such a place existed. But their orders were to check every house, every farm within a day's walk from Helvick Head.

Fenians, twenty or more thought to be off a black-hulled brigantine, had commandeered a fishing boat at gunpoint and come ashore near Baile na nGall, just hours ago. They had taken to the hills, but couldn't have gotten too far, not on foot.

"They say she's lived here alone for years now," one RIC man said to the other. "Her name is Peg Curran. Her Da was a fisherman, drowned when she was a girl, but that's been sixty years. The famine took her Ma. The publican at Murray's said the old girl must be near eighty by now."

A trickle of smoke showed them someone was at home. They first checked the barn, finding only a cow. The door to the house was standing ajar, more open than closed. Through the open door they both heard the voice, soft and then loud. It sounded more like crying than singing. They both listened carefully. It was only one voice, but having a conversation of its own, sounding as strange as any voice either had ever heard.

"What is it?" one asked.

"Don't know," said the other. "A woman, speaking Irish, or singing, or crying. Can't tell for certain."

"Hello!" the other man shouted. "You, inside. We'd like to speak to you." No response. "Hello!" he said again, even louder. "Could we come inside to speak to you?"

The lamenting went on, just as it had before, clearly not in response to their question.

"Let's have a look," the older man said.

He pushed back the door with the barrel of his rifle, taking a few cautious steps inside.

"Is Peg Curran at home?" he called. "It's the RIC. We would like a word with you if we might."

The lamenting continued. It was louder now, an incoherent mumbling. Something moved, off to the right. It was a figure, in a dress, a woman in a rocker, her face hidden by a woolen shawl. Her back was to them. She was puffing on a pipe, rocking slowly back and forth, mumbling into the fire.

"Peg Curran, is it?" he asked, getting no response.

The mumbling grew softer, then louder. He couldn't make out even a word of the Irish, if that's what it was. He stepped closer and tried again. "Good day to you," he said, shouting now, wishing he knew even a word or two of this odd tongue.

The old woman never turned her head, only rocked and puffed her pipe, transfixed on the fire, mumbling softly now, under her breath.

"What is it?" asked the other man, still standing in the doorway.

"The old woman, she's here," the first man said. "But daft with age. From the look of her she must be blind and deaf as well."

"She'll be telling us nothing of Fenians," the other man said. "Even if they did come this way."

The two men glanced at one another and then around the room. Stepping back outside, they left the door ajar, as they had found it.

In the rocker, hidden under the shawl, Sean set down the pipe and loosened his grip on the bread knife he had grabbed from the table. He mumbled even louder than he had before, sure they were gone, but making sure.

Hidden under a blanket, wearing only a shift, Peig Ni Chuirrfn could hear the Fenian lad drone on. Though she was aware any real danger had passed, she could still hear her own heartbeat.

Sean had been well into a second bowl of chowder

when he first heard the cart horse and spotted two men coming from the barn. They had weapons. Sean realized then he had none. He found the knife while the old woman took his soggy, square-toed boots from in front of the fire, hiding them beneath her bed. When she returned she began removing her clothes.

Quick, she told him in Irish, put on my dress and hide your face with my shawl. Sit in that rocker and puff on that pipe. Speak into the fire as if you were some mad old woman. I'll hide in here, in my bed.

It had been a grand plan, and her own. Peig Ni Chuirrin was old perhaps, but clever still, feeling now like a Fenian herself.

❦ ❦ ❦

Even finding the Youghal road proved a challenge in countryside as wild and untamed as this. In just a few miles the gulls and the petrels had given way to songbirds that cried out their warnings as Sean cut through the thick timber, keeping west and north.

"Tabhair t'aghaidh ar Chorcaigh," the old woman told Sean as he left her, sending him off with some bread and a blessing.

Head towards Cork.

Chapter Thirteen

June 3, 1867
Off the County Waterford headlands

Kavanagh remembered now what his father told him back in Passage East, long before he and Nel made the crossing to Boston: "You be careful what you wish for, boy, because some wishes have a way of coming true."

It had been a pearl of wisdom well hidden within a scolding, stern advice delivered no doubt as partial penance for the sin of speaking some unspeakable blasphemy. He had likely wished aloud one of his brothers dead, black and sinful thinking brought on by some brother battle over whose turn it was to muck out the barn or who last brought in the turf. His father ended such frays with blows and angry words of his own.

Though thirty years had passed, James could still hear his Da's great bellowing voice: "You be careful what you wish for, boy ..."

The only thing Joseph had wished for as a boy, prayed for in fact, was to be master of a ship, a lofty ship, a barque or a brigantine, a ship he would sail into an adventure worthy of the ballads the old men sometimes

sang after too many hot whiskeys down at Mooney's
Public House.

"...because some wishes have a way of coming true."

🐍 🐍 🐍

The urgent dispatch from Waterford County Resident
Magistrate G.V. Gould to Rear Admiral Charles Frederick
at Queenstown had twenty Fenians now in custody at
Dungarvan, with at least five others at large. All were
Americans, from the look of them.

They had come ashore near Helvick Head off a vessel
Gould reported as a brigantine, one hundred and ten tons
or more, clearly in heavy ballast. The ship was last seen
by a crew of local net-minders some considerable distance
out from Dungarvan Harbor, perhaps five miles out,
shrouded in fog, heading unknown. Two new reports from
ships recently arrived at Waterford put such a vessel
cruising east and south of Dungarvan, flying English
colours, fore main yard new and unpainted, the rest all
black.

Rear Admiral Frederick put the Coast Guard on alert
from Waterford up to Arklow: "Suspicious persons have
lately landed near Dungarvan from a black-hulled
brigantine known to be in your vicinity." Was this an
isolated incident, or could there be more ships in the
Fenian armada? "Request you exercise great vigilance as
it is not improbable that other attempts of the same nature
may be anticipated."

Frederick also ordered the Irish Station's ironclad
flagship to immediately set out toward St. George's
Channel. Should H.M.S. Black Prince encounter the

Fenian vessel she was to launch a quick and punitive attack.

❧ ❧ ❧

Kavanagh had not slept well. No one had, neither well nor long.

It was a dangerous game they were playing now, hovering off the coast, inviting trouble from faster gunboats who knew they were there and were eager for a prize.

With most of the men ashore, just ten remained to handle the watches. Kavanagh and the Druid shared the helm, eight hours on, eight hours off, though neither spent even a few hours below.

The light breeze that carried *Erin's Hope* in darkness back toward Helvick Head was building by dawn to a heavy southwest gale. First light had brightened the skies to the hue of pewter, only to be darkened by frequent squalls that passed over nearly as quick as they appeared. With the wind picking up, Kavanagh ordered Benny and the Druid into the rigging to gather sail to ease their speed. *Erin's Hope* wasn't expected off Helvick Head until midday. With gunboats about there seemed little sense in lingering.

Over crusts of stale bread and strong coffee Kavanagh and General Kerrigan spent the morning reviewing their options, discussing how best to respond to the endless setbacks the expedition had encountered since the Druid first spotted the table mountain swimming in the fog above Sligo. That had been what?, Kavanagh thought. Ten days now, a fortnight?

The General seemed hopeful those ashore could rally the local Fenian centers to action, that news of weapons arrived by sea from America would rekindle local passion for armed rebellion. If the time wasn't right, the local centers could secret away the guns, and the men. Kavanagh had his doubts, though he kept them to himself. If these Fenians' so-called rising lasted only days at most in County Sligo, why should an insurrection have fared any better at Dungarvan?

"Tell me, General," Kavanagh said. "Assuming we do make some contact with those you have sent ashore and we are in fact able to offload our cargo, what am I to do with this ship?"

Their orders were to return the Fenian brigantine to New York, but both men knew those orders were cut on the understanding that men would come aboard at Sligo, men capable of assisting in what would be a most demanding east-to-west crossing.

"It's one thing to be cruising about St. George's Channel in circles, biding our time, waiting on shore signals that may never come," Kavanagh told Kerrigan. "It's quite something else to be getting this vessel back to New York with little more than a handful of crew."

Kerrigan had no answers, only a strong determination to see that *Erin's Hope* didn't leave Ireland with her holds still packed with weapons so sorely needed on shore.

"We must find a way to get these rifles ashore, if not in County Waterford then somewhere else," the General said. "If nothing else this expedition must allow O'Mahoney and others in New York to show those who have the means to support the rebellion that it is possible to land men and supplies. Show them that the English fleet patrolling Ireland's coast is not impregnable."

"As, so far, it has been," Kavanaugh said.

"We've fared well, have we not, Captain?" Kerrigan said. "We've put men ashore and you've outrun the bastards. You've managed to keep us offshore now for nearly two weeks without being overhauled or boarded."

"We won't be boarded, General," Kavanagh said. "That our Colonel Clark will ensure. What would be worse than returning these weapons to O'Mahoney in New York would be sending them and this ship to the bottom, with us bobbing in the boats, waiting to join the others in some stinking English gaol."

"It won't come to that," Kerrigan said.

"It won't come to much of anything, General, unless this expedition finds more provisions," Kavanagh said. "For nearly a week I've been feeding both your men and my own from what meager stocks we brought aboard in New York to meet the needs of my own crew. Whatever the fate of those ashore, those of us still on board would starve if we attempted a western crossing with what little food remains."

At Kavanagh's request, Benny had inventoried the remaining provisions. Eleven barrels of bread, two known to be moldy. Two barrels of butter. One-half barrel of salted pork. Two barrels of flour. One-fourth barrel of beans. One-half barrel of coffee. Two and one-half casks of water, not counting those Kavanagh had ordered braced on deck to collect whatever rain the squalls might leave behind.

❧ ❧ ❧

Rain came in sheets and climbed by midday into the headlands, taking with it most of the clouds. The sun broke through at last in long glowing ribbons that danced along the horizon.

The wind that had pushed *Erin's Hope* west toward Helvick Head backed off by mid day, but still filled the main course and the foremast topsails as she cut through rolling swells. Benny and the Druid stayed up on the platforms, searching the headlands for any signal or sign, the light of a fire or maybe a flare.

No boats approached, not even the yawls that emerged from Dungarvan Bay to check on their nets.

Chapter Fourteen

June 4, 1867
Dungarvan, County Waterford

Páid Mór Ó Faolain had little time to be wasting here in Dungarvan. The seas were finally calm off Helvick Head, and the salmon would be running for sure.

Colin Costin had no doubt sailed at first light from the pier at Baile na nGall Páid. Mór knew that old bastard's lame excuse for a smack would be swollen with catch by now, catch that should have been his own.

The Royal Irish Constabulary didn't care a whit about this fisherman, "Big Pat" Whelan, or his problems back home. Páid Mór had been ordered to present himself with his crew of two at the Dungarvan Courthouse promptly at noon or face being delivered there in irons. The magistrates required their presence for the questioning of the Fenian prisoners.

Páid Mór cursed the dark day, Saturday last it was, the first day of June, when the lofty ship with the black hull appeared like some phantom in the midday fog. His life had been in shambles ever since these Yanks tumbled over her lee rail, demanding, in Irish nonetheless, passage

159

ashore.

A still tongue makes a wise head, his wife reminded him, as if Páid Mór had no brain at all. He had no intention of telling these English fools in wigs any of what little he knew of Dochas Eireann – *Erin's Hope* – or of these men known in Baile na nGall as na Finini.

Long before word of the rising reached the fishing villages of Ring, Páid Mór heard talk of Fenian drilling in Tallow and in the Knockmealdown Mountains beyond Cappoquin, but had heard nothing of Fenians near Dungarvan. Baile na nGall had known only little of na Finini until these Yankees waded ashore on Ring Strand in squeaky square-toed boots and sea-soaked britches.

By noon the approaches to the courthouse and the Dungarvan bridewell were blocked by R.I.C. men and soldiers, nearly all of them armed with carbines fixed with bayonets. The curious who lined the routes were surprised to see how young the Americans were. Few appeared older than twenty-five, though most were wearing chin tufts and mustaches to make themselves seem more like men than the boys that they were.

The public had been turned away from the inquiry, but not the press. Reporters came from as far as Cork, where even Páid Mór knew Fenians were as common as sinners in church.

At ten past one, the prisoners filed into the courtroom and were arranged in three groups, each group seated behind a different table. They eyed Páid Mór suspiciously, unaware that of him they had little to fear.

Big Pat Whelan had determined in his contempt that he would feign being deaf as he struggled to recall facts the R.I.C. already knew. What little they would force him to tell he would tell them in Irish, knowing few in this courtroom could understand a word.

The proceeding began with each prisoner ordered to stand and give his name and place of birth. To Páid Mór's surprise, each did so in a brusque military manner, responding quicker even than the reporters could take down each name.

The list that would appear in the next day's papers would be read aloud in more than a few of Leinster's public houses: Michael FitzGerald, Carrigaline, County Cork; Michael Green, Massachusetts; Denis O'Conor, Cork; William F. Milan, New York; Jerry Murphy, Cork; Arthur Downey, New York; James Lawson, New York; Daniel Lee, Castleconnell, County Limerick; John Haley, "from America, but that is all I will say"; Robert Kelly, "I, too, from America, but I won't say what part"; John Rooney, New York; William C. Nugent, Boston; Laurence Doyle, New York; John Cade FitzSimmons, County Longford; John Cade, England; Michael J. Green, America; Jeremiah Murray, Cork City; Sean Kenneally, Killanne, County Wexford; Sean Willian Sheehan, Nelson Place, Cork; Augustine A. Costelloe, Philadelphia, "birthplace of our great nation"; Patrick Cogan, New York; Michael Walsh, Queenstown; Patrick Roche, Cork; Andrew Leonard, New York.

Sir Nugent Humble, the chairman and chief barrister of the inquiry, explained the nature of the charges against them: suspicion of being Fenians. The prisoners glanced at each other, some suppressing smiles.

Páid Mór was the first witness called. He heard his

name and saw a bailiff motion him into a chair at the front of the room.

"Tell the court, Mr. Whelan, how you came to be here today?" Magistrate Samuel Maguire asked.

Páid Mór hadn't spoken a word of English all day and wasn't starting now. He greeted Maguire's question with a look of blank confusion, though he understood every word.

"Sean-duine mé agus tá iarracht de bhodhaire orm agus nil ao' Bhéarla agam," he said in Irish.

The prisoners whispered among themselves, the few Irish speakers among them explaining to the others that Páid Mór had said he was somewhat deaf and spoke only Irish.

Maguire looked baffled.

"My Lord," he said, turning to Humble. "It appears this common fish monger either does not know or will not consent to speak English. Can we briefly interrupt this proceeding to send for an interpreter?"

Humble and the other magistrates conferred in whispers. Humble pointed at a bailiff posted near the courtroom's front entrance and reeled him in with a finger. The bailiff spoke with Humble in inaudible mumbles, then summoned another bailiff, who received whispered instructions before disappearing from the courtroom out a rear door.

The drone of conversation among the prisoners swelled to a buzz over the full ten minutes it took for the bailiff to return, reappearing with a young man in tow. A few whispers later, the newcomer was introduced to the court, to the prisoners and to Big Pat Whelan as Liam Daly, a clerk for the keeper of the town's tax ledgers.

"Mr. Daly," Maguire said. "I understand that you have most kindly agreed to assist in this hearing by conveying in Irish the questions I will pose and repeating to the court in the Queen's English the answers that Mr. Whelan will give?"

"Yes, my Lord, if you wish," Daly said nervously.

It hadn't been a matter of agreeing to anything. Peter Powers, the dreaded tax collector for whom Liam had worked for two long months, came barging into his anteroom, demanding in a short-tempered voice to know which of the clerks spoke the Irish of the fishermen who lived along the Helvick Head.

Liam had raised his hand, foolishly hoping his command of the Irish might send him into the countryside on some tedious errand that would at least spare him another long day among these endless shelves of dusty ledgers. Now this.

Maguire approached him. "If you would, Mr. Daly, would you state your age and place of birth for the record?"

"Liam Daly, age twenty-three," he said. "Born at Whitechurch, just west of this town."

"Thank you," Maguire said. "Mr. Daly, do you know this man seated before you?"

Liam Daly was a stranger to Páid Mór, and he to him. The old man seldom ventured into Dungarvan, but knew

that Dalys were as thick as clotted cream in the hills
between here and Lismore.

"No, my Lord, I do not."

"His name, we are told, is Patrick Whelan. He is a
fisherman from the Ring Parish, who lives in a village not
far from Helvick Head," Maguire said. 'Will you please
ask him in his local tongue if he knows you?"

"D'iarradh orm a fhiafraí diot má's duine mé a bhfuil
aithne agat air," Daly said in a manner that appeared to
Páid Mór both embarrassed and apologetic.

"Tá's agam go diabhal maith cad d'iarradh ort, agus
ba cheart duit an fhirinne d'insint dóibh, ná fuil aithne
agat orm ná agam ort," Páid Mór said, trying to hide any
expression in his voice that would reveal his charade to
the English-speakers. "Ach, éist Horn, a bhuachaill. Nil sé
ar aigne agamsa aon eolas a thabhairt dos na Sasanaigh
damanta san ná fuil acu cheana fein, agus feach-se chuige
na deanfad. Ni h-aon Finin mise, ach ni h-aon amadan mé,
agus ná bí-se ach an oiread. An dtuigeann tú leat mé a
bhuachaill?"

"Tuigim go maith," Daly said, letting Páid Mór know
he would play along as best he could.

"Tá's agam go maith go bhfuil cainteoirí Gaolainne i
measc na bpríosúnach," Páid Mór told him. "Fearaibh
craiceálta iad súd agus ní h-amháin go dtuigeann siad ár
dteanga ach tá's acu cad e meas na ndaoine anso ar bhra
thadóirí."

Daly glanced over at the prisoners. Yanks though
they were, they appeared to him to be men who shared the
local feeling about what becomes of informers. One of the

older prisoners, stout with close-cropped hair, the one who identified himself to the court as Patrick Roche of County Cork, gave Daly a knowing look. There were, as Páid Mór had just told him, more than a few Irish speakers among the Fenians.

"Mr. Whelan says he and I have never met," Daly told Maguire.

"All that for 'no'?" Maguire asked, incredulous.

"He said more, of course," Daly added nervously. "He was asking if I was among the Dalys from near the Drum Hills or farther out, near Youghal," Daly said, inventing a story to cover their tracks. "He thought he might know my grandmother, but it turns out he does not. She's long dead."

"Can we move on with this?" Humble asked Maguire impatiently. "Mr. Whelan, can you tell this court where you were Saturday last, the first instant?" The question asked, Maguire shot an expectant look at Daly.

"Tá uaidh a fháil amach cá rabhais an Satharn seo caite," feeling a bit foolish in repeating to Paid Mar what he already clearly understood.

"Ag iascaireacht," Páid Mór said. "Mar a bhímíd gach aon lá dá n-oireann an fharraige. Abair leis an siabhra beag gránna go rabhas féin agus mo chriú ag iascaireacht."

"He says he was fishing with his crew," Daly said.

"And ask him how he came to be in this court today."

"Conas gur tháinig tú bheith anso inniú?"

Páid Mór pondered the question for what seemed like a full minute.

"Ar chairt chapaill, ar an mbóthar ard ar an dtaobh thiar de Chuan Dhúngarbháin," Páid Mór finally said to Daly with a twinkle in his eye. "Abair san leis agus féach cad a bhainfidh sé as."

"He says he came by cart, along the Ring strand road," Daly said, feeling suddenly like an expendable pawn in a game no one would win. The Irish speakers among the prisoners, who had been swallowing their smiles, now joined the others in laughing aloud.

"Silence!" Humble roared. "This is a court of law! You prisoners are here facing a sentence of death for treasonable acts. Save your Yankee impudence for speeches from the gallows."

"What I want to know, Mr. Whelan, is how it was you came into contact with these prisoners," Maguire said, looking through Daly to Páid Mór

"Cad ba mhaith leat a dhearfainn leis?" Daly asked.

"Abair leis ná faighinn a bheith siurálta go bhfaca mé aoinne acu dtí inniú, go mór mhór an t-é a thug dhá shabhran dom len iad go léir a thabhairt i dtír."

"He says he cannot say with any certainty that he knows any of these men," Daly said.

"That's preposterous," Maguire said, addressing Humble. "This man is here today because it was in his fishing boat that these Fenians came ashore at Ring Strand. Perhaps we should be charging this insolent fisherman with treason as well, my Lord. You tell him word for word exactly what I just said," Maguire said, turning to Daly. "And then ask him again what transpired on Saturday last."

"B'fhéidir go mb'fhearr dhuit nios mó ná séanadh a thabhairt dóibh," Daly told Páid Mór, not bothering to repeat in Irish what he had already heard in English. "Ni 'neósfad dóibh ach a bhfuil uait go ndéarfainn ach feictear dom gur baolach an cluiche atá 'á imirt agat."

Offer them more than denials, Daly had told him, feeling more than a little odd to be offering advice to such an old man.

Páid Mór thought back to Saturday last. Truth be known, it was a heavy fog that had brought him here, the fog and the black-hulled brigantine that emerged under listing sails to forever change his life. It had appeared like a vision, like a dream transformed into a nightmare in three short days.

The fog had been thick when he, Patrick Browne and Daniel Collins had left the pier at Baile na nGall to take up trammel nets. Before setting out they had huddled together around the deckhouse stove, sharing a pot of tea and a few handfuls of unbuttered bread. The seas were near calm, with only the slightest shore breeze to push them slowly through the dull light and the heavy mist toward open water beyond Helvick Head.

"Abair leó go rabhas ag iascaireacht, mé féin agus mo chriú," Páid Mór said. "Abair leó gur d' fhágamar Cé Bhaile na nGall agus gur sheolamar tré dhubh-cheó le súil a thabhairt ar ár líonta. Tá's acu san cheana féin."

"He says he and his crew, Collins and Browne, left Ballinagoul early, in fog, to check their nets."

"Are these men, Collins and Browne, in this courtroom today as witnesses in this matter?" Maguire asked.

Daly translated, and Páid Mór nodded, they were.

"And did Mr. Whelan and his crew encounter a ship while checking their nets?" Maguire asked.

Daly repeated the question, needing something to say to maintain the charade.

"Abair leis nár dheineamar, nár dheineamar fad a bhíomar ag féachaint ar an líonta," Páid Mór said. "'Sí fírinne an scéil nar shroiseamar na líonta a chuigint."

"He says 'no.' That they never did check their nets that day."

"And why was that?" Maguire asked.

"Cad a dhearfaidh mé leis?" Daly asked Pat Whelan.

"Abair leis a cheisteanna a bhramadh as a thóin," Big Pat said.

"He says he doesn't understand your question," Daly said.

"Ask him what happened at sea that kept him from tending his nets," Maguire said.

"B'fhearra dhuit rud éigin ará leis," Daly said, lilting his voice to phrase his warning to Big Pat as a question.

Páid Mór thought back to the brigantine, her copper fastening catching his eye by what little light there was to be caught. She sliced silently through the fog, coming from the west on a slow port tack, deep in the water, obviously under heavy ballast. She had no colours flying, and, when Paid Mór studied her stern for her name, he could make out none.

As the lofty ship drifted past them, she hove to, a muffle of voices on deck giving way to a single voice that cut through the fog. The speaker was lost in the mist, but the voice spoke the English in a way Páid Mór had never heard. The voice in the fog was coming from her stern from the sound of it. It asked if those aboard had fish to sell. We do not, he had shouted back in English, pumping the rudder to keep the smack clear. The big ship would stave her should she venture too close.

"Abair leis go rabhamar ar ár slí dtí'n ar líonta nuair a chonacamar an t-árthach árd seo romhainn sa chéo. Stad an t-árthach agus d'iarr duine éigin ar bord orainn blúire éisc a dhiol léo. Os rud é ná raibh dada fós againn, dúras leó ná faghaimfs."

"Mr. Whelan says he and his crew encountered a larger ship while sailing out to their nets," Daly told Maguire.

"What type of ship? What colors did she fly? Did he board her?"

"Anois má sea?," Daly asked Páid Mór. "Dé méid atá uait a dhearfainn?"

"Abair leó a bhfuil ráite agam leat. Tá's acu an méid sin cheanna féin."

"No colors. He did not board her. She might have been a coaling ship, a barque perhaps; he can't say for sure because of the fog."

"Ask him if she had a black hull? Surely he could see that, even in fog."

"Dúirt tú liom go raibh, ach b'fhéidir nach cuimhim leat?" Daly asked.

"Mar sin a bhí go deimhim," Páid Mór replied.

"Mr. Whelan cannot recall. He said it was very foggy."

"If he could see she was flying no colors, why is it he couldn't make out the color of her hull?" Maguire asked, beginning to suspect he was being toyed with.

"Deirimís leis nach ea ná raibh aon bhrat uirthi, ach ná faca tú aon cheann," Daly said to Páid Mór. "Abair san thar n-ais liom."

"B'fhéidir go raibh brat uirthí, ach ní bhfaighinn é d'fheiscint sa dhubhcheó," Páid Mór said.

"You misunderstand him, he says," Daly told Maguire. "He didn't mean there were not any colours flying, just that if there were he could not see them through the fog."

"If you will, Mr. Daly, tell Mr. Whelan that we know that men from this black-hulled brigantine, all of them the same men who are in this courtroom today on trial for their lives, wound up in his fishing smack and that he and his crew brought them to Ring strand, where they left his smack and waded ashore. What this court wants to know, and wants to know right now, Mr. Daly, is what transpired between the time that ship first appeared in the fog and the time these men went ashore. Are we to conclude that Mr. Whelan was sent out to meet this ship? Is he a party to this treason?"

"Tarraingéoidh siad tusa isteach anso muna mbíonn tú cúramach," Daly told Big Pat. "N'fheadar mé dé'n bhaint a bhí agat leis an rud seo, ach tá do lámh i mbéal an mhadra is baolach. Óm' thaobh-se de, ba bhréa liom na Puncánaigh seo agus Fínini Phortláirge a d'fheiscint ag teacht Ie chéile le ciorcail eile agus ag ruaigheadh na bacaigh seo thar n-ais go Sasana. Ach tá cuid acu seo i mbaol a gcrochta agus is baol duit féin muna bhfaighir teacht as."

"Ni Finin mi brathadóir mise. Gheobhaidh tu san ará leó," Big Pat said.

"Mr. Whelan says he is a fisherman, nothing more," Daly said.

"So how is it that some two dozen Fenians, scoundrels from the rebellious colonies sent thousands of miles on a mission of tyranny, came ashore in Mr. Whelan's smack on a day so foggy that not even the most ignorant Irish fisherman would have put out to sea?" Maguire asked, his patience now fully eroded.

"Féach, abair leó cad a thit amach," Daly said, suggesting Páid Mór tell the truth. "Cuirfidh mise mo dhath féin ar an scéal."

"Abair leó pé rod is dóigh leat ná fágfaidh im' phriosúnach mé ag na diabhail Sasanaigh ná im' chorpán i ndig éigin ag na Finini, agus ná cuir aon fhocal eile leis," Páid Mór said, asking Daly to translate only what wouldn't land him in jail.

Big Pat recalled at some length in his thick Irish tongue what had happened that day in the fog. To Daly, Patrick Roche and the few others in the courtroom who could understand his words, Páid Mór's story rang true:

"With no fish to sell, a man on the brigantine told me there were two men on board who needed to be put ashore and asked what price I would charge for the trip. I had nets to tend and didn't want to take anyone ashore, so I named a price no sane man would pay, two pounds. The voice said that price would be met and told me to come alongside. A man on deck threw down a rope that Collins used to hold our boat fast. There was some lengthy discussion on deck while I used the boathook to fend my smack from the brigantine's hull. I sent my man, Patrick Browne, up the rope to find out what was keeping them.

"All at once they all came over the side, twenty or more. I was afraid my tiny smack would be swamped. Someone handed me two sovereigns. We parted company with the vessel and hoisted our sails and made for shore. I told them I would put them ashore at Dungarvan, and they said not. The men in the boat spoke both Irish and English. One asked where we were from, and when I said near Helvick Head, he asked of the Murrays, who live on the Helvick side, near the coast guard station. He asked if they still had a long-eared ass. They do, but how he knows them I cannot say."

"What is he telling you?" Maguire asked Daly, his tone now a mix of curiosity and impatience with Whelan's Gaelic drone.

"He says when he sailed alongside a large number of men boarded his smack and demanded to be taken ashore," Daly told Maguire. "He did not know these men or of their business here, but he obliged them nonetheless as a simple act of Christian charity."

"How selfless," Maguire said with a smirk. "And did they put a gun to his head?"

"An rabih gunnai acu?" Daly asked.

"N'fheaca mé aon teidheal de ghunna d'aon tsaghas agus siní an fhírinne ghlan," Big Pat said.

"Yes they did," Daly told Maguire, which was not what he had been told.

"And where did he deposit them on shore?" Maguire shot back.

"Ca mhaith leat adearfainn gur thug tú iad?"

Big Pat remembered the man in charge said his orders were to wait offshore until nightfall so they could come ashore without being seen. But the fog never lifted. By mid-day it remained as thick as Páid Mór's Irish. The decision was made to head ashore under the cover of fog.

"Dúirt me leó go dtabharfainn go baile Dhúngarbhain ach nior theastaigh san uathu, agus dfúradar nár theastaigh uathu dul go Helvick ach an oiread nuair adfúras go raibh staisiún Bháitéirí ann. Nuair a thánagamar i ngiorracht dontalamh luiodar síos sa bhád chun ná feicfeadh na Bháitéirí iad. Fé dheireadh chuir mé i dtír i bPoll a' Phúca iad, laistiar de ché Bhaile na nGall, ach agus an taoide tráite, bhf is teach is amach le trí troithe go leith uisce mar ar chuir mé i dtír iad. Bhí orthu lapadáil tríd an usice. Bhain cuid acu a mbríste diobh."

The prisoner named Roche, who Daly knew was

among those who understood every word of Big Pat's Irish, was whispering a translation into the left ear of the prisoner seated in front of him: "He's saying we told him 'no' when he offered to take us to Dungarvan and that we didn't want to go ashore at Helvick because of the coast guard station there. He says he finally came up at Ring strand, where because of the tide we had to wade through three feet of water. He said we laid down in the boat when we passed by the coast guard."

"What is he saying?" Maguire asked, his impatience rising to a slow boil.

"He says he took them where they asked to go, ashore near the Ring strand," Daly said.

"And why not into Dungarvan city?" Maguire asked.

"Abair rud éigin, ao' rud in ao' chor," Daly said.

"Abair rud éigin, rud in ao chor," Páid Mór mimicked back.

"Because the tide was out," Daly said.

"Ask him this, Mr. Daly," Maguire said, sounding quite sure of himself. "How far out from Helvick Head was he when he encountered this lofty ship?"

"Dé'n fhaid amach chun farraige a bhí tú nuair a thainig tu ar an arthach?" Daly asked.

"Ceithre mhfle, b'fhéidir."

"Four miles," Daly repeated.

"Four miles," Maguire said. "And how large is your

174

smack?"

"Dé mhéid atá in do bhád?"

"Fiche troigh, nó mar sin."

"Twenty feet, he says," Daly told Maguire.

"And how many sails has it?" Maguire shot back.

"Dé mhéid?"

"Dhá cheann."

"Two, he says."

"And on a day like last Saturday, the first instant, given the wind, the movement of the tide and the heavy fog, how many miles would you say your ship would make in an hour?" Maguire asked.

Daly repeated the question.

"Dhá cheann, b'fhéidir," Páid Mór said.

"Maybe two, he says."

"Maybe two," Maguire said, letting the words settle into a long pause. "So, Mr. Whelan, what you are telling this court is that these men who came over the rail of this brigantine would have spent two hours or more aboard your smack as you brought them to shore. And that doesn't include the time you spent waiting to see if the fog would lift. Is that what you are telling us? Ask him, Mr. Daly."

"Tá's agat cad tá ar siúl anois aige, ná fuil?" Daly

asked Big Pat. 'Tá sé chun tú a chur ar bord loinge leis na fearaibh seo ar feadh cúpla uair a chloig agus ansan iarrfaidh sé ort méar a leagaint orthu súd a chonaic tú ar bord. Cad tá uait a dhearfaidh mé?"

Roche again was translating in whispers: "This Daly is telling him they're setting him up to identify us because we spent so much time on his boat."

"Abair leis gur bhain sé tamall dúinn casadh."

"Mr. Whelan said yes, it took some time to return."

"And throughout those hours there were twenty-six or more men on the deck of his boat, isn't that right?"

Daly repeated the question in Irish.

"Bhí," Big Pat said.

"There were," Daly said.

"Would you, Mr. Whelan, be so kind as to look around this courtroom, directing your attention specifically to the prisoners, and tell the court which of these men you recognize as the men with whom you spent hours, shoulder to shoulder, aboard your smack?"

Daly nervously translated, not knowing what else to say, adding the caveat, "Fair amach duit fein anois." Be careful now.

"Bhí forualach ar mo bhad agus shíl mé go rabhamar i mbaol, mar sin níor fhéachas ach ar na seolta agus ar chothromaiocht an bháid. Níor chuir mé aon tsuim ins na fearaibh ar bord."

"He said he was very concerned about the safety of his boat, which had been overloaded by the men who climbed aboard," Daly told Maguire. "He says he spent the passage back studying his sails and keeping his vessel in balance. He says he was too worried about his ship to pay any attention to the men who had put him and his crew in such danger."

"That's absurd!" Maguire shouted, pounding one fist on the table in front of him. "Does this common fisherman take us for fools? Though you were in a boat with these men for well over two hours, you now swear that you can't identify them?"

Daly repeated the question, this time offering no advice.

"Abair leis ná faighinn. Abair les nár fheach mé ach ar mo bheirt fhéineach agus ar na seolta."

"He says he cannot. He says he paid attention only to his crew and to his boat's sails."

"Mr. Whelan expects this court to believe that he was in a close boat with twenty or more men for all this time and he can't identify a single one of them?"

Daly repeated the question and translated Páid Mór's quick response.

"I cannot, he says."

"Mr. Whelan," Maguire said in the same threatening tone a father uses to scold a naughty child, "I want you now to stand up, walk around this courtroom and study every face you see. Please take your time. I then want you to point out to this court at least one man you recognize as being on the deck of your fishing boat on Saturday last, the first day of June. Will you do that for us now?"

"Tá tusa uaidh ..." Daly began, but Páid Mór abruptly cut him off.

"Tá's agam go diabhal maith dé ghnó atá aige dfom," Páid Mór said, his eyes glowing with anger tinged by confusion. "Teastafonn uaidh go mbeinn-se im' bhrathadóir aige. Teastafonn uaidh go ngearrfainn mo scórnach féin."

Daly shared his concern. "Scaoil liom, nó beidh mé féin ar mo thriail as camailéaracht sa chúirt. Caithfidh tú rud éigin a dhéanamh, rud éigin ará. E sin nó daorfar tú go Priosún Phort Láirge leis an gcuid eile acu seo."

Roche was whispering again: "The old man is scared that if he points anyone out he'll be branded an informer, and the young man is telling him he better tell them something or he will be going to jail with the lot of us."

Big Pat Whelan did nothing but glare at Maguire. Finally, he rose slowly from his chair, shuffling toward the first of the three tables separating the accusers from the accused.

Maguire returned Big Pat's glare with a smirk and leaned back in his chair, folding his hands over his chest and flashing Lord Humble a self-satisfied smile.

Big Pat moved deliberately from table to table, studying each man's face without any expression or look of recognition. Minutes passed like hours as he moved in a slow circle across the room. Maguire began to twist a spit curl of his powered wig around one finger out of nervous impatience.

Big Pat studied those in the gallery as well, the reporters, the bailiffs and others who by influence or necessity were able to witness the proceeding firsthand. He studied the barristers and the magistrates as well.

Finally, he glanced over at Liam Daly and gave him a slow nod.

"Can we proceed?" Lord Humble asked, growing weary of the silence.

"Please return to your seat, Mr. Whelan," Maguire said, directing the remark to Daly.

"Deir sé leat suf," Daly told Paid Mór.

"Having now closely scrutinized the physiognomies of the men in this courtroom, can you now, Mr. Whelan, point out for this court any one of the men who was aboard your boat Saturday last?"

Daly translated slowly, adding nothing, only hoping to buy Paid Mór a little more time.

"Abair leis go n-aithnfm fear amháin," Páid Mór said.

"He says he can now recognize one man who was aboard his boat that day," Daly said.

"Is he quite sure?"

Daly repeated the question in Irish.

"He says he is certain."

"At last," Maguire said, almost as an aside. "Will Mr.

Whelan please leave his seat and point out that man to the court?"

"Cad tá'á dhéanamh agat, a sheana 'mhadáin?" Daly said.

Big Pat stood and stepped toward the center of the room. He slowly turned a circle, carefully scanning each of the waiting faces. One of the prisoners ran an index finger across his own throat in a gesture of threatening contempt. Páid Mór winked at the man and then faced Maguire.

"Gheobhaidh mé méar a leagaint ar an bhfear a chonaic mé."

"He says he can point out the man he saw," Daly said.

"Then do it, man," Maguire barked.

Big Pat slowly raised his right hand and then turned deliberately toward the prisoners behind the table nearest Maguire. He swung his arm further to the right and formed his fist into a point. The man he was pointing out wore light gray trousers and a starched white shirt. He was seated just beyond the table Maguire loved to pound.

"Siné é," Páid Mór said. "Chonaic mé é siúd ar bord mo bháid."

Before Daly could begin to translate, the courtroom erupted in waves of laughter and rage.

Big Pat had identified Robert Anderson, a Crown solicitor and special investigator dispatched overnight from Dublin Castle to get to the bottom of this Fenian invasion.

Maguire was livid.

"Seize this man," Chief Barrister Humble screamed, shouting at the bailiff nearest the bench while pointing at Patrick Whelan.

"That man, too," Maguire said, fingering Daly.

Páid Mór Ó Faolain exchanged a forced smile with the prisoners as three men led him away. As he disappeared through a large oak door, the last his crewmen, Collins and Browne, saw of him was a stern fixed stare that each man understood only too well.

Chapter Fifteen

June 6, 1867
Well off Carnsore Point

Colonel Timothy Clark had been up all night, as was most everyone, what with the noise of the hammers and the stench of hot pitch.

It's all a question of buoyancy, Clark kept telling himself, as he had told Benny more than once, though the weary bos'n had yet to grasp exactly what it was the Colonel had in mind.

"I need you to disassemble three of the empty bunks and bring back the lumber," Clark told Benny. "You and I need to build boxes, three long boxes. I will show you exactly how when you bring back the wood."

Timothy Clark discovered years ago that solutions to difficult problems were usually found by not looking too far. Sending this ship and these Fenian guns to the bottom was a problem the Colonel had already solved, but it remained a task he hoped to avoid. Sooner than later, a larger, faster British gunboat would sweep down upon them, coming straight for them, faster than *Erin's Hope* could run.

Captain Kavanagh would do what he could to delay the inevitable, but a small ship with square sails, even in the best of hands, would prove no match for deckguns and steam. We must find some way to put up a fight, the Colonel thought to himself, and find it damn quick indeed.

❦   ❦   ❦

Word reached Dublin Castle that even the Queen was expressing concern about these Fenians.

London had made it Sir Hubert Longworth's personal responsibility to keep on top of seditious activity in Ireland, and now Sir Hubert found this Fenian nonsense out of hand, again. The skirmishes in March proved annoyance enough, leaving Dublin's gaols and those in Cork filled to their rafters with Fenians, professed and suspected. Now, three months later, every newspaper in London was following the "Yankee Invasion of Ireland" and speculating about "Fenian warships" cruising the Irish coastline unchallenged.

Of more than twenty Fenians jailed in Dungarvan, not even one would talk. Of three others arrested a week before by the Coast Guard at Sligo, one was badly wounded. He had sung like a meadowlark, but offered little beyond what was assumed: the Fenian brigantine was loaded with weapons consigned to the Irish Republican Brotherhod. The men aboard were military officers sent from New York to assist in the rising.

The wounded man did provide two bits of news Sir Hubert found intriguing: The captain of the Fenian brig was a Waterford man named Kavanagh, said by the informer to be the only shipmaster to ever outrun the *Alabama*. The informer also said a train had been laid to a powder magazine to send the Fenian ship to the bottom should she be overhauled and boarded.

"You tell Admiral Frederick I want the Fenian brigantine found, fired on from some distance and sunk, cargo and all," Sir Hubert screamed at an aide. "And make sure Admiral Frederick clearly understands that I want it done yesterday."

Sir Hubert would wire the formal orders. The aide's orders were to get himself to Queenstown and to keep Sir Hubert personally informed of the operation. Sir Hubert would order Frederick to send out the Black Prince.

Sending the flagship of the Irish Station after the Fenians' tiny square rigger would seem ludicrous to some, Sir Hubert knew, like swatting a horsefly with a Gutenberg Bible instead of a rolled up newspaper. Built in 1860 at the unheard of cost of nearly a half-million pounds, the H.M.S. Black Prince had been England's own iron-clad response to the impudent French, whose warship Claire could not be allowed to have her way with Her Majesty's channel fleet.

Sir Hubert believed serving up the Fenians to the H.M.S. Black Prince would provide her crew a taste for the kill. It would serve as a clear reminder to the Yanks and the French that the seas surrounding Ireland would forever remain the realm of The Queen.

"And have Frederick send the Fenian ship's captain to me," Sir Hubert told his aide. "This is one man I surely must meet before we show him his rope."

The mathematics showed the necessary displacement would require each box to be built twice as long as it was wide and deep. Each seam in the planking would have to be packed tightly with oakum and generously smeared with pitch.

"We'll need three in time, but let's build just one now," Timothy Clark told Benny. "No point building all three until we learn what we can from this first one."

When the first box was nailed together the Colonel used an awl to bore a small hole in one end, a hole precisely the diameter of the thin rope that Benny had produced on request. On each side of the hole he attached a piece of tarred leather, which served as a crude gasket that allowed some movement of a rope but still kept the box watertight.

"We need now to add enough powder to do us some good, but not so much that the weight of it pulls the box under," the Colonel told Benny. "It is critical we strike a balance, enough weight to keep the box mostly submerged, yet not so much that it sinks like it's filled up with stones."

From oilskins left behind by the others now ashore, Benny used his palm and needle to stitch together a half dozen double-seamed bags, each half the size of a seaman's duffel. The Colonel filled each one with all the paper-wrapped carbine cartridges it would hold, then had Benny stitch every bag, but one, tightly closed.

"Break into the carbines and bring me back three Sharps, a handful of linen cartridges and few bullets, fifty-two caliber," the Colonel said. "And bring back a saw that can cut through the rifle barrels."

Cut through the barrels? Don't even ask, Benny thought to himself. Even taking turns, it took most of an hour to work the saw through the heavy steel, leaving barely an inch of barrel still extending from the Sharps carbine's stock.

"We'll just do one for now," the Colonel said. "We can do the others later, once we know this will work."

He placed the stub of the Sharp's barrel into the last of the oilskin bags filled with cartridges, the one bag that Benny had left unsealed.

"Sew that last seam right up tight to the barrel," the Colonel said, watching over Benny's shoulder.

The pitch now dry, the cartridges sealed in their oilskin bags, the Colonel used the awl to force a length of rope through the tarred leather gasket into the box. He threaded the rope through the sling swivel on the carbine's butt plate and up into the trigger guard, looping it in front of the carbine's trigger. Taking the end of rope back toward the sling swivel he tied it off, using the firmest of the splicing knots he knew.

"Hand me that hammer, and a two-inch nail," the Colonel said.

The Colonel laid the carbine flat in the box, carefully aligning the base of its stock just above the hole where the rope entered the box. He drove the nail through the carbine's polished walnut stock, securing the rifle to the floor of the box.

"We should finish this job on deck," the Colonel told Benny. "No use blowing ourselves up below and leaving a mess for the others."

Their clothes reeked of oakum and pitch as Benny and the Colonel muscled the box through a cargo hatch and onto the deck. "Careful now," the Colonel warned. "Remember what's inside."

The two men set the box down on the lee quarter deck then headed back below for the box's pine lid and the five other oilskin bags filled with cartridges. The Colonel arranged the bags around the carbine before pushing in a cartridge and a bullet and pulling back the hammer.

"This thing is armed now, which is why I had you build the lid to be screwed down, not nailed," he told Benny. "Get it screwed down and then caulk and seal every seam. Whatever you do, don't tug on that rope."

Benny worked slowly, smearing each seam with the black, sticky pitch. As soon as the pitch cooled to the touch he sent for the Colonel, who was back at the helm, talking with Kavanagh.

The winds were light. With only a slight adjustment of the squares, Kavanagh had *Erin's Hope* bobbing in place, marking time as Colonel Clark shouted orders to Benny and three others lowering the box into the water with a makeshift sling Benny had jury rigged from a cargo net.

The box set deep in the water, but not as deep as the Colonel had hoped. With a little more weight such a box would prove difficult to see by anyone not right on top of it. Benny leaned over the caprail, struggling to hold the bobbing box in place with a boathook while the Colonel studied how it moved in the waters.

"Let it go," the Colonel said at last, holding onto the

long coil of rope to which the box was tethered. He signaled to the helm, where Kavanagh turned the wheel three spokes, just enough to fill the squares.

"I trust you'll be keeping plenty of slack on that rope now," Benny said with a smile as the two men joined the others watching the box float slowly astern. When the coil of rope the Colonel held was down to its last few turns, he tied off the end to a mainmast spar.

In the instant after the rope went taut a spray of water thirty feet high jumped into the sky behind them. The sea muffled the sound of the blast, but it was clear there had been a mighty explosion.

"Anchor chain," the Colonel Clark said aloud, more to himself than the others. "And a tapered leading edge."

Pulling in what little was left of the rope, the Colonel smiled at Benny.

"We've work to do, man."

Chapter Sixteen

June 9, 1867
Waterford City

The keening went on for two straight days, low sorrowful moans swelling in waves of grief that broke as piercing wails. Mary Margaret McCarty was near exhaustion, what with her only son laid out before her and she herself destined for the poor house for sure.

"They have killed my Tomás," she railed, again and again, repeating his name, over and over, at times in whispers, at times in tortured shouts.

How did this happen? Why had Tomás been there at all? Why had a Peeler singled him out and chased him down like some rabid cur? Why hadn't that wretched girl let him inside before a bayonet near cut him in two?

Many more questions than answers surrounded the untimely death of Tomás Liam McCarty, age twenty-two and the sole support of his mother and her mother, a woman said by some to be a eighty years old.

The official inquest lasted not quite eight minutes.

"My Lord," said Sergeant Kevin McCafferty of the Royal Irish Constabulary. "This death here in question was the direct result of an unfortunate and unprovoked street riot triggered by the arrival from Dungarvan of the American Fenian prisoners. The victim, one Tomás McCarty, age twenty-two, was quite clearly a Fenian sympathizer. He was seen by witnesses we are prepared to produce pitching stones at the squad of police and soldiers who were escorting the Fenian prisoners."

Tomás had a working knowledge of stones, that much was true. Of politics he knew nothing. Since the day he turned seventeen he worked as a stonecutter, as an apprentice to Miles McCracken, whose ornate headstones were in great demand among those with the means required to take their eternal rest beneath one. Since September last Tomás had been working ten hours a day, except for the Sabbath, rebuilding one stone at a time the crumbling limestone stairways the Protestant faithful climbed each Sunday to Christ Church Cathedral.

"When the deceased was ordered to submit to arrest, he fled," McCafferty said. "My men gave chase. It remains unknown exactly how this man died, or who it was who inflicted the fatal wound. Each man I have questioned denies any personal involvement. What is known, my Lord, is that the death of this Tomás McCarty was of his own doing, the direct result of a Fenian sympathizer's attempt to escape arrest for his own crimes against the Crown."

The riot had left dozens injured, but only Tomás dead. Michael Keenan, the blacksmith, took a saber wound to the shoulder. Jeremiah Sullivan, a very old man indeed, was cut twice on the hand and once on the thigh. In the chaos, a small boy found himself beneath an officer's horse and took a hoof to the face. His mother nearly lost an arm to the slash of a sword as she threw herself beneath the horse to pull the screaming boy free. Three rioters had been arrested, all of them jailed.

The Yanks had come up from Dungarvan in a string of five wagons, appearing on the Cork Road just as the evening Angelus tolled. Word of their arrival spread quickly. Forty police armed with carbines fixed with bayonets joined the cortege of wagons at the edge of the city, just up from where the road begins to follow the banks of John's River. Half the police stayed ahead of the wagons, the other half stayed behind.

The hearing at Dungarvan had ended with the filing of charges ranging from seditious activity to high treason. All of those arrested would be held in Waterford pending a decision by Dublin Castle concerning which of the Americans would stand trial. The papers said whatever trials resulted would likely be held in the fall, undoubtedly in Dublin.

The Fenians had been shackled together in Dungarvan and loaded four or more to each wagon. The thirty-mile trek to Waterford began at dawn and had taken all day. The only stops were one near Stradbally to water the teams and another at Tramore, where the prisoners, still chained, were ordered into the brush to empty their bladders and to purge their bowels.

Within minutes of their arrival on the outskirts of Waterford City the curious began lining the narrow winding route to Ballybricken Gaol. One newspaper later put the crowd at five hundred, but those at the wake, including a few who had been on the same street as Tomás, told Mary Margaret the crowd was twice that, or more.

191

Six mounted men with sabers led the way into Waterford City, flashing threatening glances at the salters, fishermen and idlers who crowded the flagways to get a close look at the Yanks. Tomás had been walking home, oblivious to the spectacle until a loud group of small boys clutching stones raced by him, as if being chased. Ahead he saw a knot of bodies, people gathered together in a clump, as if waiting on a parade.

"It's the Fenians," an old woman told him. "Up from Dungarvan to be hanged for sure."

The wagons approached. At first there were only words, taunts offered both in Irish and in English. When the wagons neared Murphy's Lane the rain of stones began.

"We were passing down a narrow street," McCafferty told the inquest. "On one side of us was a graveyard fronted by a stone wall ten feet high. It was here we were assailed by unseen stone throwers, the rocks coming over the wall at us, at the teams, at the prisoners, at everyone crowded into that street. The houses opposite the cemetery still bear the broken windows as evidence of this assault."

One large stone caught Chief Constable Robert Barry square in the back, nearly knocking him off his mount. Enraged, he ordered a flanking squad into the cemetery to give chase to those responsible. In the confusion of what quickly became a riot, the squad turned to confront the crush of men, women and children who filled the street between the wagons and the cemetery gates. Somewhere in that crowd was Tomás McCarty.

The screams grew to a deafening pitch as the police plunged into the crowd, waving their sabers and using the polished stocks of their carbines like clubs.

❦   ❦   ❦

Tomás' dearest friend, Brian McCabe, fought back tears as he took Mary Margaret aside at the graveside to tell her what he could about how Tomás had been murdered.

"The man who did it is a white-haired constable, a man whose name they say is Mercer," he said. "It was he who chased Tomás through an alleyway onto Castle Street. Tomás tried to escape into the open doorway of O'Neill's Public House, but a black-haired girl who ran inside right before him slammed the door in his face and threw the bolt, just as Tomás tried to save himself by ducking inside as well."

Brian cried openly, tears flowing freely over his ruddy cheeks. He swiped at his nose with the tattered cuff of what passed for his funeral suit.

"Tomás beat on the door. He was beating on it with both fists and screamin' to be let in. That's when this Mercer jabbed him, stuck him from behind, with his bayonet. I was across the way, a hundred feet away at most, but I could see dear Tomás turn. He had this terrible look on him, a look of confusion.

"He tried to run again. That was when this bastard, Mercer, plunged the blade into Tomás' chest. By the time I ran across the street Mercer had run off, and Tomás was slumped dead in the doorway."

Brian spared Mary Margaret the details. Death had not taken Tomás quickly. Gasping and coughing, the young stonecutter had tried to speak his last to his friend, but from his quivering lips came only a muffled rasp. The fatal wound had split Tomás McCarty from breast to hip.

Brian tried for days without success to make himself forget how his best friend's insides had spilled out of his blood-soaked shirt and onto the cobblestones, glistening in the fading light.

The inquest jury split, half putting blame on Mercer, half not.

The matter was closed, closed forever, as was Tomás McCarty's coffin.

Chapter Seventeen

June 10, 1867
Well off Helvick Head

The Fenian brigantine was hovering well out to sea, ten miles or more off Dungarvan Bay, exactly where Rear Admiral Frederick was told to expect her.

How had such a conspicuous ship, what with a black hull and rose-colored sails, managed to elude the Royal Navy, from Sligo to Arklow, for so long? he wondered. It was clear why the Admiralty was upset.

H.M.S. *Black Prince* was closing fast now. From his place at her helm, Frederick could clearly make out the brigantine's square sails just above the horizon. This entire embarrassing affair would be over in a matter of hours.

❧   ❧   ❧

The Druid climbed high into the mainmast rigging, as high as the topmast shroud would permit. Beyond the upwind horizon he studied a trail of black smoke that warned of the warship's presence long before the ship could be seen.

195

Even at this distance she seemed a behemoth, bigger than any ship the Druid knew existed. She appeared as big through the beam as *Erin's Hope* was in length. Kavanagh was below him, at the wheel, looking up at the Druid, whose hand signals made it clear the ship just over the horizon was large and quick.

Seventy feet below him, the Druid could see Benny and Colonel Clark on their knees, one on each side of the wheelbox, each hovering over one of the two wooden boxes they worked for days to build.

"When the time comes we will ease them in, one off each side of the stern, both at once, one from each rail," the Colonel explained again to Captain Kavanagh. "The rope that links them I will hurl into our wake as the boxes drift astern. We don't want the rope hanging up on our rudder."

Timothy Clark had walked Kavanagh through his plan at least three times. When the warship had closed to the point where she looked as if she would come alongside, he needed Kavanagh to tack directly through her heading, forcing the pursuer to remain straight abaft.

With only a handful of men still aboard, Kavanagh knew bringing the brigantine about as the Colonel had directed would require eight men to do the work of twelve. Fortunately those still aboard, except for the General and a few of the others, were sailors, not soldiers, and would be up to the task.

"I need you to weave a course that requires the English to be on a heading that takes them straight toward the midpoint where we lower these boxes into our wake," Clark explained. "Between the drift of the boxes and our own ship's momentum, we should be well ahead by the time the warship snags them. Once you get a good look at the type of vessel approaching, I can adjust the length of the rope between them to twice whatever you estimate is the warship's overall length."

Kavanagh had his doubts, none of which he shared with the Colonel. With this larger, faster ship now bearing down on them, Kavanagh's first concern was getting the crew over the side and safely into the boats and making sure the Colonel had sufficient time to trigger the charges that would destroy *Erin's Hope* and and send her cargo of weapons to the bottom.

The Colonel had assured Kavanagh that his new fusing device was up to the task should the need arise to scuttle the ship. It involved an old clockworks, a length of catgut, a heavy weight, a percussion cap and some copper tubing, all arranged to spark the charge in some way only Timothy Clark understood.

❦ ❦ ❦

Rear Admiral Frederick was well aware Sir Hubert Longworth wanted the Fenian brigantine sunk, either by her own hands or, better still, by the *Black Prince*, though it mattered little to Frederick which. Whatever remained of the brigantine's crew was to be fished from the sea and brought ashore for what Frederick presumed would be a very public trial.

"Do not, under any circumstances, come alongside or attempt to board the Fenian brigantine," Longworth's orders read in part. "We have learned from an informer that upon your approach a powder magazine will be detonated by fire or some other means as her crew takes to her boats."

The wind was picking up, but Frederick knew even a gale could not save the Fenians now. The *Black Prince* was making eleven knots under steam, the Fenian square-rigger barely five.

❧ ❧ ❧

"It's a very large ship indeed," Kavanagh told the Colonel, studying her bow through his glasses. "She's iron clad. She may even be the Black Prince."

"How long is she, do you think?" the Colonel asked. "I need your best guess, and I need it now."

If it was the *Black Prince*, Kavanagh remembered reading somewhere that she was three hundred eighty feet stem to stem, nearly four times the length of the Fenian brigantine.

"Three hundred eighty feet!" Colonel Clark said, alarmed and hurrying below in search of more rope.

The Colonel's experiment with the first box showed the need for more weight and less drag in the water. The two boxes now on deck were armed in the same way as he had armed the first, but weighted to their outside edges with links of loose anchor chain that Kavanagh was at first reluctant to provide.

"What use will we have of anchor chain if we need to deploy these boxes?" the Colonel had told him. "If we're overtaken we'll be putting this ship and her cargo on the bottom, not her anchor."

Watching the trail of the first box drift into the swells convinced the Colonel to reduce resistance by tapering the end of the box opposite the rope. Shaping the box like the bow of a ship would help the box cut clean through the water, providing more speed and less drag. A tapered leading edge would generate less of a wake as well, making the box harder to spot in the water.

Tethering the firing mechanisms of two such boxes with a long length of rope required some method of greatly increasing the level of force needed to trip the two triggers. Benny's solution was a length of relief cordage placed between the trigger of the carbine and slip knots tied to withstand all but a furious tug.

❦ ❦ ❦

Like a hound gaining on a rabbit at the brink of exhaustion, the *Black Prince* was closing on its quarry, now well within two miles of the Fenian ship. Rear Admiral Frederick had overseen many a sea chase, some lasting days. This sad excuse for a sea battle would end within the hour.

It had been no real contest, what with the Fenian vessel not even armed. Nonetheless, it would be in the papers, and Frederick knew it would give his men something to feel good about. Once the Fenians fired the brigantine, his guncrews could pound away at their leisure as the brigantine burned. His only regret was they couldn't target the boats as well. His orders were to bring the Yanks back, in chains, not in pieces.

❦ ❦ ❦

Benny and the Druid gathered the men amidships and explained the maneuver. Just as the English warship was upon them, they would come about and veer straight through her course. Hauling round the yards and getting them braced would need to be done quickly, mainsails first, then right smartly to the fores.

"Once the lines are tied off, it's to the boats with the lot of you," the Druid said. "The General, Benny and I will be back at the stern, giving the Colonel a hand with his boxes. But the rest of you I want readying the boats to go over the side."

The chase was over.

The Black Prince moved in close, but not too close, as Sir Hubert had ordered. The brigantine was broad on the starboard bow, sailing large on a starboard tack.

From the helm, Frederick wondered if the Fenians would heave to before dropping their boats or put them in on the run, tying down her wheel and leaving her adrift as she went up in flames. There was little point readying the guncrews. Once the Fenians took to their boats he would call the men to general quarters, using the flaming hulk for a target drill.

The brigantine was running directly ahead of the wind, maneuvering as if to come about. Though his glasses Frederick could see four men bent over at the brigantine's sternrail, lowering into their wake what appeared to be two miniature boats. What the devil were they doing?

"Now!!" the Colonel screamed.

The two boxes went into the water only seconds apart and quickly drifted astern. Between them, at the sternrail behind the wheelbox, Colonel Clark clutched four hundred feet of rope that Benny has carefully coiled to play out in the water without snag.

The Colonel counted silently to ten before flinging the coil into the sea. It struck the water flat, just as Kavanagh turned *Erin's Hope* sharply to port. The boxes drifted away and apart, trailing rope behind them.

"Hold your course, you bastard," the Colonel screamed at the warship.

"Hold your course!" Frederick shouted to the helmsman.

"What is that?" he asked his First Lieutenant, pointing to what looked to be a pine board floating a point or two off the Black Prince's starboard bow.

"Looks to be a coffin," the man said. "And there's another, Admiral, there, just to port."

Strange time to be burying your dead at sea, Frederick thought. Some Papist superstition, no doubt.

Benny and the Colonel stood side by side, peering through the swells, each hoping for some glimpse of the rope or one of the boxes.

The warship had held course as needed, crossing directly astern of *Erin's Hope*. It would be on the rope in seconds.

❦ ❦ ❦

A foot beneath her bow wake, the H.M.S. *Black Prince* snagged the rope just wide of its midpoint, her forward momentum quickly gathering up slack, the point of her bow now a fulcrum imparting a building momentum as each of the boxes moved closer to the warship's surging hull.

As the force increased the slip knots gave way, releasing the relief cordage, tripping the carbine's triggers just as the two pine torpedoes each came alongside, one slightly ahead of, the other slightly behind, the warship's massive rudder.

The explosive force of some four thousand carbine cartridges launched a spray of anchor chain that dissolved the thin tarred pine boxes as if they were paper.

Those at the bow of the H.M.S. *Black Prince* sensed nothing at all, while those at the stern felt the ship shudder beneath them.

The big ship's wheel recoiled in the helmsman's hands, only for an instant, before locking up.

❦ ❦ ❦

From the sternrail, neither the Colonel nor Benny had seen nor heard anything to indicate the boxes had worked as planned. Kavanagh watched from the wheelbox as the others aboard *Erin's Hope* made quick for the boats, as ordered. The hull of the massive warship loomed above them, seeming close enough to touch.

Colonel Timothy Clark sprinted below to activate the clock fuse, silently wondering what had gone wrong. Kavanagh's maneuvers had been brilliant, baiting the warship into holding the course required to snag the rope and to bring the boxes alongside the warship's hull.

Perhaps the rope slipped beneath her bow, he thought. Maybe the rope became tangled in the rudder, the boxes coming together two hundred feet behind her, exploding harmlessly, if exploding at all.

❦ ❦ ❦

The Druid watched in amazement as the behemoth veered sharply away, as if abandoning the chase.

The underwater blast triggered by the pine torpedoes had damaged the warship's gudgeon, bending the rudder's pivot pin and locking the damaged rudder in place. Despite all her firepower, the Black Prince could do little without rudder control but steam about in long endless circles.

The Druid climbed into the mainmast rigging. If *Erin's Hope* was destined to go down, he would see her to the bottom. Below him on deck he could see the others busy at their boat stations, the boats nearly over the side.

"Hold up," the Druid shouted, his words drifting into the wind, unheard and unheeded so far below.

At the helm, Kavanagh watched over his left shoulder as the warship steamed away. He could see men running on her deck, gun crews no doubt, moving from port to starboard stations. He turned the wheel six spokes to starboard, as much as the bracing of the squares would allow, hoping to put as much distance between predator and prey as he could without being able to come full about.

The Druid dropped to the deck as if he had wings.

"Leave the boats and get to the braces," he told Benny and the others at deck. "We need to come about again and quick!"

I must find the Colonel, he thought.

Oblivious to the chaos just above him, Timothy Clark was busy below, readying the powder train. He had already attached one end of a catgut line to a grapeshot, weight two pounds, diameter two and one half inches. The other end he threaded through an eyebolt at the top of a copper tube, hooking it with a loop to a pin on the clock cylinder placed two feet above the decking.

Five minutes should get us safely away, he thought.

As the clock cylinder turned, the loop would slip, the heavy grapeshot dropping onto the percussion cap below it and igniting the powder. It had worked every time in his trials.

Such a waste, he thought, removing the stop, setting his explosive clock fuse contraption into motion.

Rear Admiral Frederick was furious.

"Get the crews to the guns and bombard that vessel immediately," he screamed.

Having expected the Fenians to take to their boats and to fire their own ship, Frederick had failed to order the Black Prince gun crews to quarters. In the time it took to ready the guns, the brigantine was broad on the starboard beam, nearly out of range of all but the largest of the Armstrongs.

The first barrage from the sixty-eight pounders sailed well over the mainmast squares and well off to port. The second barrage fell short to starboard.

David had again felled Goliath.

Frederick knew too well that there would be hell to pay.

Chapter Eighteen

July 5, 1867
57° 20' north latitude, 46° 50' west longitude

This Brendan route seemed at first such a queer and ridiculous notion, sailing north to make west, taking *Erin's Hope* and a skeleton crew into icy waters on bitter and fickle winds.

Kavanagh knew little of the seas that they had confronted between Ireland and this pack ice rimming Greenland. He knew even less of the waters still beyond, little more than terrible tales told of ice-bound whalers who survived to tell them only by gnawing the frozen flesh of those who were the first to succumb to the cold.

Kavanagh had never been this cold, and here it was July. The sun never set, but the mercury never seemed to rise or fall, suspended always a notch above freezing. The rain came day after day in gray stinging sheets, often as sleet, sometimes as hail. *Erin's Hope* spent day and night dodging ice, tacking furiously at times among huge floating mountains of it. The helmsman's orders were always the same: make west, always west, while staying as far off the ice shelves as these strong southwesterly winds would allow.

Thick fog had required watches to be doubled. With icebergs about, sleep was a luxury none aboard a wooden ship could afford. What little sun Kavanagh had seen in recent days allowed sextant readings that put a landfall still some weeks away. *Erin's Hope* had been at sea nearly 100 days. The men, like Kavanagh himself, were exhausted.

The Druid had assured him this Brendan route was the shortest route and, given their circumstances, the safest route as well. After Colonel Clark's cleverness left the H.M.S. Black Prince steaming in helpless circles, the Royal Navy would spare neither time nor effort in throwing up a wide net of warships to prevent the Fenian gunrunners from escaping west into open seas, unchallenged. The Druid was right: the British Admiralty would never expect *Erin's Hope* to make east, straight for England.

"We must keep ourselves well to the south, as the British ships will be hugging the coast, checking the bays, but we will need to make east and then north along the Irish Sea, toward Ulster," the Druid had told him, tracing a route with his finger on the chart spread before them.

"And, along the way, would you have us drop anchor in Dublin?" Kavanagh asked, ridiculing the Druid's suggestion. "Or maybe put in at Belfast? We can lower a boat and pull ourselves ashore for a pint, perhaps, raise a glass to Her Majesty before setting off on the crossing."

The Druid had called it the Brendan route, named for an ancient Irish monk driven by a monastic vision of a Promised Land of the Saints to venture north and west from the Dingle peninsula in a curragh of oxhide tanned in wool grease, his tiny vessel rigged with but two small sails. If it happened at all, it happened a thousand years ago, maybe more. Kavanagh remembered hearing of St. Brendan as a boy, but could recall only bits of it, strange encounters with sea monsters and stones of fire raining down on the vessel from the sky. The Christian Brothers taught the fable as an allegory of faith and perseverance and as no small matter of pride in the nautical achievements of Ireland's earliest priests.

Not all who made such voyages were men of the Christian god, the Druid told him. Pagans had their legends, too, epic stories of odd adventure along a stepping stone route that took early Celtic sailors from the north of Ireland to the pine-covered shores of North America in passages that often took years. It must be the shortest route, the Druid said, as the track preferred by fulmars and guillemots and other migrating birds, creatures that could ill afford the rigors of a crossing any longer than need be. The Druid knew the birds well, and they somehow knew that north took them west as the horizon bends into frozen skies.

Their mission was over. The four Fenian officers still aboard had concluded as much within hours of the encounter with the English warship. General Kerrigan, Colonel Clark and the first and second officers, Sweetman and O'Neill, had drafted and signed rambling new orders. The General presented them to Kavanagh as *Erin's Hope* lingered once again off the County Waterford headlands, awaiting any signal from those ashore:

"We, the undersigned military and naval officers on board the *Erin's Hope*, having become satisfied that we will receive no communication from our friends on shore, and having cruised for weeks days along the coast of Ireland, almost always within hailing distance of coastguard stations, lighthouses and men-of-war, and being well beyond the time of communications appointed by Colonel Warren and Captain Kenneally, have concluded and deemed it necessary that you should, in view of our very meager supplies, and the all-important purpose of saving the arms, ammunition, and vessel for the organization, head your vessel for New York."

Easier said than done, Kavanagh told the General, as had been this entire affair. What had become of those ashore was anyone's guess. None still aboard spoke it aloud, but it seemed to them clear that the mission was over for those ashore as well. He would turn the brigantine's bow westward, as ordered, but the early summer winds would not be with them, he told the General. The spring winds came largely from the east, but shifted as May gave way to June to westerly and southwesterly. It could be a long crossing.

Provisions would a problem. The eight men left on board were too many mouths to feed with what little stores remained below, yet too few hands to properly handle the demands of a square-rigger being tossed about in the throes of a gale. "We shall do what we must," he assured Kerrigan and the others.

The Druid laid out the charts showing how a stepping stone crossing could take them from the Antrim coast to the Hebrides, north to the Faroes, west and south of Iceland and south and west of Greenland to Labrador or Newfoundland, depending on the reach of summer ice. The wind would be against them much of the way, but a strong current would help push them west from Iceland and, once beyond Greenland, into the Davis Strait, where the current would urge them south toward Newfoundland. A few days beyond Ireland they would be beyond the reach of the British, perhaps at the Hebrides, where they could go ashore and take on whatever provisions they might find. There would be no need for currency, not with guns to barter.

It was worth a try, Kavanagh decided. He had his orders, but it was up to him to determine how to carry them out, how to get them beyond a British blockade, how to keep them all a day or two ahead of the hunger and the exhaustion that would pursue them as they headed west, always west.

The first days had gone well enough, given that *Erin's Hope* was tacking through the busiest sea lanes between England's ports and those along Ireland's east coast. Kavanagh kept her well out of sight of the Irish coastline, crossing through the Dublin track in the dead of night with running lights extinguished. By day they flew the Union Jack, dipping her in mocking salute to British merchants who passed by unaware they were being hailed by the most wanted ship at sea. They made north through the Belfast track in a near gale that tested the limits of those aboard who had never sailed and likely never would again.

In the four days out from the North Channel, it had rained for three. An easterly gale kept them well west of the Hebrides, forcing them to claw up to north to reach the bleak landscape of the Faroe Islands. Pushing through heavy rip tides, Kavanagh had ducked into a cove faced with cliffs as sheer as those that rose along the west coast of Ireland, though these were nearly black, the hillsides behind them completely bare of vegetation. As luck would have it, the waters of the bay were shallow enough to accommodate what little anchor chain Colonel Clark had not appropriated for his underwater ordnance.

Kavanagh and the Druid stayed aboard, while the

others pulled ashore in two small boats, one laden with empty casks once filled with fresh water. They also took three crates of Enfield rifles and thousands of cartridges.

That half day undisturbed at anchor had been the last real sleep Kavanagh had known. The Druid never slept, it seemed, but Kavanagh found his eyes played tricks on him if he didn't close them now and then. He tried not to doze at the helm, but found himself at times nodding into sleep until the sound of luffing sail brought him back on course.

The sound of the others returning awakened him. The two boats were laden with salted cod, great hunks of mutton, more potatoes than three men could carry and large sacks of oats. All the casks, a dozen at least, had been filled with the freshest water Kavanagh had ever tasted, icy water taken from a spring which fed into a small lake in which some of the men, despite the cold, had forced themselves to bathe. The General had traded two rifles for a harpoon, a sealskin coat and two jugs of strong drink. Benny had traded a rifle and a few hundred cartridges for heavy wool sweaters and caps, one of each for himself, and one of each for his captain.

Those who they had come across on shore had been fishermen and herders living in a tiny village of small stone huts. More than a few had followed them back to the boats, helping with the provisions and curious to see the black-hulled ship they had watched approach under salmon-colored sails. They spoke but few words of English. The General made out their native tongue as some sort of Norse. Two younger men, either hungry for adventure or bored with the bleakness of the place, had pleaded through frantic gestures to come aboard, to join the crew. Kerrigan told them no, which was not the answer Kavanagh would have given. *Erin's Hope* could use two extra hands, especially men familiar with these waters and these winds.

Benny helped the cook prepare a thick stew of mutton and potatoes. The scent of it filled the deckhouse. The warmth of it going down cut the chill. When the last of it had disappeared, Kavanagh took the anchor watch, ordering all but himself below to sleep. The brightest of the stars seemed in this endless twilight only the faintest points of light as the sun barely dipped below the horizon before beginning a slow ascent. By mid-morning *Erin's Hope* was well underway, making north more than west amid bursts of southwest winds as the Faroes disappeared beneath the swells at their backs.

That was a week ago, or more, he thought, before they had spotted the first ice peaks of Greenland, before the whales had come, before he had seen the glowing rainbow of ice, thinking it a mirage of exhaustion until Benny spotted it as well. It appeared like a vision, out of a squall, a sheet of rain going silver then to shimmering red and green and the deepest of blues. It seemed alive as it neared, glowing and translucent, enveloping them both in frozen light before dissolving into nothingness as it swept slowly across the deck. It seemed magical.

Chapter Nineteen

August 3, 1867
Connacht

"Prisoners will not speak unless or until they are directly spoken to. Is this perfectly understood?"

No one answered, as if no one heard.

The rhythmic motion of the train had lulled most of the eight men in chains into a shallow, dreamless sleep. The coach's padded benches were as soft a pallet as any had seen in months. Heads bobbed as if showing agreement with orders being barked at them, though few heard even a word.

Sean Kenneally, "Captain" Kenneally to these fellow Fenians in chains, had had enough of sleep. Since early June, when this prison nightmare first began in Dungarvan, he courted sleep as an antidote to boredom, as his only escape from the numbing isolation he and the others had endured.

Throughout this pre-dawn journey from Dublin to Sligo, Sean lost himself in a waking trance of his own construction. He studied the Irish countryside, watching the cattle nose the gorse, studying the stars as they faded to nothingness in the face of first light.

As the sun began its climb above the horizon, the lakelands of Leinster became the hillsides of Connacht, damp with mist and ripe with the promise of harvest. The sweet scent of life transcended even the steam engine's acrid smoke and ceaseless rain of cinders. Sean closed his eyes and inhaled deeply. So different these smells, so unlike the damp and musty air of Kilmainham, which was all sewage, sickness and sweat. So different, he thought, from the stench of rotting tubers and the putrid gas seeping from the bloated bodies of those who had starved without them.

Sean absorbed the sights and sounds of the villages and towns through which the train passed: Mullingar, Longford, Carrick on Shannon, Boyle. Each was a familiar name, each a place Sean had never seen and would likely never see again. Sleep was out of the question.

The train took a siding at Boyle to let another pass. Sean fixed his gaze on a figure gathering firewood, a scavenger digging through brush along the track. It was a woman, young and beautiful, little more than a girl. She was the first woman Sean had seen up close in months, and she made him think of Katherine.

He couldn't look away. Red-haired and red-cheeked she was, the rest of her well hidden within a great dark shawl. Their eyes never met. Thank God for that, he thought. As the train moved on, he wished he hadn't spotted her at all.

The train slowed to a stop again at Collooney, just a few miles short of Sligo, taking on wood and water and three squads of infantry dispatched from the 72nd Highlanders. Sean and the others studied each soldier carefully, taking note that each young soldier's carbine was fixed with a sword bayonet. Dublin Castle was making certain there would be no rescue. No Fenians would cheat justice in Sligo.

Accompanying the troops was one Edward P. O'Connor, Esq., governor of the County Sligo Gaol. Red-faced and well-fed, he scowled at Sean and spat on the floor as he spoke in whispers to the sergeant of the guard.

As the train pushed on past Collooney, most of the prisoners again drifted off to sleep, impervious to O'Connor, even as his whispers gave way to shouts.

"In just a few minutes you will be put in leg irons," he said. "As this train arrives at the Sligo train yard, each of you will be chained to another, and each pair of you will be chained to another pair. On my signal, and not until my signal, you will file quickly and quietly from this coach into the train yard. Stragglers will get the boot, the butt of a rifle, the blade of a bayonet, or worse. Do you understand?"

No response.

O'Connor continued. "You will be taken by prison van from Sligo station through the city center to the Sligo Gaol. You will not speak directly to one another or to anyone else along the route as you are moved through the streets. Do I make myself perfectly clear?"

It was a question greeted only with grunts and glowering glares, at least from those few who were not asleep.

"Wake these men up!" O'Connor roared.

The sentry nearest him lifted his carbine high above his shoulder and slammed the rifle's butt down hard on the train's oak plank floor. Even those wide awake jumped in their seats.

"You miserable bastards! You will do as I say!" O'Connor screamed, his ruddy face now gone crimson. "I'd like nothing better than to show you scurvy Yanks a rope and, mark my words, after a few weeks in the Sligo Gaol, every last one of you will wish that I had."

O'Connor didn't need this commotion, much less the insolence of this rabble. He'd been up half the night, getting to Collooney from Sligo after spending most of the last week rearranging his life and his gaol to accommodate these Yanks. No trains headed south from Sligo to Collooney, not before noon, forcing O'Connor to come from Sligo by coach. He was tired and hungry. And now his temples were pounding.

Too dark to read, too early to drink, O'Connor had spent much of his long coach ride to Collooney reflecting on these ignorant fools and their so-called cause. Only the Irish. Imagine, sailing all the way from America to end up for your trouble rotting away in an English gaol. All these Paddies ever dreamed of was making the passage from what's left of Ireland to America, and now these daft bastards decide to sail back. O'Connor knew, and told anyone who would listen, that if heaven rained down loaded rifles these Fenian dreamers would wait on angels to pull the triggers.

As keeper of the kept at Sligo Gaol, O'Connor's stock and trade were common criminals, petty thieves, highwaymen, paupers turned pickpockets. Now and again there was the occasional murderer, a deranged sot in need of housing until he could be hung. Traffic in prisoners of politics was rare.

Both as a warder and as governor, O'Connor hadn't set eyes on a political prisoner for ages, none, really, since '48, when hundreds of those fingered as United Irishmen were jailed, their leaders betrayed, quickly tried and shipped in irons to Van Diemann's Land, where some of the bastards escaped.

The recent so-called "rising" of March last was too short-lived to fill many cells in Sligo. O'Connor had heard the gaols in Cork and in Dublin were jammed to the rafters. At Mountjoy and Kilmainham, Fenians had been stacked like turf, warehoused for months on end. Not so in Sligo.

Some said the handful involved in Sligo were Americans. Yanks or not, they had fled into the hills with the locals who were doing the bidding of the Irish Republican Brotherhood. Others vanished into the protective coloration of the hovels on the fringes of the city center. It was those too stupid with drink who wound up getting pinched.

The informers swear that American Fenians are no strangers still to Sligo's streets, but informers will swear to anything, O'Connor knew, for a few pence or a pint, or better yet both. The Fenians here in Ireland, they would have him believe, are men with considerable military training. Some, they said, were heroes of the Great War of The Rebellion, both Yanks and Rebs. It made no sense whatever: Irish killing Irish over the rights of freed African slaves to steal their jobs.

O'Connor had little time and even less patience for

those who preached insurrection. To him, Fenianism was only a symptom of a chronic disease of the poorest of the Irish poor. They wallowed in a popular discontent deeply seated, widely extended and, in the view of some, exceedingly well grounded. O'Connor couldn't agree. He was a religious man himself, a regular attendee at the Protestant Church of Ireland. More than once he had heard from the pulpit that a nation's greatest enemy is the small minds of its small people. O'Connor knew in his heart it was never truer than in present day Ireland. Why can't these Papists accept their lot and get on with their miserable lives?

And little of it has a bit to do with religion, O'Connor knew. To be certain, the papists and the Protestants lived in different worlds, each filled with suspicion and scorn for the other. But O'Connor believed that now, like always, the troubles in Ireland were about just thing: the golden rule. Not the Bible's golden rule, mind you, but life's golden rule: It's them with the gold who make the rules.

O'Connor wished he could take just one of these prisoners aside to study, like a butterfly pinned to a felt-covered board. Why must you bring trouble here, from America? What makes you think you can change the work of centuries? Why would you believe that overnight, with a few pikes and rusty pistols, the conquered can become the conquerors?

For those in Sligo with positions of power and prestige, O'Connor among them, the Fenians were the stuff of crude jokes. Though the people themselves would hold fast to their seditious secrets, their circles were laced with informers, toothless ferrets who would spill their guts for a handful of coppers or a splash of poteen. From such

informers O'Connor and the entire Royal Irish
Constabulary knew too well of the Fenians' heart-sworn
oaths, moonlight drillings, poetic promises and ale house
threats. They promised pikes and pistols and a fight to the
death with the Queen's militia.

And a quick death it will be, O'Connor thought to
himself. Croppies against cavalry, cannon against pikes,
hanging tree justice for those few who survive. These
pathetic peasant revolts lasted hours, at best. They were a
boil on the body politic, quickly lanced and bandaged, a
nuisance not a threat. Why they hadn't hung these bastards
straight away he couldn't say.

Word had come direct from Dublin Castle that these
eight Fenians were O'Connor's to hold in Sligo and to
present at trial. Troops, they promised, would be assigned
to guard the train and to keep the peace along the route to
the gaol, at the point of bayonets if need be. While these
Fenian bastards aren't worth spit at rebellion, O'Connor
knew they had managed to break a few of their own from
captivity, both in England and in Ireland, with damn little
concern for killing themselves, or anyone else, in the
bargain.

There would be no rescues in Sligo. "If there's
trouble," O'Connor told the troops as they formed in ranks
at Collooney station, "shoot the bastards dead. I'll answer
to the Castle."

The truth of it was O'Connor and his troops had
nothing to fear. Captain Kenneally and his men harbored
no delusions of escape or rescue. Sean knew he and the
others now headed to trial in Sligo were pawn pieces, at
best. The Fenian Brotherhood might plot with the Irish
Republican Brotherhood to stage daring rescues of the
likes of its founder James Stephens or its chief executive

Colonel Thomas Kelly, but not risk any necks for the likes of him or the others on this train.

Had they not, after all, failed? Had they not been captured with hardly a struggle? And their cargo? What became of their cargo? And what had become of *Erin's Hope*?

When Sean's thoughts turned to Stephens, which was hardly at all, he pictured him back in Paris, living the good life on greenbacks stolen from the cause, sipping fine brandy and passing the time by teaching the Queen's English to Parisian whores and the pampered sons of French aristocrats. Or maybe Stephens had returned to America. After being smuggled out of Richmond Prison by Colonel Kelly, Stephens was sure to be far from Ireland and the certain execution that awaited him there should the Chief Executive of the Irish Republic ever again fall to capture.

And Kelly? Who knew where he was hiding? Not the British, to be certain. The Colonel was said to be a master of disguise, quick to perfect an accent or affect a limp. As Sean and the others endured this sham of a trial, Kelly might very well be at Buckingham Palace, taking tea with Queen Victoria herself.

Since wading ashore at Helvick Head in June, Sean had seen his fill of the likes of O'Connor, little men with little concern for little more than keeping their hands in Her Majesty's pocket. Sean had seen nothing much at all except a numbing array of Her Majesty's prisons, filled with prisoners like him and men like O'Connor, little men who took great pleasure in making other men miserable.

In Dungarvan Gaol, the men off *Erin's Hope* had numbered more than twenty. After three weeks at

Waterford, all but the officers were sent to Cork to be put on ships bound for America, at least those who could raise five pounds for their passage. Before deportation each man was required to swear his oath, both to God and to Her Majesty, to never in his lifetime devote another thought or deed to the cause of insurrection.

Sean was among the others, shipped on to Dublin to await trial and sentencing. He was locked away at Kilmainham before being moved across the Liffey to Mountjoy Prison, himself now three stone lighter and barely able to catch a breath. A bail hearing sent him back to Mountjoy to await his fate in Sligo at what the newspapers would call a trial.

The procession through the streets of Sligo station held no surprises. The leg irons raked at Sean's ankles as he and the others stumbled down from the train and shuffled through the yard. What O'Connor had called a prison van was a horse-drawn bus, commandeered for the task from the Victoria Hotel. It was flanked by a platoon of Royal Irish Constabulary. Armed with carbines, the Highlanders followed close behind.

The bus and its cortege moved slowly down the depot hill and east toward the River Garavogue bridge. More than a thousand people had gathered at the Sligo station for a chance glimpse of the Yanks. Many tagged along behind. The crowd swelled in numbers at every street through which the procession passed. Gulls circled above, hoping for a scrap of bread, lighting on rooftops of the shops and tenements that lined the narrow streets.

As the bus crested the bridge, Sean smelled the sea. It

sent his mind reeling back to those long weeks under sail. Those thirty-one days had forever changed his life, if not for the better. Off to his left, well beyond the first hills that rose from the east banks of the Garavogue, was Benbulben. It made him think of the Druid. A welcome sight Benbulben had been last May, rising from the morning fog, the sow swimming in the sea to welcome this one-ship Fenian armada to the shelter of Sligo Bay.

From the storefronts and market stalls, the curious glares of Sligo greeted Sean and the others as the bus moved through the city center diamond and up the Barrack Street hill. Up ahead, at the crest of the hill, Sean spotted the spire of what must be the courthouse.

🐚 🐚 🐚

From a high window in the building's clock tower, Daniel Buckley looked down on this spectacle of these Fenians in leg irons being carted through Sligo's streets like so many wild circus beasts. Buckley had made the crossing with Captain Kenneally and the others, but his life was now his own, no longer the Fenians, no longer O'Connor's.

While those below faced a long, cold night in the Sligo Gaol, Buckley had made arrangements to spend the night burrowed in a stranger's bed. He would bury himself in her breasts, busy himself between her thighs before having his way, come morning, with these Fenian fools.

Chapter Twenty

August 4, 1867
The Summer Assize, Sligo

"If you please, state your name for the court."

"Buckley, my Lord, Daniel Joseph Buckley."

It was a lie, the first of many those assembled would hear today from this man now calling himself Buckley.

He had been up all night and looked it. Officially he was under confinement at the Sligo Gaol, charged like the other eight with conspiracy under the treason felony act, the Eleventh of Victoria.

Truth be known, and there would be little of that this day, he had spent last night and the previous three hidden away in one of the more ordinary rooms of the Victoria Hotel. He had planned to spend his last night before the trial once again dipping his quill into Peg O'Shea, a buxom young whore who charged only a quid to raise more than his spirits. Dublin Castle had other ideas.

Sir Robert Anderson, the British Secret Service's new Special Advisor on Fenianism, dispatched to Sligo

223

the Crown's most experienced felon setter, John Joseph
Corydon. Once a trusted Fenian officer in England,
Corydon was now the quarry.

A month ago in Dublin, Corydon testified that
Colonel John Warren was the Fenian leader known to him
personally to have planned the landing of weapons at
Sligo from a brigantine that had sailed to Ireland from
America for that seditious purpose. Warren had been
convicted, but Corydon's credibility had been seriously
undermined, both in court and in the newspapers. He had
proven himself in Dublin to be a man whose reputation,
even for an informer, was well beneath contempt.

"Is it true, Mister Corydon, that you have lately lived
in a brothel in Liverpool with a prostitute and that you
paid for her services with Fenian money?" he was asked in
Dublin.

"I did live in a house in Liverpool."

"And what room had you in this house?"

"The best room."

"And the best girl?"

"No, I cannot say that," Corydon said with a sneer.
"She was an Irish girl."

Anderson agreed with the Crown's solicitors that a
new, less roguish informer would better serve the Fenian
trials in Sligo. Who better, Anderson figured, than one of
the very Fenians who had made the crossing? While the
Crown had yet to capture the ship or its cargo, it had
managed to lay its hands on most of her crew. With
Corydon's help, surely one of these Yanks could be

persuaded to tell a credible tale of this scurrilous expedition.

Anderson found the task of persuading Buckley to turn on his shipmates a remarkably easy affair. Anderson had Corydon dressed in prison garb and placed him in the Fenians' cellblock at Kilmainham to learn what he could of the expedition and the men involved. Corydon quickly spotted Buckley as a lamb awaiting slaughter.

Six weeks later, in the lamplight of Sligo's Victoria Hotel, the two informers spent the night over strong tea and cheap cognac, polishing Buckley's betrayal. There were to be no surprises for Lord Rupert Trimble, the Crown special prosecutor assigned by Dublin Castle to make examples of these Yanks.

Not just the courtroom, but the entire massive courthouse was packed to the rafters. Even the hallways and anterooms were jammed with the curious. Admission to the main gallery had been strictly by favors owed. The landed gentry of County Sligo had flocked to the city to see these caged American tigers, these insolent Yanks sent up by rail from the dungeons of Dublin to be sentenced at last.

The trial opened promptly at ten with Lord Rupert Trimble reading aloud a twenty-part indictment alleging multiple crimes. Together, the court was told, these eight Fenians had "conspired with James Stephens, the Head Central Organizer for the Irish Revolution, and with Fenian leaders John O'Mahoney, Colonel Thomas J. Kelly, Colonel William R. Roberts and other evily disposed persons to raise, make and levy war, insurrection and rebellion against our said Lady the Queen within this realm."

They were further charged with acts designed to subvert and destroy the constitution and government, including participation in an invasion of Ireland as oath-sworn members of the Fenian Brotherhood, a subversive organization with origins in Irish-American communities throughout the United States.

The Brotherhood's stated purpose, Trimble reminded the court, was and remains driving the British government from Ireland through the force of arms. Its efforts on this soil to achieve that goal have been undertaken with the assistance of the outlawed Irish Republican Brotherhood. All charges fell within the legal parameters of the Treason Felony Act.

"I should state for the record that the object of this act, my Lords, was to mitigate the extreme penalty, to reduce the penalty of capital punishment to imprisonment for a term of years, or for life," Trimble said. "We have for the last two years, unhappily, too much experience with this Treason Felony Act to render it necessary for me to dwell at any length upon the subject.

"The indictment at hand charges those before you with twenty-two overt acts of furtherance of a treasonable design, acts which would indicate a criminal intention to execute these treasonable acts. It is not necessary to prove all of these overt acts, but only some of them to show that the parties charged took action to carry out their criminal intention."

The outcome was a given. Just six months ago, these Fenians would have hung. But times had changed. Dublin Castle required no more martyrs, especially not citizens of

America, a nation with whom England shared a very tenuous alliance. Executions had only fanned the fires of Fenianism, both in England and in Ireland. Hanging these Yanks would only ignite a firestorm in New England and would surely test the patience of an American president who had family still in County Antrim.

Trimble wasted little time in laying out his case.

"Please tell this court, Mr. Buckley, your age and your place of birth."

"My age is twenty-five. I was born in Munster, near Barraduff, in the mountains east of Killarney."

"Then you are an Irishman?"

"I am," Buckley said. "Or I was. I emigrated to New York City in '48 as a young boy. My brother and I were orphaned and sent to America during the famine. We lived for a time with an uncle, our dead mother's brother. He had made the crossing before us, in '46."

"So are you an American, or are you an Irish citizen and a subject of the Queen?" Lord Trimble asked. It was a point of law he knew would muddle this trial.

"Both, I suppose. I joined the Federal army in '61 and fought for the Union in the 69th New York State Militia."

"The 69th New York? Was that not the so-called Irish Brigade?"

"It was. The 69th and other volunteer regiments as well."

"And how long were you in the Federal army?" Trimble asked.

"Until 1865."

"That's a lie," a prisoner shouted from the bench behind the barristers.

It was Costelloe, here on trial out of stubbornness mixed with pride. Those not fingered in Dublin by Buckley as expedition leaders had been set free on a promise to immediately sail home to America. All were required to sign a confession and a formal apology to her Majesty for their insolence. Costelloe had refused to leave and refused to sign.

"He's a feckin' deserter, a grave robber and a liar," Costelloe screamed, waving a fist at Buckley. "Every bloody word this feckin' Judas speaks is bought and rehearsed. It's the thinnest tissue of perjured lies."

"Silence!" Chief Justice FitzGerald shouted. "One more outburst from you and I'll order you and all of your comrades as well to be gagged for the duration of this trial."

A murmur went through the gallery.

"May I proceed now, your honor?" Trimble asked.

"If you please, Lord Trimble," FitzGerald said.

"When you, Mr. Buckley, first arrived in New York as a child, did you then swear an oath of allegiance to the United States?"

"I did not." That much was true.

"And when you became a soldier, did you swear an oath then?"

"No."

Another lie, one concocted by Trimble who knew allegiance and citizenship had become an important legal point. It was a point lost on Buckley, but hardly on the defense and those dispatched from the American consul in Dublin to monitor and report back to Washington on the status of the trial.

Lord John Wodehouse, referred to derisively by the Fenian newspapers as "Wood-louse," was then The Earl of Kimberly. He had been appointed by the Labour Party to keep a tight lid on Ireland. Both he and Lord Clarendon, the British foreign secretary, firmly ascribed to the legal theory of indefensible allegiance: Once a Briton, always a Briton.

Many of the Fenians now on trial, Buckley not among them, had been born in Ireland but naturalized in the United States. As American citizens, they claimed alien rights. Under British law they were entitled to a trial by a jury *de medietate,* a jury comprised of aliens such as those on trial. Wodehouse was adamant. "The consequences would be obviously disastrous," he told Trimble more than once, "if Irishmen could return from America to plot against the Queen as filibusters and then, when discovered, shelter themselves in our courts under letters of naturalization."

The nuances of international law be damned. The British courts, both in Ireland and in England, would treat Fenians as traitorous British subjects. To hell with diplomacy.

"Tell me, Mr. Buckley, why would you join the Federal army if not for some heart-felt allegiance to the government of the United States?"

"For the money, my Lord. There was no work to be had in New York, none for the paddies at least. Most Irish, myself to be certain, were worse off than the coloreds. I was ready to head west, to lay rail in Missouri. Then the word on the streets was that Colonel Meagher was forming a brigade and was promising enlistment bonuses to all able-bodied men."

"This Colonel Meagher you speak of. Is this not Thomas Francis Meagher of Waterford?" Trimble asked. "Was he not the seditious Young Irelander leader sentenced to death and then banished to Van Diemann's Land for his role in the rising of '48?"

"One and the same, me Lord," Buckley said. "He escaped and was exiled in America. I heard he ran a newspaper before the war."

Corydon had done his job, Trimble thought. This Buckley, or whoever he was, had a better memory than most.

"And how much did this Fenian criminal, Meagher, pay you to join his Irish brigade?"

"There was a federal enlistment bounty of three hundred dollars."

"That was the equivalent of two hundred English pounds, was it not?"

"I cannot say, but I do know it was more money than I had ever seen at one time," Buckley said.

"And did you swear an oath of allegiance?"

"I did not. Not then. When I left the army in '65 I was sworn into the Brotherhood."

"You swore an oath to the Brotherhood but not the United States? By 'the Brotherhood' do you mean the Fenian Brotherhood?" Trimble asked, already knowing it so.

"Aye."

"And do you remember this oath to which you swore?"

"I do. And I remember that it was called then a pledge, not an oath. It went something like this: 'I, Daniel Joseph Buckley, solemnly pledge my sacred word of honor, as a truthful and honest man, that I will labor with earnest zeal for the liberation of Ireland from the yoke of England and for the establishment of a free and independent government on Irish soil.' There was more, something about pledging not to divulge the objects for which the organization was established. That's all I can remember now."

Corydon's coaching had served Trimble well: memorize this oath, word for every last word, he had told Buckley. But, when you're asked to repeat it back to Trimble, say only the first of it. Pretend you can't recall the words in full. It will sound less like an actor on a stage.

"So this oath pledged you to support an armed insurrection, a foul conspiracy to deprive or dethrone the Queen from the government of Ireland?" Trimble was playing to the crowd. "To put it more palpably, Mr.

Buckley, you are admitting here today in open court, in front of God as your witness, that you were a party in a conspiracy having as its object to upset the existing government and to institute in its stead what has been called an Irish republic?"

"I was."

"And tell the court, if you will, Mr. Buckley, what brings you here today to Sligo? What brings you to be here on trial for your life as are these others seated here before us?"

"Last year, or the year before last it was, I joined an expedition," Buckley said. "I was sent with other members of the organization to the Maine frontier, from which we were to cross over into Canada."

"For what purpose?"

"To invade New Brunswick."

"To participate in an armed invasion of a province within Her Majesty's sovereign domain of Canada?"

"Aye. We were sent by the Brotherhood to the settlement at Eastport, across the border, in Maine. Our orders were to link up with a steamer, which was bringing weapons up from New York. We were to use the weapons and the ship in capturing the island of Campobello in the Bay of Fundy."

"And what became of this Canadian invasion?"

"Damn little," Buckley said.

A titter of laughter swept through the gallery.

"By the time the steamer arrived, six British warships were protecting the island. An American naval vessel intercepted our steamer and confiscated our weapons. The American government sent General Meade, the hero of the Federal Army, and a company of artillery to put a stop to the whole affair. That he did, even before it began."

"And how did that fiasco bring you to Sligo aboard the Fenian brigantine?" Trimble asked.

"Some months later, after we came back to New York, I was in a public house, where I was met by that man Costelloe," Buckley said, gesturing toward the prisoners. "He heard me talking about having once worked aboard ship, as a cook's helper. He later introduced me to a Colonel James Kelley, who was head of the military department."

"The Fenian Brotherhood's military department?" Trimble asked, again knowing the answer to his question.

"Aye. Kelley brought me to the Fenian headquarters in New York, somewhere on Chatham Street. They said they were assembling a ship's crew and would have orders soon. After months of waiting, he finally asked me and some others to meet in connection with another expedition."

"How many others?"

"Maybe forty. We met on the tenth of April at the Chatham Street headquarters. There had been news on the underwater cable of a rising. The New York papers all said an Irish Republic had been established but was in need of reinforcement. "

"What happened then?"

'We were told by Colonel Kelley to pack sea trunks with warm clothes and to bring with us enough food for a month. He told us to report back in two days to a house somewhere on East Broadway. When I did I was told to follow the others, all with baggage, to the foot of Canal Street. We got there in the morning and waited until late afternoon, when we went aboard a steamer."

"And where did this steamer take you and the others?"

"The steamer left the quay and went to an outer bay of New York, a place called Sandy Hook, a distance of fifteen or twenty miles."

"And what happened next?"

"We stayed anchored there from the twelfth to the thirteenth. Kelley had spoken of a vessel, which was to convey arms and officers with military experience, but the vessel not appearing we intended to go back to New York."

"A vessel to convey arms to Sligo?" Trimble asked.

"We did not know then where the vessel was destined or what its cargo was," Buckley said. "Because of the news of the rising and them telling us to pack food for a month, we all thought we would stand east toward Ireland. They told us only that we would set sail and receive our orders at sea."

"Then what happened?"

"We began steaming back toward New York when we were met on the way by a two-masted vessel. We steamed close to her and jumped aboard. She was called

Jacnel. She was a brigantine, and the men among us who knew about ships said she was not very well rigged. Her crew consisted of just four sailors, two officers, a cook and meself, beside the captain. She had no papers."

"And this brigantine faced directly for Ireland?"

"No, not at first. I learned from the first mate that we were on a tack usually pursued by West Indiamen, in order to avoid capture. I don't recollect seeing any colors. During the voyage she hoisted the English colors, especially when hailing vessels or being hailed herself. The West India tack was changed after the fourteenth, and, on the fifteenth, we pursued the ordinary European tack, but a little more south."

"And who, if you know, was in command of this treasonous expedition?"

"A man named James Kerrigan. He had been a colonel in the Federal army."

Trimble had done his homework, too.

"Is this James Kerrigan not the same man who was also a congressman of the United States of America?" he asked.

"Aye. I knew him from the papers but I did not know he was connected with the expedition until I was on board."

"An American congressman, a member of the federal parliament of the United States of America, was himself in charge of this seditious expedition. Is that correct?"

"He was."

"And what was your rank in this army of Fenian rabble?"

"None. I was taken aboard only as a cook's helper. Some of the others obtained commissions in New York from Colonel Kelly, others on board the brigantine from General Kerrigan."

Trimble interrupted. "A general is he now?" His tone and accompanying sneer sent more snickers through the gallery.

"Aye, a general," Buckley said. "The commissions I saw were on paper, in print, signed both by Colonel Kelley and Captain Hogan."

Buckley thought hard, trying to remember all the names on the list that Corydon had provided him the night before. He knew their names and faces from the crossing, but not their ranks.

"There was Colonel Kenneally, Colonel Warren, Colonel Taylor, Colonel Prendergast, Colonel Cedlian, Colonel Jerein, Colonel Doherty, Captain Costelloe, Captain Greene, Captain FitzSimmons, Captain Kane, and Captain Leonard. The rest were lieutenants - FitzGibbon, Roche, Liam Nugent, Lawless, Doyle, Lee, Thomas, Fernen, Patrick Nugent and James Goffey."

Warren, Taylor and Prendegast had already been tried last month in Dublin. Taylor was acquitted on an alien rights technicality and deported back to the U.S. Warren and Prendergast were locked up in Kilmainham prison. It was before Anderson had broken Buckley at Richmond, so Corydon had played the role of fingering the conspirators.

"And do you today in this courtroom see present any of those who you have named?" Trimble asked Buckley.

"I do."

"And who might they be?"

Buckley pointed to each, naming them, one by one. "Colonel Kenneally, Captain FitzSimmons, Andrew Leonard, Patrick Kane, Augustine Costelloe, Frederick FitzGibbon, Patrick Nugent and Daniel Lee."

"And these eight men, like yourself, were all conspirators in this gunrunning expedition?"

"They were."

Kenneally glanced at FitzSimmons. They shared a knowing look. Buckley was a dead man. Maybe later, maybe sooner, but a dead man either way.

"So at this point you are on the packet *Jacnel* and you have abandoned the West India tack and are steering northeast toward Ireland, is that right?"

"Aye."

"And what happened next?"

''There was a furious gale on probably the seventeenth. Few of these men were sailors. Most had never sailed before. We were lucky to get her through without losing a man overboard or even the ship itself. The seas finally calmed in a day or two. By then most aboard were exhausted or sick. Then nothing happened, not until Easter Sunday, the twenty-first, when before noon we were all summoned on deck by General

Kerrigan."

"For what purpose?"

"We used a capstan to haul up from below three small artillery pieces, which we braced on the quarterdeck. We didn't know why at first. Then we were ordered to stand at salute. A green flag, the Fenian colors with a harp and a sunburst, was hoisted above the main t'gallant. Rifles were fired in salute. The ship's captain, a man named Kavanagh, announced that he was re-naming the ship. He said *Jacnel* wasn't a proper name for a Fenian boat. He said he was rechristening her Dochas na hEireann."

"Meaning what?" Trimble asked. Gaelic was a language beneath him.

"It's Irish. It means 'Erin's Hope.' After that the salute was fired. This Kavanagh then presented the orders he had been given in New York. They were signed by Colonel Kelley."

"And what were those orders?"

"To land the arms in Ireland, if possible at Sligo, or if not here then wherever else might prove convenient."

"Aside from the rifles used to salute the Fenian flag, what other arms had you aboard?"

"We had arms of different kinds. The men spent much of the voyage, when not on watch or sick in their bunks, unpacking and repacking them. They used oil on the barrels to keep down the rust from the salt air. In New York the guns had been packed in large crates labeled sewing machines and pianos and in hogsheads labeled wine. They were stored between decks. The officers used carpenter's tools to build smaller crates, using the wood of the larger crates. They said smaller crates would be easier to get ashore."

"And what types of munitions were in these crates?"

"There were Spencer repeating rifles, seven shooters. There were Enfield and Austrian rifles. We had some breech loading rifles. Those were the larger arms. We also had revolvers, a few small field pieces. There were about a million rounds of ammunition."

"One million rounds of ammunition?" Trimble asked in mock surprise. He could see the Sligo Champion's front-page headline already.

"A million rounds for how many weapons?" Trimble asked.

"I should say there were some five thousand stand of arms on board, as well as some swords and pike heads. I was told there were one thousand swords, as well as some bayonets. We drilled some with pikes on deck to learn how to fend off boarders."

"And there were field pieces as well?"

"Only three small cannon. They fired only three-pound shot. There was shot and powder for the cannons as well, though not much."

"After the sailing orders were read, what happened next?"

"There was nary a wisp of wind that day, so after the ceremony the order was given to heave to and splice the main brace."

"Meaning what?" Trimble asked, a bit irritated at being thrown by this ignorant paddy some nautical phrase he didn't understand.

"We slowed the ship and broke out a hogshead of whiskey and had ourselves a ceili, or as much of one as one fiddler and one old penny whistle would allow."

"A sea lee?" Trimble asked. More Gaelic, no doubt. "What, please tell us, is a sea lee?"

"Not a sea lee, a ceili. Music. Dancing. 'Twas a christening, after all, so they made a grand time of it. The cook and I boiled ham and potatoes for an Easter feast, and they used the potato sacks for races on deck. They learned right quick it's no small feat running in a sack race on the deck of a ship."

Trimble was quickly losing his patience. Buckley was drifting away from his task. He was there to demonize the conspirators, not to humanize them.

"So, in other words, Mr. Buckley, the conspirators on board this Fenian vessel of war got roaring drunk. Is that what happened?"

"Yes, my lord, that they did. All except the captain and his own crew. Captain Kavanagh didn't abide spirits while under sail, but exceptions were made for the rest, under the circumstances, given that we were nearly becalmed."

Trimble had heard enough for now. Buckley was beginning to romanticize sedition as adventure. It was not what Trimble had in mind.

"Justice Keogh, Justice FitzGerald, I have no further questions of this prisoner at this time," he said. "But I do plan to recall this witness at a later point in this trial."

"Very well," Keogh said. "Mr. Heron, as counsel to these defendants, do you wish to ask Mr. Buckley any questions at this time?"

"I do, indeed, my Lord," Richard Heron said.

Heron had waited for weeks to get his shot at Buckley, or this man who pretended to be Daniel Joseph Buckley.

After last month's trial in Dublin of Warren and the others, Heron had been hand-picked by the American Counsel in Dublin to defend those to be tried at the autumn assize in Sligo. Heron had received the imprimatur of C.F. Adams, the American Foreign Secretary in London. In lesser cases, or at least those of less interest to the newspapers, Heron had proven himself a bright and capable barrister, with skills that belied his youth. A Presbyterian trained at Queen's College in Cork, he had promised to tie this court in knots with points of international law that he knew were as clear as mud.

"Please proceed."

"Daniel Joseph Buckley, is it now?" Heron asked, affecting an air of scorning bewilderment.

"That I am," Buckley said.

"That you are not, sir. What you are, I fear, cannot be spoken in open court, in front of the women in the gallery. Who you are is James Patrick O'Boyle, a fraud, a war criminal, born not in Munster but in Massachusetts."

241

"That's a lie," Buckley said. "All of it."

"Is it now, O'Boyle?" Heron said, taunting him. "And is it a lie that you are wanted still in America for desertion under fire and for conduct unbecoming a soldier during the War of the Rebellion? What was it again? Stealing gold teeth from the charred remains of your own comrades of the New York 69th, the wounded left in the woods in the heat of battle and consumed by fire in the conflagration at Chancellorsville?"

Heron knew all about O'Boyle, including the fact he'd be hung if deported. The court would know, too, if Heron had his way.

Chapter Twenty-one

August 6, 1867
The Summer Assize, Sligo

Sean Kenneally never expected to see the old fisherman again. This old man they all called "Big Pat" had been jailed with Sean and the others after the hearing in Dungarvan and was taken with them in chains to Ballybricken Gaol in Waterford, where they were kept for weeks. Big Pat had been freed, set loose with others determined by Dublin Castle not worth putting on trial. That had been months ago, many miles away.

Sean watched as the old man stumbled into the courtroom, one staggered step ahead of a bailiff nudging him forward. He stared at the floor as he made his way toward the table reserved for Crown witnesses. He looked to Sean even more ancient than he was, shoulders hunched, hair unwashed and in tangles, a stubble of beard hiding hollow cheeks the color of tallow. His arms were chained together at his wrists.

He finally looked over at Sean and the others, his eyes empty and lifeless.

Why was he here? Sean wondered. Why had they

brought him to Sligo? He had refused to cooperate early on in this madness. Why would he choose to now?

Lord Rupert Trimble, the Crown's special prosecutor, tugged on the old man's tattered sleeve. "This way if you please," Trimble said, towing Big Pat to the witness seat before placing himself in front of the bench.

"May I proceed, your honor?" Trimble asked Chief Justice FitzGerald.

"You may," FitzGerald said.

"Tell me, sir, and this court, what is you name?"

Big Pat looked at him and mumbled quietly, as if to himself.

"Speak up, man!" Lord Trimble barked.

"Paidraig," the old man said slowly, "Paidraig O Faolain."

"And why are you here?" Trimble asked.

"Because you have brought me here," the old man said.

"And from where have we brought you?" Trimble shot back.

"From Cork," he said. "From a prison cell in Cork."

"And why are you in prison?"

"Because you have arrested me."

"On what charge?"

"Murder."

"And who was it that you murdered?" Trimble asked.

"I have harmed no one."

The old man's appearance now in Sligo as an apparently unwilling witness caught Richard Heron by surprise, too. As the Fenians' barrister, he had been told of an old fisherman who had brought the Americans ashore, apparently against his will but not, as alleged more than once, at the point of a gun. The old man's imprisonment at Waterford had been payment due for his lack of willing cooperation in Dungarvan, for pretending he understood and spoke only the Gaelic of the region where the Fenians had come ashore. Of this murder charge, Heron knew nothing.

"Not only have you harmed someone, but you have killed a man, killed a friend," Trimble said. "And for taking this life I expect you will hang, unless, of course, you have the good sense to redeem yourself in the eyes of this court by cooperating with us now. We know you are a Fenian."

"I have harmed no one," Big Pat said again. "And I have never been a Finini."

Heron was on his feet. "Your honor, this man is not on trial. Whatever charges he may face elsewhere have nothing whatever to do with the legal issues under scrutiny here today, which I might remind the court include the fact that, as American citizens, this court has no jurisdiction over these defendants, who are citizens of the United States of America, and as such not subject to the charge of treason against a nation to which none owes any allegiance."

"Enough of that, Mr. Heron," FitzGerald said. "You have already wasted too much of this court's time in raising this jurisdictional objection. As far as this court is concerned these matters of citizenship, allegiance and international law have been resolved, apparently to everyone's satisfaction but your own. Please take your seat, Mr. Heron. Lord Trimble, please continue and please get on with how this man's arrest on another matter has some bearing on the case at hand."

"If the court will grant me a moment to explain," Trimble said. "This is the man, your honor, who, according to oath-bound testimony in an earlier trial, brought more than two dozen American Fenian gunrunners, among them those on trial here today, ashore from their American brigantine as it lay in wait for him off Helvick Head in the fog on the first day of June. This is the man who, when asked under oath in Dungarvan to point out one or more of the men who had spent more than two hours face to face with him aboard his tiny fishing smack, could identify not even one of them. This is the man who undermined those official proceedings by pretending at the time that he understood not a single word of the Queen's English, which as you see in this courtoom today was the boldest of charades."

Heron was on his feet again.

"None of this is relevant to the matter here at hand, your honor," Heron said. "As this fisherman has not been charged as a Fenian or with felony treason, as have these other men here, all of what Lord Trimble alleges is the thinnest of speculation and all of it clearly beside the point."

"Please sit down, Mr. Heron," Judge FitzGerald said. "Proceed, Lord Trimble. "

"Did you know a man named Daniel Collins, late of the fishing village Baile na nGall, near Dungarvan?" Trimble asked the old man.

"I did," Páid Mór said.

"And how did you know him?"

"He tended nets for me, on my smack."

"And where is Daniel Collins today?" Trimble asked.

"He drowned, just a few weeks ago, the seventeenth of July," Páid Mór said. "Disappeared over the side in a storm. A terrible tragedy, it was."

"Was it now?" Trimble said, mocking the old man's answer. "And wasn't that quite the coincidence, given that only days before your boatmate Daniel Collins tumbled over the side he had returned to Dungarvan from Dublin, where he had testified in the trial of the American Fenian leader Colonel Warren, testified that the Colonel was among the Fenians you brought ashore on the first day of June."

"I know nothing of that," Páid Mór said. "Daniel Collins was lost overboard in a gale."

"These men here today, Kenneally, Costelloe, FitzSimmons, these others," Trimble said. "You have seen these men before?"

"Only in a courtroom, the courtroom in Dungarvan," the old man said. "There and exercising in the yard, at Ballybricken Gaol."

"Never aboard your own fishing boat, after climbing over the side of a black-hulled brigantine?"

"Not these men, no," Páid Mór said. "The men who put a gun to my head and ordered me to take them ashore were other men, not these."

"Enough," Trimble said, exasperated by the old man's willingness to be hanged for something he hadn't done, to protect men he didn't know and a cause he didn't understand. "Take this lying fishmonger out of my sight. He is a murdering Fenian sympathiser who will be shown a rope once we have dealt with these others."

❦   ❦   ❦

Sean had seen this man before, but couldn't remember where. Two months in English prisons had taken their toll on his senses.

"Your name please," Trimble asked.

"My name is Andrew Roche, a farmer, from Ring Parish, near the town of Dungarvan, in County Waterford."

The young man seemed very nervous, pulling on his tuft of beard. Still Sean couldn't place when he had seen him before.

"Tell this court, Mr. Roche, where were you on the morning of June the first of this year, if you recall?"

Trimble knew he would recall. He had walked him through this testimony many times.

"I was working in my garden, behind my house, near Milenahorna, a townland toward the western edge of Ring Parish," Roche said.

"And what time was that?" Trimble asked.

"Early afternoon," Roche said.

"And did anything unusual happen while you were tending to your garden?"

"Yes, my Lord," Roche said. "Two men appeared out of the woods and approached me, men I had not seen before."

"And do you remember what these men were wearing?"

"I remember not so much what they were wearing, my Lord, but what seemed odd to me then was that they were both wet up to their middles, their trousers and their shirts were wet, or had been," Roche said. "I noticed, too, that they both wore square-toed boots."

Sean remembered him now. After leaving the old woman's house in search of the Youghal road he had stumbled onto Colonel Warren, making his way east as well. Together they had followed the road, keeping to the woods.

"And did these men say anything to you?" Trimble asked.

"Yes, my Lord," Roche said. "One asked me how far

it was to Youghal, and I told them it was twelve miles. The other one asked me if there was anyone about with a wagon that could take them, and I said I had a pony and a cart and would take them for five shillings."

"And did you take them?"

"Aye, my Lord, in my cart."

"And did they speak to you while you drove them to the Youghal crossing?"

"Only a little, my Lord, though I did ask them how it happened they were on their way to Youghal."

"And what did they tell you?"

"That they were Americans, which I could tell by their queer way of speaking. They said they were off a fishing vessel that had caught fire at sea off Helvick, that they had been rescued by local fisherman and brought ashore in their smack."

The man was telling the truth, Sean knew. It was a story he himself had contrived and shared with Warren. They had practiced it aloud while heading east through the woods.

"Did you not think that odd?" Trimble asked, forgetting not to ask any question for which he hadn't already provided the witness an answer.

"No, my Lord," Roche said. "Ships are lost all the time, especially to fire."

"Tell me this," Trimble said, walking toward the table where Sean and the others sat. "These two men you say you drove to Youghal. Do you see them here in this courtroom today?"

"Only one of them, my Lord."

"And which one would that be?"

"Him, my Lord," Roche said, pointing at Sean. "The one there, on the end, the man closest to your Lordship."

❦   ❦   ❦

Sean knew this constable. He was the one who arrested him and Warren, just outside Youghal. His name was Norton, or North. Something British.

"Your name and residence, if you please?" Trimble asked him.

"Norris, my Lord, James Robert Norris of Youghal, County Cork."

"And you are in the service of Her Majesty?"

"I am, your lord, as a Constable with the Royal Irish Constabulary, stationed at the Kiley's Cross barrack."

"And were you on duty on the afternoon of June the first?"

"I was, my Lord," Norris said. "We had been alerted to keep a sharp eye, as Fenians were reported about. I was assigned with others to watch the Youghal road."

"And did you encounter any Fenians that day?"

"I did, my Lord, two of them."

"Please tell this court of this encounter."

"Well, it was half three, maybe a bit later, when I saw them on the bridge which crosses the Blackwater, about a mile east of Youghal," he said. "I noticed there were two men, both hunched low in a common cart being driven by a countryman, a man I had seen before, coming from the Waterford side of the bridge. I stopped the cart and noticed they were strangers and that their clothes were wet, their trousers and boots, they were wet and spattered with sand."

"And did you speak to these strangers?" Trimble asked.

"I did, my Lord. I asked them how far they had come. One said from Dungarvan. I asked them where they belonged, and the other said Cork City."

"And did you ask them their names?" Trimble said.

"One said he was called John Donovan, and the other said his name was William Palmer."

"Tell us, Constable, do you see these men here, in this courtroom, today?" Trimble asked.

"Only one of them, my Lord, the one who said his name was Palmer. That man there," he said, gesturing toward Sean.

"Let the record reflect that the witness has identified the Fenian officer Sean Kenneally," Trimble said. "And tell us, Constable, did this man who that day identified himself as William Palmer say anything more to you?"

"He said that he and his companion were crewmen on

252

a fishing excursion aboard an American fishing vessel and that she had been scuttled by fire and that they had recently come ashore after being rescued by fishermen who saw their plight and came to their aid from the piers along Dungarvan Bay."

"Did they say they were aboard a schooner?" Trimble asked.

"No, my Lord," Norris replied. "They said the ship that had burned at sea was a brigantine."

"And what did you do then, Constable?"

"I searched their cart and found no weapons, but told them they would have to come with me now to the police barrack and allow me to search them."

"And did you?"

"I did, my Lord. They offered no resistance."

"And when you conducted this search of their persons, what did you find?" Trimble asked.

"On the one who called himself Donovan, only a pin and a scarf and some money, American money. On the other, the one who called himself Palmer, I found some scraps of wadded paper with penciling on them and a collar marked 'Kenneally'."

"And what became of these wadded scraps of paper?" Trimble asked.

"I turned them over to the Crown's Fenian investigator."

Trimble gathered up some papers from his table and handled them to the Constable. "Are the scraps of paper now spread flat and attached to these pages the same scraps you took from the man here today who identified himself to you then as John Donovan?"

Norris gave them a glance. "They are, my Lord."

"And will you tell the court what is written on them?"

"There is a list of names, two lists actually," the witness said. "One is headed with the word 'officers', the other is headed 'privates' and each has men's names and notes behind each name."

"What type of notes behind each name?" Trimble asked.

"Let me see," the Constable said, studying the notes more closely. "After the officers' names, it says either 'infantry' or 'artillery', while after the privates' names, it has their trades, such as 'carpenter' or 'bricklayer' or 'baker'. Also, some have notes that say 'infantry' or 'cavalry'."

The Fenian's barrister, Mr. Heron, was suddenly on his feet.

"Enough of this, your honor!" he said. "There is no proof that these notes are authentic, or that they were ever in possession of any of the men on trial here today. This should not be allowed!"

"I will allow it," Chief Justice FitzGerald said. "Sit down, Mr. Heron. It is my intention to see this case to its conclusion before this day is out, which will not be served by your impudent interruptions. Please take your seat. Proceed Lord Trimble."

Trimble's glare followed Heron into his seat.

"What else do these notes say, Constable Norris?" Trimble asked.

"There are notes that appear to be an inventory of a ship's provisions," he said. "It is dated May the twenty-sixth and says eleven barrels of bread, two barrels of 'but', which must mean butter, one-half pork, one flour, one-fourth 'bns' which might indicate beans, one-half coffee and one and one half casks of water."

"Anything else on those scraps?" Trimble asked.

"Aye, my lord, notes of a ship."

"And would you read to this court the words written?"

"It says the words 'Brigantine, register one hundred fifteen tons, burden two hundred tons, length eighty-one feet, beam twenty feet, hold nine feet' and then it has a list of types of sails: 'one mainmast, one staysail, one middle, one gaff topsail, one top staysail, one foresail'."

"I see," Trimble said. "And tell us again, if you will, Constable, you took these scraps of paper containing these penciled notes from whom?"

"From the man who called himself William Palmer," Norris said. "From that man, there!" Trimble said, pointing straight at Sean.

"Yes, my Lord, from that man there."

Chapter Twenty-two

August 7, 1867
The Summer Assize, Sligo City

Word that the juror panel reached verdicts of
guilty came as no surprise to Sean Kenneally, nor to
anyone else, it seemed. Though a guilty verdict would
likely cost Sean his life, it came as something of a relief.
He and the others might hang, but at least, by nightfall,
this sham of a trial would have come to an end.

The last day began with Chief Judge FitzGerald
belaboring points of law intended to rationalize what was
about to be done to Sean and to the others. In reading the
verdicts, FitzGerald announced the prisoner Daniel
Buckley had been absolved of all guilt in the matter and
had been released earlier that morning.

"Mr. Heron, before I proceed with sentencing, let me
reiterate again for the record that it has been held from an
early period that an alien whose country is at peace with
our own may be indicted and convicted of high treason,"
FitzGerald said.

Heron sprang to his feet, eager to again argue the
point on the Fenians' behalf. FitzGerald was having none

of it.

"Sit, Mr. Heron," he said. "I will not allow you to speak. I have heard all I am willing to hear from you on this subject. You have defended your case and these clients valiantly, but whatever the beliefs of the American government in this regard, they cannot have the slightest influence on my judgment. Your only task this morning, Mr. Heron, is to sit quietly and listen and perhaps to console your poor desperate and misguided clients."

FitzGerald looked directly at Sean and the others.

"It is impossible for anyone listening to this trial to not feel regret," FitzGerald said, "and not for the punishment that I am about to inflict upon you. What it is I lament is to see the amount of intelligence which you have certainly exhibited so misapplied in your futile efforts to raise, make and levy war, insurrection and rebellion against our said Lady the Queen within this realm."

"Feck the bloody Queen!" Augustine Costelloe said from the prisoners' bench in a voice loud enough to send gasps through the gallery.

"Silence!" FitzGerald roared. "Another insolent remark from you, Mr. Costelloe, will force me to have you gagged or removed from this courtroom entirely."

FitzGerald continued. "It is clear from all we have heard in this trial and from the guilty verdicts I have now received from the juror panel that your sworn intention was to subvert and destroy the constitution and government of this realm, that your intentions were to invade Ireland, that you are all members of the Fenian Brotherhood, and as Fenians did attempt to bring thousands of guns, muskets, pistols, swords, pike heads, pike handles, gun powder and leaden bullets to these shores in accommodation of rebellion. Luckily, Providence intervened and these treasonous actions were precluded. It is my duty here today to deal out stern punishment for your foolish and seditious actions."

Sean barely listened. He was distracted by the understanding that he must be given a chance to speak, before he was sentenced. He would be allowed, as they had allowed Robert Emmett, before being hung and quartered, to make his dock speech. Emmett's had been a long and eloquent speech, but not so long that one man Sean knew in the Irish Brigade hadn't memorized every word and, if you asked him, would recite it to the very last phrase: 'When my country takes her place among the nations of the earth, then, and not 'till then, let my epitaph be written."

Like Emmet, Sean would be put to death, but, like Emmett, Sean would have his say.

"It is my imperative duty to not falter in the administration of the law," FitzGerald said. "However, before I proceed with sentencing, I must ask each of you if you have some final remarks to make to this court, some opinion you wish to share as to why you should not be sentenced to a punishment most severe. "

"I do indeed," Sean said, rising to his feet. He suddenly felt energized, better than he had felt in months, even though these past months had been the worst of his life.

"I must warn you, Sean Kenneally," FitzGerald said. "I have a great difficulty in preventing you from making any observations that may occur to you to be of service, but I shall not allow you, nor the other prisoners here who may wish to speak some final words on their own behalf, to cast imputations or obloquy upon the law officers of the Crown. Such treasonous pleadings this court will not permit."

Sean stepped forward and took his place in the dock. The courtroom was thick with the curious, a sea of stern faces staring at him without expression, as if studying some rare beast on display in a cage.

"I must say to all of you here within the reach of my voice that I have been a great many places, but never so flanked as in this instance," Sean began. "I am an American citizen, and I owe my allegiance to the government of the United States. I protest the jurisdiction of this court and have perfect confidence in my own government that they will see justice done. I will stand or fall not by what passes as law and justice among you English and you Irish here, Irish who are too willing to become as English as the English themselves, but by the constitution of the government of the United States, which will not, I would hope, permit England to abuse loyal American citizens in the manner in which is being done here today. And if America will not resent England's conduct toward one of her own and protect his allegiance to her government, the only allegiance he has ever acknowledged, he would call on thirteen millions of Irishmen to take up arms ....."

FitzGerald interrupted. "I will not allow this," he said. "I will not allow you to use the position in which you stand here as an arena for such seditious observations. "

"What shall I refer to then?" Sean asked, confused.

"My business is not to tell you what to refer to,"

FitzGerald said. "My business is to tell you what you cannot refer to. Proceed with care, Mr. Kenneally, or remove yourself."

"With respect to what has been presented here as proof against myself and the others, I submit that there is not a shadow of evidence to prove that there was any intention of a hostile landing," Sean said. "These thousands of weapons to which your Lordship makes reference are but figments of a perjurer's imagination. If we are to be sent to our deaths for putting guns into the hands of beleaguered Irish peasants, then where is even one of these guns? Why have they not been produced here as proof of our intent?"

It was a question Sean longed to have answered. What had become of *Erin's Hope*? Of her guns? Of those he had last seen months ago, peering over the caprail at him and the others before evaporating into the fog?

"There is not a particle of evidence to show that the brigantine your coastguards claim appeared in Sligo harbor was the same black-hulled vessel that we are told appeared in the fog near Dungarvan. You have only the perjured statement of a war criminal who now calls himself Buckley, who is a liar and worse. This so-called evidence as to the identity of this vessel would not stand for a moment where either law or justice would be regarded.

"And as to the old fisherman," Sean said. "I ask any man of intelligence in this court, if there are any here to be found, to look at me and see if I am scoundrel or idiot enough to place a pistol to a boatman's head and compel him to take myself and others ashore and then afterwards set him free? I ask you: Am I such a scoundrel, such an idiot? I tell you as I am on the road to my grave, I never set eyes upon that man until I first saw him in a courtroom in Dungarvan.

"And as to this Constable who has laid fresh stress on the fact that I have traveled under different names and that therefore I am guilty of some great crime," Sean paused, selecting his words carefully, "I have precedent. I have read in the papers that some Continental monarchs travel under an assumed name. And I hear the Prince of Wales does so as well whenever he thinks it proper to visit the London brothels."

"Enough of this!" FitzGerald stormed. "I cannot allow this!"

"I understand," Sean said, well aware he was testing the patience of a man with none to test. "I would feel much obliged if your lordship would permit me to utter but a few more words as to my motives through this affair."

It sounded to FitzGerald like an admission of guilt. "Proceed," he said, reluctantly.

"I left Ireland not because I disliked this country," Sean said. "I loved Ireland as I love myself, and I love her still. I left Ireland as a boy for the very good and cogent reason that I could not live here. And why? This government has ruled this people by starvation, in poverty. I went as a boy to America and there became an American citizen. I was a soldier in America, a member of the national militia. Now, in case war broke out between the two countries, and the army of England took me prisoner, they would have you believe it would be proper not to treat me as an ordinary prisoner of war, because for the quirk of fate that I drew my first breath in Ireland. They would instead hold me guilty of high treason and would string me up from the nearest oak. Is this not the position of England toward the United States in this instance? Is England in such a hurry to fill the hanging trees of Ireland with American citizens that it would risk war with a great nation whose President's own grandfather was an Irishman?"

"I cannot allow you to proceed with any reference to what has been done by any government," FitzGerald said. "We have nothing here to do with the conduct of government. We are only here to administer the law we have sworn to administer. I will hear your final words, Mr. Kenneally."

"I stand in this dock proudly and defiantly, as an American citizen of Irish birth confident, your lordship, that the position which I have taken in this regard will be sustained," Sean said. "I know that the imperfect verdict of this jury panel will be reversed, if not by your law by a higher law. And while returning your thanks, my lord, for your many kindnesses throughout this trial, I fear you are taking from me this privilege to speak openly to which I am entitled. I stand before you, convicted of treason while owing no allegiance to this country I have been convicted of betraying. Were I a free man tomorrow, I would sooner swear allegiance to the King of Abyssinia than spend half an hour's allegiance to the government of this country, a country that has blasted the hopes of half the world and disgusted it all."

"It is impossible for me to allow you to proceed with this line of observation," FitzGerald said.

"Let me just say this, your lord," Sean said. "I look to another place, another government and another people to see that justice shall be done to me. This outrage offered to me and others who claim, as I do, to be citizens of the United States, will be gladly submitted to if they only have the effect of making the sword of justice spring from its scabbard."

"I cannot," FitzGerald said, "suffer you to make this a place of appeal to persons in this country or in America."

"I am not making an appeal to any man," Sean said. "Although I have been found guilty by a jury of this court, I deem my conduct above reproach. I know I have been convicted, and I will still assert that the first gun fired in anger between this country and America will be a kind of comfort to my ears for I shall be hearing the death knell of this infamous government. And though I myself may not, I am sure the cause of freedom will live longer than the bloody British constitution."

"That is all I shall put up with," FitzGerald said. "Return to your place, Mr. Kenneally. Are there others who would speak?"

As he stepped down from the dock, Sean was surprised to see that none of the others, not even Costelloe, would take their turn in the dock. There was so much more to be said, Sean thought, so much more these solicitors of perjury needed to be told.

"Very well," FitzGerald said. "In conformity with sentences pronounced in this court for similar offenses, the sentence I am now about to award you will withdraw you all for a long period of time from all you may hold dear in this world. It will be the means of immuring you in a living tomb."

Sean realized at that moment he would not hang, though he was not certain being returned in chains to a vile hellhole like Kilmainham was preferable to the eternal rest awaiting beyond a hangman's rope.

'We feel we cannot pronounce on each of you a sentence less severe than that you will be kept in penile servitude within this realm for a period of fifteen years."

Lord Trimble had spent months contriving this case, as had Sir Robert Anderson, the British Secret Service's special advisor on Fenianism. Both men argued long and hard for death sentences. Dublin Castle, too, was convinced of the necessity of making an example of these men to any others in the festering Irish ghettos of New York and Boston who might harbor romantic notions of an Irish insurrection. It was said even the Queen herself wanted at least one of these men hung. But diplomacy had prevailed over even Royal contempt. Lord Derby, the British Prime Minister, had convinced the Queen that what England needed least was to provide the Americans' Irish president with any excuse to call for war with England. What Ireland needed least, Derby knew, were fresh martyrs to the Fenian cause.

Costelloe jumped to his feet, more agitated than relieved that his life had been spared. "It may be fifteen years more, my Lord, if you like!" he shouted. "I will take fifteen more for Ireland any day, I will."

"I cannot allow this," FitzGerald said, pointing to a bailiff. "Take this man off."

It required not one, but three, burly bailiffs to drag Costelloe from the courtroom, kicking, flailing, bellowing.

"I would not given even a shilling for the lease of the

British rule in Ireland," Costelloe screamed as they carried him off. "Watch your backs, you British bastards!"

Chapter Twenty-three

October 31, 1867
Quincy, Massachusetts

The message reached Colonel Clark as he was about to speak to a roomful of Fenians gathered from throughout New Jersey. "B. spotted in Boston," the note read. "Come to C. St. at once."

The dock watches had paid off, at last.

He read the note and folded it into his vest pocket as he walked from the head table to the dais draped in green and gold.

"Gentlemen," Colonel Clark said in a bellowing voice. "It is with great pleasure that I find myself among you here this evening. In fact, after what I have endured in recent months aboard the Fenian brigantine *Erin's Hope,* it is with great pleasure that this evening finds me anywhere at all."

Word reached Chatham Street by messenger that afternoon that a man with an ugly scar from his forehead to his left ear was seen emerging from a Liverpool steamer that tied up in Boston Harbor on Wednesday last. For

266

nearly a week now this man who appeared to match a sketched likeness of the informer Buckley had been staying in a small hotel near Quincy, usually alone, sometimes with one whore, sometimes with two. He left his room only now and then to take a meal, and he appeared stupid with drink whenever he did.

He often left the hotel clutching a brown crockery jug that he took every day or two to a neighborhood public house. The barman there, a friend of the Brotherhood, said this man who called himself Kevin always bought rum and always payed with two silver dollars.

Just as Dublin Castle was eager to make examples of Colonel Warren, Captain Kenneally and the others they still held, the leadership of the Brotherhood wanted nothing more than to make an example of Buckley, or O'Boyle, or whatever he was calling himself now. O'Mahony himself ordered the man killed, and Colonel Clark volunteered his assistance.

The Colonel and the others involved in the expedition had been in great demand since *Erin's Hope* limped into Long Island Sound on the first day of August, all of them half-starved, unwashed and in rags. The brigantine had lost much of its foremast to lightning in a relentless storm off Labrador, but what fire the strike sparked was quickly doused by the driving rain. The worst of it was the Druid, who had vanished during the storm. Benny last saw him high in the foremast rigging, trying to salvage the tattered remains of the fore topgallant. There was not a sign of him when the storm lifted. In waters so cold, the Druid could not have lasted long.

The Brotherhood put a best face on the whole sorry affair, spreading word among the centers that the expedition had been a brilliant success. The weapons hadn't been landed, true enough, but neither had they been seized, and not from lack of trying on the part of the damnable British. Some of the men were arrested and jailed, but *Erin's Hope* proved to the doubters that a Fenian vessel could make such a crossing laden with guns and that a Fenian vessel could cruise the Irish coastline at will, having its way with the Royal Navy.

It was a grand tale, more grandly embellished with each public recitation by Colonel Clark and General Kerrigan, who both agreed to present lectures designed to pry open the pocketbooks of chambermaids and millionaires being courted by the Fenian Brotherhood to provide the means for a proper ship. What was clearly needed, they would tell those who attended, was a steamer, a proper ship properly outfitted to handle the task of taking men and guns to Ireland more effectively than a square-rigger ever could. It must, they said, carry deck guns heavy enough to defend both crew and cargo from onrushing British rams.

Captain Kavanagh refused to be a part of it, staying in New York only long enough to collect the gold owed him. He missed the Druid terribly and wanted nothing more to do with the Brotherhood or with those who pleaded that he tell his tale to an Irish newspaper or agree to make a speech at the Brotherhood's next national convention. He wasn't a hero, Kavanagh told them, he was a fool, but not fool enough to listen to another mention of "the cause," as they called it. Kavanagh was through with causes. He knew he was lucky to have survived the experience, damned lucky to have taken this ship some nine thousand miles through waters he planned never to set eyes upon again.

By the time Kavanagh reached Chatham Street to

collect his gold, so had word of Colonel Warren's conviction in Dublin on a charge of Treason Felony. Fifteen years of penile servitude seemed to most preferable to death, though some close to the leadership would have preferred a hanging for its ability to generate both sympathy and funds. Word came, too, that Sean Kenneally and the others convicted in Sligo had received the same. Many of the those released at Waterford were by now back in New York, though some who agreed to return failed to appear at the Queenstown docks as ordered, disappearing into the hills beyond Cork, where the Irish Republican Brotherhood remained strong.

Kavanagh returned to Baltimore and slept for what had seemed a week. The last thousand miles of the crossing had left him a shell of himself, both in body and in spirit.

The assembled faithful cheered Colonel Clark wildly, raising their glasses in a toast to their noble cause. The Colonel went on for more than an hour, describing in minute detail the Easter Sunday christening, how *Erin's Hope* had evaded the coast patrols, how his floating torpedoes had disabled Her Majesty's most massive iron warship, how when the food ran out he fabricated underwater bombs to stun the cod that sustained a hungry and desperate crew as *Erin's Hope* emerged from the ice into the Grand Banks.

"At the close of the Great War of the Rebellion," he told them, "there were some two hundred thousand disbanded Irish soldiers, many like those of you in this room tonight veterans of the Irish Brigades, fighting men still eager for the fray, most eager to be tightening their grip around the throat of England. As Frederick the Great once said: 'L'Irlandais se battle pour le plaisir de se battle', which means the Irish fight for the pleasure of fighting."

The room erupted in liquored cheers from a crowd that included men dressed in the manner of Fenian officers, their dark green coats decorated with epaulets embroidered with sunbursts and shamrocks, their black trousers set off by green silk sashes.

"It was the proud and not undeserved boast of the Young Irelanders who gave birth to the spirit of Fenianism and the reality of the Irish Republican Brotherhood that they brought a soul back into Eire. But before Fenianism that soul had fled Ireland's shore, as had so many of her loyal sons and daughters. Aboard *Erin's Hope*, American Fenians brought it back again, brought it to the very shores of Ireland, teaching men again to sacrifice themselves for Ireland instead of selling themselves, and Ireland, to the English. Some now say our grand expedition failed, that as our ship fled the shores of Ireland, with it fled our spirit from the land, leaving us as far as ever from freedom that we deserve. It is not so.

"The love of home is deeply implanted in the heart of every Irishman," the Colonel continued. "Wherever he wanders, whatever sky looks down on him, his soul turns with intense longing to his own beloved island of sorrow. Hence it is that he ever cherishes the hope of seeing his native cot again and ever dwells with anguish upon the dark and cruel fate of his country. Give him but half a chance, and he will risk his all, as did those of us aboard *Erin's Hope*, to free the aulde sod from the foul grip of the hated oppressor."

Colonel Clark checked his pocketwatch. It has nearing half-ten. He needed to get himself across the river and back to Chatham Street to make arrangements for what he would need to bring with him to Boston. He must pick these pockets and be on his way.

"Such men have been tempted into futile efforts at rebellion, without any of the means, except their own near-naked bodies, to ensure success, each new failure making their condition worse, were that possible, dulling the edge of hope, generating distrust in the cause and in each other. I shall ask you now: What shall be done? Must Irishmen like ourselves abandon a cause so sacred, a cause so interwoven in our very hearts and souls? I answer no."

"And so shall we," came a voice from the crowd, followed by cheers.

"Let us then join together in unified and generous support of the Fenian Brotherhood, which if properly supported and silently, vigorously and wisely conducted will, in due time, accomplish the desired result. But with a view to this end, the magnitude of the task must be fully appreciated and it may be necessary to work keenly and incessantly for years."

O'Mahony had told Colonel Clark and General Kerrigan to make no specific promises at such events. "Appeal to their guilt, to their memories of those they have left behind in Ireland," he had said. "We want not so much to open their hearts, as their wallets." The Canadian invasions had shown him that a physical force movement that ends without a fight has a more demoralizing influence than a fight that fails.

"*Erin's Hope* has given us a taste of what is possible," the Colonel said. "As it's been said, men and money are the sinews of war, and so they are. In the case of Ireland's freedom, men can be had in any number, but without money nothing whatever can be done in these modern times. It is therefore very evident that the creation of a large fund should be the Brotherhood's first concern. It is also evident that such a fund must be raised by individual subscriptions. And it is to you the Brotherhood now turns in this time of desperate need."

As Colonel Clark left the hall, men were lining up to put their signatures to subscriptions. They clapped him on the back, welcoming him home, thanking him for his remarks. He mumbled his thanks, though his thoughts were far from this banquet hall in Hoboken. Had the chemicals smuggled from the West Point Armory arrived in New York City? Had the men he had hand-picked to bring them followed his careful instructions? If not, there may hardly be enough of them for a proper Christian burial.

❦ ❦ ❦

Jimmy O'Boyle knew he shouldn't stay long around Boston. Too many Paddies about and too many of those loyal to the Fenians.

Dublin Castle suggested he not return to America at all, and if he did that he put in at Quebec or perhaps even Galveston, any port but those along the New England coast. Before he sailed from Dublin to Liverpool, Corydon brought him a change of clothes and a red velvet pouch containing fifty English pounds and three hundred American dollars. He also gave him papers that made Jimmy out to be one Kevin O'Meara, shipwright, last employed at the Belfast docks. Ten pounds, Corydon said, would find him a gun in the backstreets of Liverpool, a small gun he should hide in his boot or his belt, for protection.

As Kevin O'Meara he had come straight away to Boston. It was a place that Jimmy knew well, as well as it knew him. He would have himself a few drinks and a few women to recover from the crossing. He swore to himself to never again set foot on a ship.

The rum in Boston was plentiful and cheap. So were the women, Jimmy soon discovered, though not even two of them could please him quite like that chesty young redhead Corydon had sent to him in Sligo. The very thought of her had made the long crossing less of an ordeal.

He would go west to Cincinnati, then by paddleboat down the Ohio River to St. Louis, where he would head west again. Surely there could be no Fenians in Kansas. He would stay in Boston only a day or two, or so he had told himself a week ago on the day he arrived.

❦ ❦ ❦

The trunk was filled with thick glass bottles packed in cotton. It had cost the Brotherhood four hundred dollars to smuggle it out of the West Point Armory, but Colonel Clark had assured O'Mahony what it contained was worth its weight in gold. There was no sense trying to explain glycerol trinitrate to the military men who oversaw the Brotherhood's affairs. They would see soon enough what this substance could do.

On the overland trip to Boston, the Colonel devised a plan certain to accomplish the mission at hand. When the train arrived the two men who accompanied him would

carefully load the trunk into a carriage. One was to take it
to the hotel near the Charles River, where Clark said he
would join him later. "Never, not for even a moment, lose
sight of this trunk," the Colonel told the man. "And mind
you, what's in it is breakable, so see that it's handled as if
it were your own grandmother's place settings."

The other man he directed to take him to the same
public house where Buckley had been spotted buying rum.
Yes, the barman said, he had crockery jugs exactly like
those in which this man kept his rum. The Colonel bought
two, paying extra to have one half-filled with rum, extra
still to ensure the barman understood the entire transaction
never occurred.

Back at his own hotel, the Colonel ate a bowl of soup
and made quick work of two drams of fine Scotch
whiskey before getting down to the task at hand. He had
read in scientific journals at the New York Public Library
of the methods required to mix the oily, colorless liquid
and to combine it with a highly absorbant material. Back
at West Point they called it guncotton. Clark had hoped
some of it could be smuggled out with the chemicals, but
it would be easy enough for a careful chemist like himself
to fabricate his own.

Three men had been keeping an eye on Buckley in
shifts, noting his movements in and out of the hotel on
Dorchester Street. Over most of the past week he left each
night about eight, returning by half-nine, sometimes alone,
sometimes with a woman, though never the same one.
They followed him from some distance to a sleeping room
on the second floor, a room off a rear stairwell, a room
with windows overlooking the bay.

It would be simple enough, one man told Colonel

Clark, to sneak inside and wait with a gun for his return. "Too simple," the Colonel told the man with a smile. "This is a problem with young people today; you seem to lack any sense of the dramatic."

It was half six when Colonel Clark told the man to bring round a hack just before eight and then come up to his room to fetch him. They would ride together to Quincy and join the other lookouts.

Once the man had gone, the Colonel carefully unpacked the trunk, lining up the bottles of liquids before him. Into the chamberpot hidden beneath the bed he poured two different liquids, blending them with a wooden spindle he ripped from a chairback. Into the mix he dumped two great handfuls of cotton, swirling it about with the spindle until all of the liquid was absorbed.

He removed the cork stopper from one of the crocks he had bought from the barman, the one still empty. Using the spindle, he forced the damp cotton inside through the neck of the crockery bottle. From the other crock he added some rum, giving it some weight and the feel of the crock it would replace. He knew the nitric and sulfuric acids now embedded together into the cotton fibers would not break down in either water or alcohol.

With any sort of spark, this makeshift guncotton would prove deadly enough by itself, but the Colonel felt strongly the need to make a point. He mixed up what was left of the nitric acid with the glycerol compound smuggled from the armory, carefully pouring all but a few drops into the crock already swollen with cotton reeking of chemicals and rum.

What was needed now was a detonator. With a penknife he went to work on the crock's cork stopper. Into the cork he carved a series of deep grooved rings, one just above the other, top to bottom. He also cut a deeper, vertical groove that ran from just above the base of the cork to its porcelain pull.

Using his thumb he carefully pressed what little remained of the nitrated glycerol mix into the rings carved into of the cork. Once sparked, it would ignite the rest. The spark would come from a mix of ammonia and iodine. The mixture was harmless enough when wet, but as it dried it created a deep red powder of highly explosive salts sensitive to even the slightest friction.

The Colonel slid the cork into the neck of the crock, inserting it nearly all the way. Using a syringe he brought with him from New York, he filled the long vertical groove carved into the cork with the liquid mixture of ammonia and iodine, then pushed the cork tightly into the crock, setting it solid with a slow and deliberate twist.

❧ ❧ ❧

Jimmy packed the last of his things. He never planned to stay beyond a day or two and it had now been more than a week. He would have a bite, get some sleep and leave for Cincinnati at first light.

From the shadows across the street, Colonel Clark saw this man he recognized as Buckley leave the hotel and head down Dorchester Street. He wasn't carrying a crock. It was past nine. The salts hadn't had much time to dry, but perhaps Buckley wouldn't return right away.

One of the two others standing watch knew the room that was Buckley's and offered to make the switch. "Whatever you do, man, don't drop this crock," the

Colonel told him. "Leave it precisely where you find the other crock, which you must take with you as you leave the room."

Within ten minutes the man was back. Buckley's room had not even been locked. He had hurled the other crock over the sea wall beyond the back door.

By half-ten, Buckley still hadn't returned. The others were nervous, but the Colonel Clark relieved. The amonium triodine salts needed time to dry.

Jimmy had enough drink for one night, even for him, but there was no point leaving this rum behind. He wasn't about to be hauling this heavy crock to Ohio.

The stopper on the crock was tight, so tight Jimmy put it his mouth and bit down on the stopper, throwing back his head to yank it loose with his teeth.

A harbor pilot rounding Thompson Island a mile offshore saw the fireball erupt on the distant Quincy shoreline a moment before hearing the blast. The back wall of the hotel disappeared in a hot wind of flaming splinters.

This excuse for a man so quick to betrayal was one of four to die in the blast. More than thirty others were forced into the street as fire consumed the entire block.

Powerful rum indeed.

Epilogue

November 29, 1867
Kilmainham Gaol, Dublin

We Irish never think in shades of gray. Life to us seems all black or all white, never darkness softened by light nor brightness tempered by shadows.

Those without souls have found a way to live among the English, with never a worry about this day or the next. These live in the grays, condemned to sleep with dogs and to rise with fleas. What proverbs are there for the likes of me, Sean Kenneally, condemned by dogs to sleep with fleas?

Word came at last of *Erin's Hope*, sea-worn but safe in New York, the Druid lost at sea, her cargo of weapons never landed. Some nights behind closed eyes I see her listing, in the fog off Helvick Head, black-hulled and copper-clad, those few left aboard waving from the shrouds to us who were more hungry than afraid as we set off to take our chances on shore.

I dwell as well on those hours of freedom, those few hours on the run through the green hillsides rising above Dungarvan Bay. Ever since it has been nothing but chains and cells, warders and misery. Dungarvan Gaol, Waterford Goal, Mountjoy Prison, Kilmainham Gaol, Sligo Gaol and then back again to Kilmainham. There's no white to be found in Her Magesty's gaols.

They just hanged the martyrs, Allen, Larkin and O'Brien. Innocents all they were, men who saved many a Fenian neck by offering up their own. All Ireland prays for their souls, these Manchester Martyrs, as do I. It passes the time.

They tell us again and again that we have failed, but it's only another lie. In spite of ambition, in spite of selfishness, in spite of the follies of our leaders, there is one grand element of Fenianism that endures. There is the intense devotion, the ever-ready pluck and the noble heroism of those drawn to the task. Therein lies the power of the Brotherhood, not in its numbers, but in those within the ranks who fear not, who shrink not from sacfice, who dare anything and dare everything for the cause.

England may hang us by the threes if she likes and fill her cells with us, but she will not extinguish the spirit that motivates and animates us. Nor will she deter others from filling our places, whether in the dock or on the gallows.

Do these November rains never cease? It is soft all day, buckets all night. How many days now? Four, five, eight? The midnight winds drive the damp off the Liffey right through these stone walls and those entombed within. The fog and mist roll through these cells as if

sliding down Benbulben's backside into the streets of
Sligo. Back there at least, when the winds were fair and
the nights clear and the cellblock long asleep, I could
listen for the sea. The sound of the pounding surf marked
those silent hours, a timepiece always wound.

In time sleep would wade ashore to douse even a
patriot's rage, once a blinding blaze reduced now, I fear,
to embers amid ashes. Dust unto smoldering dust, swept
into my own forgotten corner of Kilmainham Gaol.

Acknowledgements

Given that the process of researching and writing (and re-writing and re-writing) Erin's Hope transpired over 20 years, there are two decades of folks whom I need to thank for their support and encouragement, both in the U.S. and in Ireland.

At the top of that list is my long-suffering spouse, The Lady Beth, who has made this book and everything else possible, having once endured a month with three kids – two of them teenagers – while I abandoned her to help sail a tall ship from Boston to Ireland.

The financial generosity of Joy Smith and David Rust made much of my extensive research in Ireland possible, and John Horgan's insights and advice have proven invaluable throughout the project.

Special thanks, too, to Tom and Bonny Curran and countless others who call Ring Parish in County Waterford home for sharing with me over many stays the rich history of the Gaeltacht where most of those aboard *Erin's Hope* waded ashore in 1867.

On the production side of this project, many thanks to my publisher, Patrick Walsh, and to my editor, his child bride Carol Ann Riordan. Thanks, too, to Catherine Walker McKinney, Maria Dunne, Dick Blazek and others like Jeanne Anderson who reviewed early drafts and weighed in with many useful suggestions.

I'm also indebted to the late Tim Clark, whose enthusiasm for this project never waivered.